'Tis THE Damn Season

'Tis THE Damn Season

KIMI FREEMAN

Library of Congress Cataloging-in-Publication Data
Library of Congress Control Number: 2023911783

First paperback edition October 2023

ISBN 979-8-9880004-0-2
ISBN 979-8-9880004-1-9 (ebook)

Interior Design and Formatting: Sabrina Milazzo, www.sabrinamilazzo.net

For Mom,
Thanks for being a superwoman,
and teaching me that I could be one too.

PLAYLIST

The Story of Us (Taylor's Version) – Taylor Swift ❄
Counting Stars – OneRepublic ❄
I Almost Do (Taylor's Version) – Taylor Swift ❄
Sparks Fly (Taylor's Version) – Taylor Swift ❄
So Much More Than This – Grace VanderWaal ❄
Fifteen (Taylor's Version) – Taylor Swift ❄
When We Were Young – Adele ❄
Enchanted (Taylor's Version) – Taylor Swift ❄
Clarity (feat. Foxes) – Zedd ❄
Treacherous (Taylor's Version) – Taylor Swift ❄
This Is Why We Can't Have Nice Things – Taylor Swift ❄
bored&blind – Ella Jane ❄
New Romantics (Taylor's Version) – Taylor Swift ❄
Untouchable (Taylor's Version) – Taylor Swift ❄
The Greatest – Sia ❄
Miss Americana and The Heartbreak Prince – Taylor Swift ❄
ivy – Taylor Swift ❄
Ribs – Lorde ❄
Chasing Cars – Snow Patrol ❄
Feels Like – Gracie Abrams ❄
Brave – Sara Bareilles ❄
400 Lux – Lorde ❄
Pompeii – Bastille ❄
Young Volcanoes – Fall Out Boy ❄
Battle Scars – Lupe Fiasco and Guy Sebastian ❄
Die Alone – Ingrid Michaelson ❄
Otro Atardecer – Bad Bunny & The Marías ❄

Wake Me Up – Avicii ❄

The Lucky One (Taylor's Version) – Taylor Swift ❄

coney island – Taylor Swift ❄

Bad Liar – Selena Gomez ❄

The Other Side of the Door (Taylor's Version) – Taylor Swift ❄

Elastic Heart – Sia ❄

Run (Taylor's Version) (From The Vault) [Feat. Ed Sheeran] – ❄
Taylor Swift

Nothing New (Taylor's Version) (From The Vault) ❄
[Feat. Phoebe Bridgers] – Taylor Swift

Let Somebody Go – Coldplay & Selena Gomez ❄

gold rush – Taylor Swift ❄

Never Forget You – Zara Larsson and MNEK ❄

Christmas Tree Farm – Taylor Swift ❄

Holy Ground (Taylor's Version) – Taylor Swift ❄

mirrorball – Taylor Swift ❄

I miss you, I'm sorry – Gracie Abrams ❄

Sign of the Times – Harry Styles ❄

Come Back...Be Here (Taylor's Version) – Taylor Swift ❄

Beautiful Lies – Birdy ❄

Would've, Could've, Should've – Taylor Swift ❄

Superheroes – The Script ❄

Box of Memories – Georgia Webster ❄

'tis the damn season – Taylor Swift ❄

Karma – Taylor Swift ❄

King of My Heart – Taylor Swift ❄

CHAPTER
one

"The Story of Us" (Taylor's Version) by Taylor Swift

November, Present

Nothing screams, "Welcome back to LA!" like a scathing text from your best friend telling you she'd rather gouge her eyes out than ever see you again. I guess in her mind, it's well deserved, but in reality, it hurts like a bitch.

I try calling Sierra for a third time, but I know it's probably useless. Just thirty minutes ago, the paparazzi spotted her and her boyfriend, Cane, walking into Nobu for their first date after our North American tour. She clearly won't be interested in talking.

"God, Sierra!" I shout at no one in particular, collapsing onto the couch closest to the elevator. "Why can't you just answer the phone?"

Paul, the doorman to our luxury Los Angeles apartment building, doesn't even flinch at my outburst. I guess working in a building that houses some of the biggest young adult stars in this city, he's gotten used to strange behavior. People in LA have a way of acting totally off the rails, then pretending like no one has a right to be upset about it. But I'm still embarrassed that I'm losing my cool like this when I usually try to come off so calm and collected.

Pretending everything's okay is getting increasingly harder the longer I stare at the wall, unpacking what's just happened. Unpacking what the entire world now believes. Unpacking what threatens to wreck my career if I don't get this situation under control.

This was *not* the way I wanted to return home from touring in support of my debut album. My ideal homecoming would have involved a box of sausage and onion pizza, cream soda, and watching chick flicks with Sierra on our couch. The only other person I would want to spend time destressing with after a stressful tour lives three thousand miles away and is painfully unavailable.

I jab at Sierra's phone number once again and finally hear her voice at the end of the line.

"Aspen!" she whisper-shouts over the hum of the restaurant's patrons in the background. "You need to stop calling me! We're not friends anymore. You betrayed me. We're done. Over!"

I quickly stand up and rub a hand over my miniskirt. "If you would just let me explain, you'd know that that's not true! Cane is a liar. He's lying to you and—"

She cuts me off in a clipped tone. "Why would he lie to me? What reason? You must have done something."

"I don't know!" I reply frantically, asking myself the same question. "I don't know, but—"

I try to think of a concrete reason to supply her with, but nothing comes to mind. I don't know why Cane is doing this to me. I don't know why he so suddenly decided to blow up my life.

"Goodbye, Aspen. You're blocked."

"Shit!" I shout as I slink back to the couch.

There's not much use in discretion, anyway. By now, the entire city has heard about the love triangle of the century. And who's the main event? *Me*, Aspen Moore, the American Television Network actress turned mega-popstar turned homewrecker and skank.

And which home did I allegedly wreck?

My own. And that of my best friend and world-renowned supermodel Sierra Wong and her boyfriend, Cane Dawson, lead singer of the indie rock band the Disasters.

Me being the music industry's shiny new toy, having just come off a massively successful first album, more people care about this situation than I ever could have imagined would. Back when I was on my television show, *Soon After*, a killer soap opera about a sorority girl serial murderer, people only cared about my drama if they watched the show. But now it feels like I'm a spectacle for the whole world, a trainwreck they just can't miss.

Sure. Cane was nice. He always knew the right joke to tell and a way to charm people into feeling exactly how he wanted them to. Not to mention, he has an incredible voice. When his band signed a record deal with the same label as me, I couldn't help but want to see him succeed. I even requested to have his band open for me on my recent tour. By the time it rolled around, we'd become friends. I'd go so far as to call him a confidant. Life on the road can get rough, and it was nice to have someone to talk to.

Now he alleges I came onto him?

We've never gotten physical. Not even once.

And yet, of course, the media can spin anything. Make any story seem bulletproof. And suddenly, I'm the diva home-wrecker who'd stoop so low as to sleep with her best friend's boyfriend just because he was convenient.

If Sierra would give me five seconds to explain this all to her, she'd realize that it was once again just the media blowing smoke and messing with our lives.

I open a group text with some of my other friends. I can't say I'm genuinely that close with anyone I've met over the past seven years I've lived here, aside from Sierra, but we share a few friends we hang out with and invite over occasionally. They were always more her friends than mine, but it beats having no one—like I did in high school.

I anxiously type their names into my phone. Darcy Brine, a model like Sierra. Hailey Trent, a former reality TV star turned actress. Aubrey Lark, a social media influencer turned reality star. And finally, Ophelia Hunt, the socialite daughter of the Oscar-award-winning actress Scarlett Frazier.

> **Aspen:** Hey, guys. I need some help dealing with the situation. I've tried to reach out to Sierra and tell her the truth of the matter, but she's already blocked me and moved my stuff out of our apartment. If you guys could text her for me, I'd really appreciate it!

As if she'd been waiting for this moment, Hailey shoots me a text that causes my heart to drop.

> **Hailey:** Hey, Aspen. It's been decided amongst the four of us that we can no longer maintain a friendship with someone like you. I mean, how dare you break girl code like you have?! Despite what you told us after your NYC show, Cane has told us otherwise. Sierra is so heartbroken over what you've done, and we can't betray her by continuing this friendship. Besides, you're all over the media right now, and not in a good way. How could our careers ever survive if we associated with you? We wish you the best of luck sorting out your new living arrangements, though!

Oh my God.

Sierra has meant more to me than anyone other than my parents since I left Fertsville all those years ago. Since I left Roman Torres all those years ago. And it's hard to believe that I've lost her. And no one cares about me enough to have my back.

I was planning to go home for Christmas. But it seems like my trip back to Fertsville might come a lot sooner than that.

With no other choice, I whip out my phone and text my team, asking them to book me a hotel room for the night and a flight to Philly in the next few days.

Then I text my parents, telling them I need a break from LA and that I'm heading back to stay with them for a while.

CHAPTER
two

"Counting Stars" by OneRepublic

November, Seven Years Ago

They may as well have shoved my head in a locker or poured their lunch over my head. While on the outside, it may seem as though high school bullies have gotten classier, in reality, they've just become sneakier about their bitchiness.

My days at Fertsville High School are nothing like the movies. It's my senior year, and I still haven't found a solid group of friends. I don't focus on much other than my schoolwork, and let's face it, I haven't got much going for me when it comes to sports or athletic ability.

All I have is my singing. My voice. And now I'm not sure I've got anything at all.

I stupidly decided to sign up for our school's talent show on a whim. I'd been practicing my singing and acting skills because I wanted to audition for the school musical, and I thought this would be a good way to break out of my shell.

Little did I know Margo, Rina, and their entire posse would be sitting in the front row, unable to keep their negative commentary to themselves.

I heard them over the background instrumental, laughing at me as I sang. I tried to focus and assure myself that I knew what I was doing, but it was impossible.

So, I forgot the words. Made a fool of myself in front of half our school and the directors of the musical I so badly wanted to impress.

I don't understand why these girls have to target me. Rina, Beatrice, and Laura have made it their personal mission since freshman year to make my life hell.

Maybe it was the fact that I was at the peak of my awkward phase. Braces, bad bangs, acne, and all. They stole my middle school best friend, Margo, successfully, leaving me friendless. But why do they have to torture me too? I can still imagine them snickering and whispering about me with her as I ate lunch alone on the first day of school.

God forbid I try to do something for myself. Break out of my shell. Do something that makes me happy. What could a poor mechanic's daughter ever have to offer the world?

Not a beautiful voice or even half-decent singing ability. Absolutely nothing.

Letting out a deep sigh, I remove the last of the smudged mascara off my face before leaving the bathroom and deciding to head to the library. Maybe I can actually get some peace and quiet before fourth period. Plus, I can start that history assignment I have to finish for tomorrow.

I begin to make my way down the hall, but someone calls my name from a distance.

"Aspen!" a male voice shouts. "Hey!"

I turn around to see Roman Torres trying to catch up to me. Why would he be talking to me? I've only ever seen him from afar. And even then, it's been brief. I'm surprised he even knows my name.

"Hey," I reply wearily.

I can't help but notice how good he looks, even in jeans and a tee shirt. His hair is dark brown, almost black, complementing his tan skin well. It's also curly, falling slightly onto his forehead. Not that I have a type, but if I did, it would definitely be him.

The hall is nearly empty as most people are either eating lunch or have just started their afternoon classes. It feels like it's just the two of us in the room. And for some reason, it's kind of daunting.

"Are you okay?" he asks me, which throws me for a loop.

"Why would you ask me that?" Embarrassment washes over me as I wonder if he was in the auditorium to witness the disaster.

He takes a step closer to me. I almost think he's going to do something random, like put a hand on my shoulder or something. "I heard what they said to you during the show."

I want to die of shame. Right here in the hallway.

Rina and her friends said a lot of things after that dreaded performance. That I should have never signed up for the talent show in the first place. That I'll never make it in music. That I was making their ears bleed.

Did I really sound that bad?

I sang a cover of one of my mom's and my favorite songs, *Dreams* by Fleetwood Mac. I thought it sat nicely in my alto range, but now I'm not so sure.

"Oh, that?" I shrug it off like their words meant nothing. "It's okay."

"No, it's not," he insists. "They're assholes. I'm sorry they treated you like that." I'm surprised he's calling them out like this, considering he eats at their lunch table every day.

"Thanks. But it's nothing new," I reply.

"Well, I'm sorry to hear that, Aspen," he tells me. "You should stand up for yourself."

I scoff. Who the hell does he think he is?

"Thanks for the unsolicited advice, Roman. I never even thought of that. I'll be happy to try it out sometime."

I turn on my heel and begin to walk away. I'm normally not this abrasive, but honestly, is this guy serious?

"I'm sorry. Wait!" he calls. "That's not what I meant. I'm just a little nervous, that's all."

I can't help but blurt out exactly what I'm thinking. "Nervous? Why?"

"I'm talking to a pretty girl," he begins meekly. "And I'm pretty sure she hates my guts."

"Oh."

Is he hitting on me right now? I mean, *horribly*, but is he hitting on me? Half of me thinks he's joking, and the other half has no idea what to say.

"Tell me now," he demands. "Did I already fuck this up?"

"Fuck what up?"

"My chance with you."

He's hardly spoken to me in the past few years. We've never had any classes together or really seen each other around. How can he know enough about me to ask me out?

"You want a chance with me?" I ask him.

"Did I not make my intentions clear enough?"

No. Not at all.

It's hard to believe that he could want a chance with someone he barely knows. Someone he hasn't really taken the time to get to know since he moved to town in seventh grade.

"So. Are you going to answer my question?" He repeats after my long pause. "Did I ruin my chances with you?"

"No. I wouldn't say so."

He lets out an audible exhale. "I meant what I said before."

"About what?"

"When I asked if you were okay. I genuinely want to know. Are you okay?"

"Yes," I reply. "I'm okay."

I usually don't let what they say affect me this much. I know most of it is bullshit. But when they start to come for the things I really care about, attack the thing I put everything I have into, day in and day out, I can't pretend it doesn't hurt. For some reason, getting a solo in choir convinced me I'd be good enough to try out for the lead in the school play.

Roman seems sweet. And nothing like how I thought he'd be.

But then again, Rina, Margo—they're all a part of his friend group. Those are his people. And no matter what he seems like, I can't let myself forget the fact *those* are the kinds of people he likes to keep around.

I start to walk away, but Roman stops me.

"Aspen, wait."

"Yes?"

"Will you come to my game on Friday?" he asks. "Please?"

A football game.

Not really my scene. Actually, not my scene at all. I've never been to any football games, and I've never intended to.

"I'll think about it."

"Wait, I—"

"Bye, Roman. I'll see you around."

I turn and stalk away, leaving a speechless football player in my wake.

CHAPTER
three

"I Almost Do (Taylor's Version)" by Taylor Swift

November, Present

$\mathcal{A}$fter a five-hour flight to the Philadelphia Airport that felt like forever, I finally arrived in my hometown. There were some paparazzi crowded outside my terminal today, but I hid behind my regular security team and tried my best to block them out as they shouted at me.

"Aspen!" one had called as I made my way out of my driver's car. "Why did you try to sleep with him? The other guys in Hollywood weren't doing it for you?"

I shuddered a little as I tried not to internalize his crude words. He doesn't know me. He shouldn't mean anything. But every time I see these people following me around with their stupid cameras, trying to get a response out of me, it makes me wonder whether any of this was even worth it in the first place.

I'm glad I rented a car from the airport instead of getting a ride home from my parents. The fifty-five-minute trip was meditative. Besides, it's nice to drive on my own for once without the lingering threat of being ambushed by the paparazzi.

I love my parents more than anything, but I'd never want them to clue into the severity of all that's happening right now. Sure, they watch the news and see the tabloids in the grocery store. But Fertsville isn't like LA. They probably see the rumors as no more than stupid small-town gossip, not something that threatens to ruin my career if I can't get my image back under control.

"Penny!" my dad exclaims as he opens the front door. The worries melt away with the sound of his tender voice, loving and filled with genuine excitement to see me.

"Hey, Dad!" I exclaim, wrapping my arms around him with my duffel bag still slung over my shoulder. He squeezes me tight and gently kisses my cheek.

"Come on in!" he says, ushering me past the door. "Your mom's not home yet, but there's someone here you'll want to see."

We walk through the entrance, past the staircase, to find a familiar face sitting at my parent's kitchen table.

The ground shakes beneath me. My heart pounds. The lights flicker off. Mountains move for Roman Torres.

Or at least that's how it feels.

"Pen," he breathes.

"Rome," I say back, unable to conceal the warmth and surprise in my tone. I knew I'd have to see him at some point. I just figured I'd have a little more time to prepare myself.

Slowly but surely, he gets up from his seat, crosses the room, and wraps his arms around me. I don't fight his embrace. I welcome it. There's no point in fighting it now, anyway.

His arms feel like home. They always have.

"What are you doing here?" I ask as I pull away.

Dad replies, "Rome's been helping me out at the auto shop lately. We've seen a big change in revenue with him around."

"Oh!" I reply, a little shocked. "I didn't know you were into that kind of stuff."

Growing up, he always wanted to be a teacher. To be exact, he wanted to teach math and coach football, but that was no longer in the cards after his mom got sick.

Rome and Dad share a laugh. "I'm learning a lot."

Rome opens his mouth to add something, but Dad says, "We can talk about that later. Let's bring your bags in and let you get comfortable."

Both men follow me back to the entrance and bring my suitcases from my car to my room upstairs. I tried to pack as lightly as possible, but considering my current living situation, I ended up having to bring most of the contents of my apartment, which was enough to fill five suitcases. It was a hassle to get them all paid for and into the rental car at the airport, but I managed to make it work.

It had taken me a little less than a week to wrap things up in California. I'd had to meet with my public relations agency as well as my management to discuss our plan of action after the scandal. I put out a statement from the Notes app, telling the world that I'm "listening to how they feel but maintain that I'm innocent in this situation." My team told me it was worth a shot and that I needed to give things time to blow over. I boarded my flight the next day, perfectly content to let things do so. And to try to get some relaxation over the next few months.

"Thanks, guys," I tell them as I follow them into my room. "You didn't have to do that."

"Nonsense," replies Rome. "It was no problem."

After a long beat, Dad clears his throat. "I'll let you two catch up. Your mom wants me to prep for dinner."

"You're staying?" I ask Rome. I don't mean to come off so rudely, but the words tumble out of my mouth before I can stop them.

"That a problem for you, Pen?"

"No, of course not!" I answer quickly. "I was just wondering."

I've never not loved having Rome around. Not since I was seventeen years old. I was heartbroken when we'd have to spend just a few weeks apart, like when he went to visit his family in the Dominican Republic for three weeks.

Ever since I left for LA seven years ago, coming home has meant coming home to Rome. But after everything that's gone down lately, I'm not sure how I'll handle losing someone else when I have to leave him all over again.

Dad smiles at me. "Well, I'll leave you to it."

I kick off my boots and flop backward onto my old twin-sized bed in my airport clothes: a comfy sweater and flared leggings. I would normally change first, but I'm just too damn tired to care.

"Rough week?" Rome asks while taking off his shoes, then sitting down on the bed next to me.

I let out an audible exhale. "That would be the understatement of a lifetime."

I've been receiving hate mail and death threats all week. Other celebs receive this kind of treatment all the time. Aubrey was canceled just a few months ago for doing a brand deal with a company whose CEO made insensitive remarks about feminism. But everything feels different now that I'm the one in this awful position. And it's not just about brand endorsements. It's about Sierra and Cane's fans thinking I'm a terrible person who would intentionally try to break up their OTP.

He scoots in close and puts an arm around me. "I'm sure things aren't nearly as bad as you think."

But that's not true. If anything, they're much worse.

"You've seen what they're saying about me?"

Rome shakes his head. "Not exactly. But I did see a few tabloid covers in the grocery store yesterday."

I saw them too. *Aspen Moore: Serial Killer or Serial Heartbreaker? Moore goes from sorority girl serial killer to best friend-betraying relationship killer.*

I turn over and bury my face into my pillow, not wanting him to look at me anymore.

People already assumed I was a bitch, given my character on the show. But I thought my music was finally causing people to see me in a different light.

"You know none of that's true, right?" I ask, looking at him once again.

"Obviously, it's not. You'd never do something like that to someone you love."

At least there's one person on planet Earth who doesn't think I'm totally awful. And I suppose he's more important than most of the people who think that anyway.

"I just can't believe how fast the world turned on me. It's like one day, I was selling out huge venues and performing for thousands of screaming fans, and the next, I'm the most hated person on social media."

"But you chose to move there for a reason. You choose to do *this* for a reason."

"I know."

I love my job, and I'd never trade it for the world, no matter if it means living in the city and working in an industry that's cutthroat, to say the least.

Seven years ago, LA became my fresh start. The way to make my dreams come true. I could be bigger than I was back in Fertsville. Bigger than any of the kids who made my high school years a living nightmare.

"It's just too much for me right now," I tell him, my voice breaking. "What if I'm not meant for this life?"

Sierra and Cane are the golden couple of social media. Each day Sierra uploads a new video or story showing them in a cute pose or doing some cringe dance. The internet eats them up. And there is no room for my truth in this narrative.

"Don't say that, Pen. That's not true. I've never met someone more deserving or talented. I've known you were going to be big from the day we met." He touches my arm, once again sending heat throughout my body.

There goes my shield of protection. It falls down when I'm around him. Every. Single. Time.

How do I tell the man who's been rooting for me from day one that I made a mistake?

"There's so much about the industry you don't know," is my sad reply.

Once the words leave my lips, I regret saying them in the first place. I can practically see the hurt register on his face. I should call him more often. He wants to know more about my life. He wants me to cross the barrier I've built between us. But I can't. And we both know that.

Rome lets out a heavy sigh. "I don't need to know the industry. I know you."

I stiffen. His words cause my heart to squeeze. Rome knows me better than anyone else on the planet. I've hurt him by keeping my distance, but he's better at moving on than I am. He's better at the goodbye. It takes me what feels like years to let go of the memories. To stop thinking about his touch.

Yet there he goes. Always saying the right thing. Always finding the perfect words. Reminding me why I'm still enchanted by him, even after all of these years.

"Thanks, I really appreciate that."

"Don't say that like you don't believe it's true. It is."

Not wanting to face any of this right now, I switch topics. "Be real with me. Why have you actually been working at my dad's?"

"I like working with cars now."

"I don't believe you for a second."

"I needed a job, Pen. That's all it is. A job."

I don't know what I expected to find him doing, but this certainly wasn't it.

"You don't need to do anything you don't want to do, Rome. You can always come to me. Besides, you've never been interested when Dad had spots open before." I know for a fact my mom's brought it up a few times around him.

He grimaces. "Let's not talk about that right now."

I nod my head.

"Are you still taking classes at the community college?" He mentioned taking a few classes in education briefly when I was with him last April.

Rome nods, laughing. It's nice to see him smiling again. "Yeah, it's going pretty well. I'm surprised you remembered."

I scoff, only half kidding. "Of course, I remembered. Do you seriously think so little of me?"

"It's just been a long time," he answers. "That's all I meant."

I hate that he reminds me. No matter how awful it makes me feel, I can't reach out to him. The game we play every time I come back here is bad enough. But if I start talking to him while I'm in LA, I might do something utterly stupid. Something that will ruin the weird kind of friendship we've built over the years.

"I'm sorry," I blurt. "You know how it is."

"Yeah," he says dryly, moving closer to me. "I know how it is."

I don't know why I let him. I see it coming. I see his hand inching closer to me. I feel my heart lift as he tucks a strand of my long brown hair behind my ear. I feel the bed shift beneath me as he leans over.

We jerk apart the moment we hear my dad's voice booming from the kitchen downstairs. "Aspen! Roman!" he calls. "It's time for dinner!"

It's hard to believe we've been up here for so long.

Slightly embarrassed, I hop off the bed and start toward the kitchen, but Roman grabs my arm and pulls me back toward him.

"Hey," he says softly, planting a kiss on my forehead. "I missed you."

I can't help but smile. "I missed you too." I always miss him.

My mom's lips are quirked up into a warm smile as she opens her arms toward me while I make it down the stairs. I wrap my arms around her. "Hey, Mom. I didn't even know you'd gotten home."

She sighs. "I didn't want to interrupt. You're staying here through the New Year, right? We'll have plenty of time to catch up."

My cheeks are now a bright shade of pink. "Thanks, Mom."

I can't imagine the look on her face if she had come upstairs to see us all over each other. Mom's always been cool about us, but definitely not that cool.

"You guys about ready to eat?" my dad calls from the kitchen.

"Coming!"

Dinner with my family is nice. Casual. A change of pace from my typical routine. Being back here is starting to feel a little more normal after being on the road for so long.

"So," my dad says as he interrupts a conversation between Rome and me, "I have something I want to ask you two about."

"Of course, Mark. Anything," Roman says.

Mark? They're on a first-name basis now?

"Well, as you guys know, every year, I like to put together a production at the church...."

A smile spreads across my face as I anticipate what he's about to ask.

The church he's referring to is the old Methodist he's spent every Sunday and Thursday attending all my life. While my father has limited experience in acting or singing, he always recruited the best he could find to put on a production of the first Christmas for the families of the church every year. It's never been in the budget to hire official staff or anything, but Dad always finds a way to make it work. It's so sweet how important this is to him. I'd performed in his shows as a kid, playing Mary when I was twelve.

"Well, I was thinking maybe you guys would be interested in helping out this year?" he asks.

"Of course!" I exclaim immediately. "I'd love to!"

Rome shoots Dad a humongous smile. "It would be my honor, Mark, though I'm not sure what I bring to the table."

I smack him on the shoulder. "You're great with kids!" He was the best assistant football coach Fertsville High had ever seen.

"She's right, Roman."

He nods solemnly. "Thank you for putting your faith in me. I won't let you down."

"I know you won't," Dad replies.

"What will we be doing exactly?" I ask.

"Directing," he states. "Running auditions, staging, helping the kids nail down their lines."

"When will we start?" I ask.

"Thursday, if you're willing? I've invited any child interested in participating to the church for an introductory meeting."

"That works for me." Two days from now is plenty of time to prepare.

"My schedule's clear," adds Rome.

My dad looks over at my mom and then back at me lovingly. "Thank you so much for doing this, sweetheart. I know you've got a lot on your plate."

"Of course, Dad," I say, running around to his side of the table to give him a quick hug. "I'm really excited."

"That's great, Penny. I'm happy, then."

And at this moment, I feel happy too.

CHAPTER
four

"Sparks Fly (Taylor's Version)" by Taylor Swift

November, Seven Years Ago

$\mathcal{I}$'d debated coming to this game. I knew I'd have to sit alone, and Roman might not even want to talk to me anymore. But I did it anyway, against my better judgment.

After my run-in with Roman on Wednesday, I had a lot of time to think about the situation. It took me by such surprise I couldn't decide what I should do. But when I'd casually mentioned to my mother that I might be interested in coming tonight, her face absolutely lit up. I would have been rotten not to.

She was so happy to see me out of my room and doing normal high school things. Mom's constantly worried about the fact that I spend most of my time on my own. She works a part-time job as a substitute teacher at Fertsville Elementary and feels like I should be going out more at my age. It makes sense. She was a popular cheerleader in high school and has probably attended more parties than I can count. The worst she's ever caught me doing was pulling an all-nighter playing guitar in my room.

By the time I arrive, the game has already begun. Surprisingly, there is just enough space for one more person toward the end of the front row, and I sit, neglecting to take a second to scan my surroundings. Big mistake.

I can feel the stares from Rina, Margo, Beatrice and Laura, even without having to look to the side, but I glance over at them to confirm my suspicions. They're probably wondering why I'm here; I never show up to things like this.

Since I don't know much about football, I simply stare at Roman. I watch the way he glistens in the moonlight through his sweat and tiredness. I watch as he lifts his shirt up to wipe his face, and I stare right at his abs, shiny from perspiration.

I love the way he smiles as he runs and looks as if he's genuinely enjoying himself. I love his smile in general, though I don't think I can ever admit that out loud.

He doesn't notice me at first. But during a timeout, he scans the crowd. When his eyes land on me, he smiles that goofy grin of his and waves, and I can't help but admit I melt inside.

"Hi," I mouth, not even sure if he can really see me from down there.

As the game continues, I mindlessly watch, unable to distract myself from thoughts of Roman and that smile.

In just a few days, I've thought about him even more than I did my first crush, Harry Coven, in freshman year. We dated for about a month before he broke things off. Sure, I found him attractive. But he never gave me *butterflies*.

I've never felt this way before. And I'm not sure I ever want to again. It's scary to put myself out there. Especially when it comes to someone as popular as Roman.

Falling for him seems like the kind of recklessness that should send me running far away, but for some reason, I want to do just the opposite.

I let my mind race throughout the entirety of the second quarter. By the time it's halftime and the cheerleaders are performing, I've already pulled out my notebook, pen in hand, and a melody in mind. I've been writing songs in this notebook for about a year, as it was a Christmas gift from my mom. She painted the cover just for me with music notes and fun designs.

You can't escape my mind
Though I wish you would sometimes
You take up too much space
Make me second-guess
Everything
Everything

I'm lost in my head for a while until I see that the cheerleaders' performance has wrapped up. I shove my notebook and pen back into my bag as the players return to the field. I try my hardest to pay attention, but inspiration strikes again.

I don't want to fall too hard

I'm scared that
You'll pull away and it'll all stop
And I'll curse myself stupid girl stupid girl
It's all a lie more often than it's not

But you're
But you're
In my dreams
In my dreams
I'm dreaming of you

I put down my pen, reading over my work a few times. To get a full picture, I'd need to put it to guitar, but so far, so good.

I've been writing songs since I was ten years old. One of my dad's friends taught me how to play guitar when he came to visit, and from then on, I became obsessed. I'd always loved to sing but writing my own music was taking it to a new level.

My heart races and my mind snaps into focus the moment I see Roman running at lightning speed down the field, holding the ball. Players from the opposing team are chasing him, but they're not even close. Our side of the crowd whoops and cheers, but I'm frozen in silence.

Rome sprints to the end zone, still with the ball, as time is running out. He accelerates faster and faster until he makes it to his destination. The crowd around me erupts in wild applause. Rome just scored a touchdown. And we totally just won!

"Oh my God," I whisper.

The team begins to crowd around Rome, but he's not looking at them. He's looking at me. I see him walking toward me, and I jump up from my seat.

And before I can even mutter something congratulatory, he does the unexpected. The unthinkable, really.

He picks me up and holds me tight. In front of everyone.

Despite my shock, I settle into his arms as he spins me around.

"You came," he whispers.

"You thought I wouldn't?"

He puts me down and smiles. "I wasn't sure. But I'm glad you did."

CHAPTER
five

"So Much More Than This" by Grace VanderWaal

November, Present

The next day I sit at my desk, notebook in hand, as Rome and I brainstorm ideas on how to spice up the production this year.

"What if we add more music?" I ask. "Maybe Mary can sing a little song at the end?"

The script my dad normally uses is fine, except there's only one song in the whole show. Music has always been my first love, way before I was interested in acting.

"Good idea," Rome replies as he sits on my bed. "I know you'll be a great vocal coach."

He says this as if I've coached anyone in my life. I never even had a formal voice lesson until I was twenty.

"So will you," I say, but we both know he can't sing to save his life.

"What are you thinking about for auditions?"

"Maybe everyone should audition with either a Joseph or Mary monologue, and people who want to try for Mary can sing a song?"

He nods. "Sounds good to me. I give you total creative control."

"Stop! I know nothing about children or directing."

"Yes," he responds. "But you're an expert on singing and acting. Directing will be a breeze for you. I can feel it already."

I'm glad at least one of us can.

"You think so?"

"I don't think so," Rome tells me. "I know so."

I don't welcome the feeling this evokes in me, but I melt anyway. It's been too damn long for me to still be affected by his charms.

"Thanks," I reply weakly.

"No problem," he says back. "I mean it."

"I know."

We iron out more details and objectives for the upcoming show. I'm enjoying the process and letting it ground me a bit. Maybe this is what I needed.

"*Mi cielo*," Rome whispers, pulling me into him a little. "What happened over there to make you so insecure? I mean, besides the obvious love triangle gone wrong."

"What?" I say, shocked.

"You were so confident before you left," he answers. How can he always read me like a goddamn book?

I was always insecure, even as a kid. The high school bullying certainly did not help with that. But things changed when Rome and I got together in junior year. Thanks to his confidence and encouragement, I started to come out of my shell a little bit.

But LA can change people.

"Young," I correct. "I used to be so *young*."

He gives me a look that tells me he's not buying my shit.

I sigh, telling him a bit of the truth. "Things change. I was a big fish in a small pond. Now I'm not."

Rome grabs my hand. "That doesn't make you any less you."

"That doesn't mean others aren't better at doing what I do," I reply.

"But no one is you."

He still doesn't understand. He doesn't understand what it's like to book a project, feel on top of the world, and then have everybody criticize you and compare you to dozens of other actresses or say you don't deserve it.

Riding the waves of your career, knowing that at any moment, it could all be taken away from you. At any second, you could become the star that once was. In the eyes of the entire world, just a shell of your former self.

"The media invades my privacy. They criticize every aspect of my life. And there's nothing I can do to stop it. Nothing besides giving up everything I've worked so hard to accomplish."

And I refuse to do that. Not just because some people on the internet decided I'm a homewrecker and the biggest slut on the planet. This is not the legacy I want to leave on this Earth. I've come so far already. I refuse to allow my career to fade out this way.

"I came to Fertsville to get away from the drama of LA. Not relive it again. Why are you trying to turn this into a therapy session?"

"I'm not going to..." His tone sharpens, "...*apologize* for caring about you, Pen."

I let out a loud groan, but the look in his eyes makes me soften my expression and apologize. I know he cares about me.

Maybe a little more than he should. It's impossible not to let him in when he cares the way he does.

"I'm sorry. I'm just a bit on edge right now."

I can't afford to lean on him any longer, not knowing when he's going to move on. When he's not going to want to hear from me because he's being there for someone else.

Someone who can give him more than I ever could.

His lips quirk upwards into a smile as he gets up and lifts me out of my chair, throwing me onto the bed and following me down.

"Don't worry about it," he replies, laughing. "You're all good."

I turn over, trying to push him off me, but this only makes him strengthen his grip. I smile at him, throwing him off guard, before pushing him again. He only lets me win for a moment before resecuring his place on top of me.

"Get off!" I whisper-scream, urging him not to take things to a place I know we shouldn't go.

He just laughs again. "No."

"Please?" I ask, giving in slightly, a huge smile beaming across my face

He stays put. "No."

"Rome…"

"Yes?"

I just look at him.

He shoots me another award-worthy grin before pressing his lips to mine.

I'm going to be working with him. Seeing him every goddamn day. No matter how much I want him, I can't have him this time.

I'll never be able to let him go. Not if we get this close.

"Rome," I say. "Rome."

"Yes?" he answers, his voice breathy.

"We can't," I tell him.

"We absolutely can," he replies.

"Rome," I rasp. "Stop."

That's all it takes. He rolls over immediately.

"What's wrong?" he asks, visibly concerned. "Did I do something to...?" I don't even want to think about what he's insinuating. Or else the memories will slowly creep back in.

"No, no. You did everything right."

"Then what is it?"

He doesn't need my chaos. And he doesn't want my drama. The paparazzi, the city, the culture, the lack of privacy. It'll always be too much for him. He could never deal with the drama, and he's made that clear.

But I don't want to return to my past. This small town, the people who remain here. The ones who made me feel like I was nothing. Fertsville was my home, but it will never be enough for me.

Despite how much we care about each other, we can't keep falling into our old patterns just to leave each other all over again. I know the heartbreak that causes all too well.

"I think we should just be friends."

He laughs, but not lightly, confusion crossing his face. "I am your friend."

"No, you're not." I huff, begging him with my eyes to see my side. "You've been so much more than that."

"I don't see the problem."

"Yes, you do!" I reply. "This game we play. It's not good for either of us."

"This is a game to you?"

"You know what I mean."

I can't stay. Fall back in love with him, have him for the next month and a half, just to go all over again. I won't be able to handle it. Not another time.

He breathes out deeply, exasperated. "You're always good for me, Pen."

"What happens when I leave?" I ask him. "We both know how this goes."

"Why are we talking about this now?" he mutters, choking up.

"I'm staying for a while this time, Rome. I can't have my heart broken again. I won't be able to handle it another time around."

"I didn't *mean* to hurt you," he says, sitting back down on the bed next to me. "This was best for us. I never wanted us to be this way."

"I know," I answer softly. "I'm not denying that."

"You know," he whispers, his hand reaching for mine. "It broke me too."

"That's my point, Rome."

He shakes his head and runs a hand through his curly hair. "I'm happy with where we are. I'm happy to be here with you whenever you come back. You're always good for me. We're good together."

"And I'm happy to be with you too. I'll care about you for the rest of my life. But I can't live here. We can't do *this* forever. I can't keep learning to forget you over and over again. Don't you see what's going on now? My life is a mess. I can't afford to fall apart any more than I already have. So please. Just give me this."

Sanity. Space to put distance between us. A fighting chance at not leaving Fertsville an even bigger mess.

"Okay," he finally says, his tone unhappy.

"Okay." I add, "Friends?"

"Always. You'll always be my best friend."

CHAPTER
Six

"Fifteen (Taylor's Version)" by Taylor Swift

November, Seven Years Ago

$\mathcal{I}$ can hear people murmuring about me. About Roman. About that damn hug from across the bleachers.

"Come on!" Rome says. "You should meet the team."

No, I really should not. I haven't spoken to any of them before, but I see them around all the time. If I had to pick one word to describe them, it would be unapproachable.

"Oh, I don't want to impose."

"No, I'm serious."

"Maybe next time," I say gently.

"Please?" he asks me again with puppy-dog eyes. "I deserve a gift for winning so hard tonight."

I smack him on the shoulder. "You can't be serious."

From the look on his face, I can tell. He totally is.

I let out a defeated sigh. "I guess I could say hi for a minute."

"I knew you'd come around, Pen."

"Pen?"

"As-pen. Get it? Pen?"

"Yes, Roman, I got it," I reply lamely. "I just didn't know we were wandering onto nickname territory just yet."

"Oh, Pen," he teases, wrapping his arm around my shoulder. "There's so much about us you don't know yet."

"Care to enlighten me, Rome?" I ask. "Get it? Roman. Rome?"

"Yes, I get it. But I have no interest in enlightening you about my master plan. A man's gotta keep some cards to his chest, you know?"

"Oh my God," I mumble, trying my hardest to stifle a laugh. It doesn't work.

I could really fall for this guy. If I let myself, that is.

"Follow me," he says, as he takes my hand. "The team's waiting."

Blinded by my infatuation with Roman and his need for nicknaming me, I almost don't see who is standing right in front of me when we reach the field.

Rina, Margo, Beatrice and Laura, along with a host of their friends, stand talking to the players.

How could I be so stupid? Everybody knows that Beatrice is casually talking to Derek, the wide receiver. And Rina's been on and off with Kevin, the running back, since sixth grade.

"On second thought," I say, pulling out of Roman's grasp, "I think I'll head home now."

"No!" he replies, pulling me back. "It's too late. You've already agreed."

"I can't go over there! Why are you tormenting me?" He must have heard the way the girls were harassing me during my talent show performance. It was impossible to miss.

45

"I'm not tormenting you. I'm helping you face your fears. Besides, these guys are important to me. I really want you to meet them."

Oh my God.

"You know what they'll say," I tell him, referring to Rina and her friends.

"Fuck what they'll say," is his angry reply. "And I can assure you, they won't say that shit around me."

I follow him, dreading each and every step I take.

"Hey, guys!" Roman calls out.

The guys murmur various greetings, seeming way nicer and more welcoming than I expected.

"I want to introduce you to someone," he says, his hand on the small of my back, guiding me. "This is Pen." I find it a little weird that he's introducing me, considering I know most of these people already.

"Aspen," I correct. "My name is Aspen."

"Like the place," Roman adds.

The guys all shoot me variations of "Hey Aspen" and introduce themselves. If they'd seen me around before, they didn't make that obvious. The girls are all silent, but the looks on their faces tell me everything I need to know. They don't approve.

Seeing Margo like this hurts especially. She's acting like we weren't best friends just two years ago. I used to tell her everything. We used to have sleepovers at my house almost every weekend. And now…

We're just nothing.

"I don't remember the last time Torres introduced us to anyone," says Kevin. "This must be serious, then."

I blush.

"We're taking things slow," Rome says.

"News to me," I mutter, just loudly enough for him to hear. We never even established there was anything to take slow. He smiles at me.

"Well, that's good to hear, brother," says John, another one of Roman's friends from his team.

"Thanks, man."

Rina finally speaks up. "I'm surprised to see you here, Aspen. Seeing as you've never been to a single game before."

I open my mouth to speak, unsure what to say, but Roman cuts me off.

"Football's not really her thing. She's willing to put up with it, for me, of course."

All the guys laugh.

"It's not that," I explain. "I just don't know much about the game."

"Well, if you're looking for a crash course," Derek adds. "Torres will be a good teacher. He's one of our best. After me, of course."

Roman slaps him on the back. "Well, it's been great, guys."

"Heading out already?" asks Jeff, who I believe is a kicker. "I'm hosting an after-party at my house tonight, and you, my friend, are the guest of honor."

"I would if I could, but I'm not feeling too well. Besides, I should probably get this one back home."

Everyone's gaze falls on me.

"No, it's okay!" I say quickly. I don't want him to feel like he's responsible for me or anything. "Please, stay with your friends. I'll walk myself."

"No, you live at least fifteen minutes from here. It's late. I'll come with you."

How does he know where I live?

"Or you could both come to my party," Jeff adds.

"No, it's fine, really," I respond. "I'll see you guys around."

I start walking away, but Rome pulls me back toward him.

"Rome, I—"

"Stop," he whispers in my ear. "You'll only make it worse. Come with me."

I feel his breath hot on my face, tickling my skin, his hand now on the small of my back, holding me to his side.

"Okay," I reply, absolutely melting.

"Okay," he whispers to me again before turning back to the group. "Bye, guys! I'll see you on Monday."

Rome drags me along with him as he walks in the opposite direction of my house.

"Where are you taking me?"

"The locker room. Give me a few minutes to shower and grab my stuff."

"Oh my God," I say on a groan. "I'm gonna be late for curfew. I have to go." I know that if I explained it to my mom, she probably wouldn't care, but I've already had enough of breaking out of my comfort zone tonight.

"Give me five. Please."

"Okay," I tell him. "Five minutes."

"Great," he says, smiling. "Thanks."

He returns in about ten minutes instead of five. His hair is slightly tousled and wet, and he's now changed into school sweatpants and a black tee. He's the first out of the locker room, so I can tell he was rushing.

"Come on!" he shouts, rushing me toward the gate. "You're gonna be late!"

CHAPTER
seven

"When We Were Young" by Adele

November, Present

The next two days seem to fly by, and suddenly, I'm gearing up to begin our first day of rehearsal.

I already see Rome's truck in the parking lot as I walk toward the entrance of the church. I quickly run my hands over my bright blue sweater before making my way inside the auditorium.

"Hey, Pen!" he calls out from the stage.

"Hey, Rome." He matches me today in a navy-blue crewneck and black jeans. "I brought you a coffee," I tell him as I place it on the folding table beside him. I didn't want things to be weird between us after our conversation the other day, so I decided a coffee would be the best peace offering.

I got his usual, coffee with a splash of milk, and mine, the sweetest coffee they offered. I had trouble falling asleep last night; caffeine is the only way I'm going to make it through my day. In LA, I'd normally go for an iced coffee, but I can't bring myself to drink anything cold now that the weather is cooling down.

He offers me a small smile. "Thanks, *mi cielo*."

God. Does he have to call me that swoon-worthy nickname *all* the time?

I know my heart shouldn't skip a beat, and my blood pressure shouldn't rise every time I'm going to see him. But old habits die hard, and being infatuated with him has been a habit of mine since I was seventeen years old.

"How's the setup going?" I ask.

Rome insisted on bringing snacks and games for the kids to celebrate being a part of the show on day one. It warms my heart to see how much he cares about making this fun for them.

"Pretty great, actually. I can set up the games myself, though I could use some help with the variety packs." He points to the boxes of chips on the tables he set up.

"No problem."

I lay the chips out on the table, sorting them by brand. *Everybody Talks* by Neon Trees plays in the background as we work. Rome likes to make playlists for almost everything.

"Should we turn this off before the kids get here?" I ask. Some of the music he normally plays is quite explicit.

"No, don't worry," he replies, putting his right hand to his heart. "All the music is child-friendly. I swear."

"Awesome," I say. "Thanks."

It's definitely strange coming back to this church. I usually don't come here on my visits home, especially considering its location next to my old high school. My dad doesn't mind this much, especially considering my mom doesn't really go either, but some-times I come with him. Whenever I can tell he needs me to.

"I'm so excited for the kids to get here," Rome says.

"Yeah?"

"I've thought of so many games we can play with them."

I smile. It makes me so happy that he's able to do something like this again. "Such as?"

"Handball, cornhole, kickball…"

I laugh. "You do realize we're in an auditorium, right?"

"Yeah, obviously," he says. "My bad."

"No, no, I'm happy you're excited!" I tell him. "It's kind of sweet, actually."

Coaching young boys in football was one of the main things that got him out of his depression when his mom passed five years ago. Helping kids and getting to be a part of their growth and training really helped him in his grieving process.

I know he doesn't do it anymore, but a part of me is hoping he'll go back to it someday.

By the time kids start piling into the auditorium, it looks more like a carnival. Candy and decorations are scattered throughout the room. Games are sprawled all over the stage, and tables of food line the walls across from the seats.

As the parents start to file into the auditorium with their children, it's clear that nobody told them Rome and I were go-ing to be taking over the production. Though they're attempt-ing to be discreet, I can tell they're talking about me. About my damaged reputation. About how someone like me isn't a good fit to direct their young children.

Oftentimes Fertsville feels like my normal, while LA is just some strange sort of alternate reality where everyone has an ulterior motive. Everyone knows everything about you and is constantly judging you for it. Nothing there is real. But Fertsville is when the universe returns to its typical world order.

Today is knocking that whole balance out of whack.

Rome is too busy greeting parents to notice. And he's so excited about doing this production. I don't want to bring his energy down. Plus, I can't bring myself to back out of the show and let my dad down. But standing here, in this corner by myself, it's all too clear what even people in my hometown think of me now.

"Welcome, everyone!" Rome says once everyone has made their way in. "Thank you so much for coming."

"Yeah," I add. "Thanks so much for being here."

"We want today to be about you guys having fun and getting to know each other better, so we've brought some games for you all to play and snacks. Auditions will be held later this week. We'll keep you posted on the time. But don't worry—everyone who signs up will get to be part of the production."

I've done so much auditioning in my life up to this point, far more than I could even begin to quantify. It feels so weird to be on the other side of it.

"If you or your parents have any questions about the show," Rome continues, "let Pen or me know."

"Yeah, guys, this production is going to be super low-stress. Have fun and enjoy yourselves!"

The small crowd bursts into applause and high-pitched cheers.

Some kids scatter to try out different games, but many of the girls approach me to ask questions like, "Do you write all of your own songs?"

"What is it like to go on tour?"

"Were you really with Cane Dawson?"

"What was it like working with Keith Haverton?"

"Is he a good kisser?"

I inwardly cringe at the mention of my former costar but try my best not to show my true emotions in front of the kids. They don't know what happened to me, and I intend to keep it that way.

I'm a good actress. I can handle this.

"I co-write some, but I mostly write them myself. It's super fun! I was never with Cane. And Keith was nice. No comment on any kissing!"

Once the awe wears off and the kids go off to play together, I take the time to watch Rome. He's teaching a group of little boys to play kickball. I don't like to admit that I've thought about it, but I've always pictured what it might be like to have children with him.

A miniature Rome roaming the earth, knocking things over, playing football with his dad.

What would have happened if I had never left? If he had never told me to go. If I had put my foot down and said that I wanted to stay here and be with him?

I wouldn't have made a TV show or launched an album. Maybe I'd be working for my dad now, too...

But back then, there was nothing I wanted more than to support him through what ended up being the hardest two years of his life. I want to imagine a life with the man I've never been able to forget, but doing so is a death by a thousand cuts.

I don't know who I'd be without my music or acting career. I'm not sure I can stand to give it up.

I'll never forget how I felt when I opened my first show. I couldn't believe that all of those people had really come to see me. Sure, my album had soared to the top of the charts due to my name being a constant fixture in the press. Sure, I broke records and won numerous awards. But I didn't really believe in my success until I heard all of those people singing my lyrics with me. It was unimaginable.

An absolute fairytale.

"We don't want to play with you."

I turn to see a small group of four girls over by the cornhole. They look around eleven or ten, though I'm not quite sure.

Three are similarly dressed in flare leggings and sweaters. The fourth girl, a really cute kid, is wearing matching sweats and white sneakers, her black hair braided loosely over her shoulder.

"Hey!" I call out to her, making direct eye contact. "Do you want to come sit with me?"

The rest of the girls' mouths hang open as she nods her head and sits down next to me on the edge of the stage.

"What's your name?"

"Ella," is her sheepish reply.

"Hi, Ella," I say. "I'm Aspen."

She whispers, "I know. Am I in trouble?"

"No! Why would you think that?"

A small tear rolls down her cheek. "I wasn't trying to bother them, I swear. I didn't know they didn't want me around."

"Oh my goodness. Ella, I would never punish you for something like that. Or at all. You did the right thing by putting yourself out there. Some people just don't treat others how they should." I pause. "Do you know them from school?"

I assume they've probably interacted before. There's only one elementary school, and Fertsville's a small town.

She nods. "They're in the other class, but I used to talk to Mille sometimes last year. I thought she'd want to be friends with me."

"Don't worry," I reply. "That has nothing to do with you."

"So why does it feel like it does?"

I hesitate. "That's how it always feels. Like you should be ashamed for putting yourself out there. Like you should have to make yourself small in the presence of others, fearful that they might judge you. But that's not true. Sometimes people are struggling within themselves and take it out on people around them."

I study her, and she seems to understand what I'm saying.

"Come here," I say, wrapping my arms around her. She leans into me, hugging me tight. We stay like this for a long while.

"You okay?" Rome mouths to me from across the room. Forever the protector. Forever reading my mind.

"Yes," I mouth back.

"How old are you?" I ask Ella when we finally pull apart.

"Ten."

I look back at the group still over by the cornhole. They're only in fourth or fifth grade? They're laughing, looking to be having a wonderful time, while Ella sits here, sad and alone.

"Can you do me a favor?" I ask. I'm not licensed or her parents or anything, but what the hell.

"Sure," she answers me.

"Don't worry about those girls, okay? They might have a reason for treating you badly that has absolutely nothing to do with you. What they said to you wasn't right, but I'm sure you'll find tons of other kids in the cast who will want to play with you and make you feel welcome in their group."

"You think so?"

"I don't think so," I tell her, taking a phrase from Rome. "I know so."

"Okay. Thank you."

"You don't have to thank me, Ella. I'm here for you. Anytime."

There's a long pause.

"You know," she begins, "my mom and I play your music in the car sometimes."

"Really?" I ask. "What's your favorite song?"

"'Dreaming of You.'"

My heart swells. "Dreaming of You" was the lead single off my first EP. The project came out just six months after I signed my record deal, and much of the music was written during my high school years. It also happens to be the first song I ever wrote about Rome.

Most of the stuff on that EP doesn't really feel like me anymore. Pop music isn't necessarily what I feel captures the new person I've become since I've spent time in the spotlight. But my old music encapsulates a fond moment in time. A simpler time. Parts of my high school experience I genuinely enjoyed. My relationship with Rome.

"I'm so happy to hear that," I tell her. "That's one of my favorites."

"Singers have their own favorite songs of theirs? Aren't they all your favorite?"

I laugh. "I'm not sure about all singers, but I know I do."

We spend a long while talking about a ton of things while the rest of the kids play. She asks me what it was like growing up in Fertsville and what I like about living in LA. I tell her all about my "awesome" life now that I've moved to Cali, even if most of it's not true. I just like the way it makes her smile when I tell her about all the cool things that exist outside of this bubble of a small town.

"Do you have a boyfriend now?" she asks eventually.

"No," I answer lightly. "No boyfriend."

"Why not? I'm sure sooo many boys want to date you. You're Aspen Moore!"

"You can't date just any guy," I inform her. "You have to wait for the right one."

"Who's your right one? Have you found him yet?"

What a loaded question from someone so young.

I look over to Rome, who's still playing games with the kids. "I'm not sure. I think so."

"So why isn't *he* your boyfriend?" Ella asks, pointing over at Rome.

"I don't know," I respond honestly. "Life is complicated, I guess."

"It doesn't sound complicated to me."

Of course, it wouldn't.

"Adults are weird," I admit.

"Yeah," Ella agrees. "Even famous ones."

"Come on!" I say, laughing. "Let's go find you a snack."

"Hey, Pen," Rome greets me at the snack table, putting his hand on the small of my back. "How's it going over here?"

"Great," I reply. "Rome, meet my new friend, Ella."

"Hi, Ella," he says. "I'm Roman." At six foot two, he practically towers above both her and me at five foot six.

Ella waves. "Hi, Roman."

"Are you enjoying your first day so far?" he asks her.

"Yeah… I've made a whole new friend, and these are my favorite chips!"

My heart melts. Literally.

"I'm glad to hear you're enjoying yourself, Ella," Rome says.

"Thanks, guys!" Ella says, wrapping us both up in a hug. "I'm so glad my mom signed me up."

As much as I was scared of it before, maybe this directing thing might not be so bad after all.

CHAPTER
eight

"Enchanted (Taylor's Version)" by Taylor Swift

November, Seven Years Ago

The fifteen-minute walk to my house after the game feels more like five. The cool breeze makes me wish I'd brought a jacket. Though it's early November, it was fairly hot and sunny out when I left. But you never know with Pennsylvania weather. It can never decide which season it wants to be.

"This is mine coming up on the right," I tell Rome as we approach my house, pointing toward it.

"I knew you lived on Reeder Street, but I wasn't sure which was yours."

"How did you know that?"

"Margo lives down the street from you. She said you used to walk to school together in middle school?"

"Yeah, we did."

Back when she still wanted something to do with me.

"What are your plans for the rest of the night?"

"The rest of the night?" I ask. "It's almost ten-thirty! I have to be home by then."

He smiles. "You don't strike me as the type of girl who's asleep by eleven."

"Okay," I reply, not quite sure what he means by that.

I am the kind of girl who goes to sleep by eleven. Unless I'm songwriting, of course, then I just fall asleep whenever my fingers are too tired to keep playing.

"So, what are your plans after I drop you off?" Rome asks.

It feels strange to share with him so much about my personal time.

"I'll take a shower. Eat some more food. Play my guitar—"

"You play guitar?" he asks, eyes widening.

"A little bit. I'm not very good."

He shrugs me off. "I'm sure you're amazing. What songs do you play?"

"You know," I mutter. "Songs."

"Come on, give me an artist. I already know you like Fleetwood Mac."

God. There he goes reminding me of that dreaded talent show performance.

"If I'm being honest—"

"As I'd expect you to be," he says.

"I usually write my own," I finish.

He stares at me. "You're a songwriter too?"

"Well, I wouldn't go as far as to say that..."

And after the embarrassment I faced at the talent show, I don't think I'd go as far as to call myself a singer either.

"Okay," I say, changing the subject. "It looks like we're here."

"That we are."

We turn and stop at the gate to my backyard, just steps away from my front porch. The streetlights are off, but the small lamp on my front lawn remains lit as cars pass us by. The lights are off in my house, though, signifying my parents already went to bed.

Guess they weren't too concerned about my curfew, after all.

We stare at each other for a while as the energy shifts between us. There's a slight heat and intensity now behind his eyes, drawing me in. I want to go inside so I can escape the burn of his gaze, but he takes my hand in his, pulling me closer, releasing butterflies in my stomach. My breath quickens as the warmth of his hand in mine takes away a bit of the cold.

He brings his other one up to my cheek, cupping my face. I look down at his hand, but he brings my face back up to look at him.

He leans into me. Closer. And closer.

"You know what I think," he whispers.

"Another one of your brilliant ideas?"

"I think you should take me inside and play me a song."

Moment officially ruined.

"You're kidding, right?" I ask him, pulling away.

"Why would I be kidding?"

"It's almost eleven o'clock!" I whisper-shout. "Don't you have somewhere else to be? Like, I don't know, home? Jeff's?"

"Nope," he replies coolly. "I've got nothing but time."

I give him the death stare. "If my parents find you in my room at this hour, they're gonna kill me."

Sure, my mom was happy that I wanted to go to a game, but I definitely don't think she'd be happy to find a hot football player in my room past curfew.

"Uh-huh," he responds.

"Ground me for life, actually."

"Do you usually stay up late playing guitar?"

"I mean, sometimes," I reply.

He nods. "Perfect. They won't suspect a thing."

I hesitate.

"Come on, Pen. I'm dying to hear your beautiful voice."

His words ignite a thousand little flares throughout my body, and it feels like it's just us alone in our own little world underneath the starlight.

"You're out by midnight," I tell him.

"Scout's honor," he says, a smirk on his face.

I shove him but don't actually manage to move him much. "Just shut up and walk quietly."

Rome locks his lips and throws away the key.

CHAPTER
nine

"Clarity (feat. Foxes)" by Zedd

November, Present

There are ten more minutes until auditions start, and I'm more nervous than I'd care to admit. In a regular audition, I recognize that whether or not I get cast is largely circumstantial. Everything isn't up to me. But now? I'm in full control. And it's nerve-wracking, to say the least.

Rome and I have set up a table in front of the stage where auditions will be held. Parents and children arrived at the church around twenty minutes ago, anticipating when auditions are set to start. I mingled with a few of them and tried to be as nice as possible. And most were kind to my face, which I appreciate.

I anxiously fiddle with my pen and paper from my seat.

Rome leans over and whispers softly in my ear, sending goosebumps all over my body. "Don't stress, *mi cielo*. It's all going to work out great."

"How do you know I'm stressing?"

"Because you're making the cute little scrunchy face."

"I do not make a scrunchy face." Although I'm aware I most definitely do.

He simply smiles at me.

I recognize the first little girl to audition almost immediately. Her bright, shoulder-length auburn hair and emerald-green eyes make her easily recognizable.

She's the girl who was mean to Ella.

Sporting shimmery gold eyeshadow and bright red lipstick, she adorably matches her hair color. Her clothes are the kind I wish I could have afforded at her age, a Burberry top, and Prada sneakers.

Smiling at me now, she seems sweet. But I can't seem to get what she said to Ella out of my mind. The awful way she made her feel. Despite this, I swallow it down. I'm a director and an adult, meaning I have to treat her the same as I would the other kids.

"Hi," Rome says as she walks through the stage door. "What's your name?"

"My name's Millie," she responds cheerfully.

I love her enthusiastic energy. I appreciate a break from the nervous energy of the kids and parents in the lobby. No amount of cookies and hot chocolate was going to fix that.

"Hey, Millie. Will you be singing for us today in addition to performing the monologue?"

"Yup! I'm a shoo-in for Mary."

"Well," he responds, smiling. "I appreciate your confidence."

"Yes," I add with as much cheer as I can muster. "Start whenever you're ready."

I watch her performance intently. Though I love her vibe, this monologue is about Mary finding out she's having baby Jesus, and Millie gives us Hollywood drama queen.

"Thanks, Millie, that was great!" I say as she takes a dramatic bow.

"Should I sing now?"

"Yes," Rome replies. "Go for it."

Millie sings her rendition of "O Come Little Children," and she's definitely got raw potential. With a bit of breath control and coaching, I could make this number really good.

Rome beams next to me. But something about casting her as Mary doesn't feel quite right to me.

"Thanks again, Millie," I say once she's finished. "That was wonderful. We'll let you know in about a week."

"Yup. Thanks for sharing your talent with us," Rome chimes in. "Head into the lobby. We'll call the next person out in a few minutes."

As the next few kids audition, I take notes on each performance and mark down if anyone strikes me as fitting for a certain part. A boy named Brody seems like a good fit for Caesar Augustus or Gabriel, and there are a few other little boys I flag for Joseph or Gabriel.

There are a bunch of super-talented little girls I think will be perfect to play angels. A few have similar mannerisms and ways of performing their scene, which makes me think that they may have practiced together. Evie and Grace were so alike that I immediately want them to be angels together. Many of them didn't audition for Mary, which makes my life a lot easier.

There are a few things I think everyone needs to work on, obviously, but I think that will come with knowing the script better and a brief discussion on character choices.

It's toward the end of our day when Ella finally comes in to audition. She's wearing pigtail braids and a huge smile. I can't say I wasn't most excited to see her today out of all the other kids, but I am trying to be fair.

I greet her with a warm smile. "Hey, Ella."

"Hi, Aspen…Roman."

"What part will you be auditioning for today?" I ask.

Her face lights up. "Mary."

Oh my God. It makes me so happy to see that she's putting herself out there like this.

"That's wonderful, Ella," Roman says. "Let's see what you've got."

I want her to be amazing. I want her to do well. I already have all these plans for her circling around in my head. And I don't have anything to worry about, at least not in the acting department.

Ella is magic during her scene. Honestly. And it's not just because she's my favorite or anything like that. She's special.

When she's done, I clap enthusiastically. "That was amazing, Ella! Thank you so much for sharing your talent with us."

"Yes," says Rome. "You were terrific."

"Thank you so much," she responds. "I was nervous."

"We couldn't tell," I answer. "It was awesome. Really."

She smiles, but after a moment, it disappears, and worry filters through instead. "Is it time for me to do my song?"

"Yes!" I encourage. "Go ahead."

She starts the song, and I can read the concentration on her face. Subsequently, her voice cracks on the opening note. I'm immediately crushed for her, knowing this will affect her confidence going forward.

"It's okay," says Rome. "Start again whenever you're ready."

She takes in a deep breath, collects herself, and starts again.

Though soft and breathy, unlike Millie's, her voice holds a lot of power. She's a beautiful singer. And honestly, a little confidence and a few voice lessons might be all she really needs.

When Ella gets to the chorus, she fumbles and trips over the words. Rome and I look at each other, unsure of what to say. I think I've heard all I need to hear. I already know she'll be perfect.

"I'm sorry!" Ella cries, clearly on the verge of tears. "Can I do it again?"

"Yes," I say back, a little too quickly. "Of course. Just take a deep breath."

She starts again and opens her mouth, but she just can't seem to do it. She starts and then stops continuously, forgetting words or getting ahead of herself.

"It's okay," says Rome. "Take your time."

But now I can clearly see that the situation has gone from bad to worse. She's crying, hyperventilating, and almost inconsolable to the point where I wonder if I should call her parents.

It breaks my heart to see her this way, upset over something so insignificant in the grand scheme of life. I want nothing more than to make her understand that it will be okay. My opinion of her hasn't changed. Not in the slightest.

During my first few months in LA, there was no one who understood the industry to tell me that I would recover from the multitude of rejections I received. No one to tell me that one mistake wasn't going to make or break my career.

Those nights involved a lot of loneliness and crying to myself, just wanting to pack my bags and go home. Stay in the comfort of the arms of the man I was still so in love with.

But I couldn't do that to me.

I couldn't give up on my dream to make something of myself.

"Ella," I say gently. "Don't cry. Not over this."

"I messed everything up," she replies. "I wanted this part so bad…"

"Aw." I can hardly hold back the emotion myself. I want to cry just looking at her. Stressing about auditioning for me? "You were wonderful. You are so talented."

Ella sniffles. "I wanted to prove to everyone that I could do it."

"I know you did, but their opinions shouldn't matter to you like this. In the long run, this won't matter as much as you think it will. These people won't matter as much as you think they do. Besides, who's to say you won't get it?"

"Okay," she says, hope in her eyes.

"Okay," I say. "Take a deep breath and grab some water from the fountain. Good job. You were great today."

"Thank you," she says, wiping her tears before walking out the door.

"Wow, Pen," says Rome after she leaves.

I stand up and brush off my jeans. "What?"

"Who told you that you weren't good with kids?"

CHAPTER
ten

"Treacherous (Taylor's Version)" by Taylor Swift

November, Seven Years Ago

Thank goodness my parents have gone to bed by the time we arrive. I'm sure they'll be up bright and early to ask me about my night, though. I take Roman by the hand and lead him up the stairs extra cautiously.

When we make it to my room, I sit on my bed and motion for him to join me. I'm glad I cleaned it last weekend, so nothing is really out of place aside from a small pile of clothes by my closet door.

"If they hear me talking to someone, they're going to come to see what's going on."

"Trust me, Pen," he says in the gruffest whisper I've ever heard. "I've got this."

It melts me to my core.

I sit on my bed and grab my black acoustic guitar off its stand. "Okay. What do you want to hear?"

"One of your songs, obviously!"

I groan. "I have a lot of songs."

"Okay," he says, considering. "Play me your favorite song to play alone in your room."

I smile. "Wow. Specific."

"First, I was too broad, and now I'm too specific?"

"No, no, I can handle this," I say.

So many choices are circling around in my head. But I decide on a song that's special to me. And since I wrote it about a year ago, it's easy to play without stressing too much about it.

I introduce the song as if I'm on a stage. "This is called Dead Plants."

"Dead plants? How morbid."

I smack him in the chest. "Are you listening or not?"

"I am," he tells me, his tone suddenly intensifying. "I promise."

I take a deep breath and grab my pick before strumming out the short intro. I take in another quick breath. Then I begin.

The little things seem harder to shake
Your memory I cannot erase
But you know that I hoped for my sake
I'd move on

I guess I should've seen the signs
I know what I said last time
that I would wait for right
I'd stay strong

I overwatered you over eager that you'd grow
You know I never thought that you'd leave me so
I poured it all into you
You were my favorite plant that never grew

I stop abruptly as my last chord rings out. "That was just a verse and chorus, but…."

"Holy shit!"

I immediately want to hide. "That bad?"

"That amazing. How long have you been hiding that beautiful voice?"

"Thank you," I say.

"No. Thank you for playing that for me."

His words warm my chest. "It was my pleasure."

"Who'd you write it about?" he asks uncertainly. "Was it an ex or…?"

"A friendship breakup," I say quickly. "They say those are the worst ones, so…."

"Yeah, I get that," he replies, sounding oddly relieved. "You want to talk about it?"

"I'm kind of over it now," I tell him. "I put all my emotions into the song."

"Well, I'm always here if you do."

I think about what he's offering me. I haven't had someone my own age to talk to about this sort of thing with in a while.

"I've never been the best at keeping friends," I say.

"You think it's something about you?" He looks confused.

"I don't know. It just happens a lot, I guess. Can it always be about the other person?"

"Who did you write the song about?"

I hesitate. I can't decide if telling him is a good idea. I don't want to talk poorly about someone he considers a friend. A small part of me is also scared that he'll tell her and their entire friend group and cause them to treat me even worse than they do now.

But I feel like I can tell him anything. I want to tell him anything.

"Margo," I say. "I know you eat lunch with her and her friends."

"Margo, Yeah," he replies. "Her mom and mine are friends. We're not super close or anything, but I see her a lot."

"Oh," I respond, immediately regretting saying anything. "Well, I don't want to skew your perception of her or anything."

"No, please. Tell me the story," he pleads. "If you want to."

I suck in a breath. "There honestly isn't much to tell. Hanging out with me brought down her popularity, I guess. By the end of eighth grade, she'd decided she couldn't handle it anymore."

We'd been friends since sixth grade when we were paired together for an art project. We immediately bonded over our love for the Cheetah Girls movies and decided we *needed* to go as them for Halloween.

The rest was history.

"She dropped you just like that?"

"I mean, she started responding to my texts less and less. She stopped eating lunch with me after a while and started eating lunch with Rina and her friends. And then eventually, we just faded away."

"I'm so sorry, Pen," he says in a voice so deep and sincere, I can tell he means it.

"Don't be sorry. You don't need to feel sorry for me. I'm perfectly fine, as you can tell."

"Yes," he says, laughing. "In peak condition… I can't really say I know too much about losing friends, but things definitely changed a lot for me when I moved here."

Though I'm not really friends with Roman, I do know that he moved here in seventh grade. Fertsville is such a small town everyone notices when a new kid joins our grade.

"You lost touch with your friends from home?" I ask, moving the guitar strap off my shoulders and placing the instrument back onto the stand.

"Sort of. They started seeing me differently after I came here, and after a while, they stopped visiting as much. Or calling."

"Where did you use to live?"

"Cranfeld," he replies.

"Oh!" I tuck a strand of hair behind my ear. "That's not too far from here. Did you go back often?"

Rome grimaces. "Yeah, for a while."

It's so strange to realize we have more in common than I previously thought. The "popular" kids always seem like they have no problems. Like the world is constantly in their favor. But Rome is so different. And it makes me feel strange that I judged him for so long.

"Why'd you stop?" I ask.

"We grew apart, I guess. People change. I got caught up in football and the crowd here."

"Do all your old friends still hang out?"

He nods. "They do."

"That sucks, Rome. I'm really sorry." And I really mean this. I know how much it hurts to lose a friend.

He shrugs but then gives me one of his stares. The kind where I don't know what he's about to say, but I know it's going to make me melt. "I like it when you call me that."

"What?" I laugh. "Rome?"

"Yeah," he says. "I like it." And I like his smile.

"Okay," I reply, getting butterflies again. "I'll bear that in mind."

I can't get over how new and exciting this all feels. I get this sort of bubbly feeling in my chest, like a million little sparks flying whenever he smiles at me.

"Can I try something?" he asks, an intensity in his eyes.

"What?" I say, slightly nervous. My stomach drops as I prepare myself for anything.

His face is just inches from mine now. My head is telling me to shift away, but my body won't allow me to do this.

He presses his lips to mine in a gentle kiss. It shocks me for just a second, but eventually, I'm able to lean into it. He takes the lead, and I give into that, feeling completely hooked on this foreign feeling. Sure, Harry and I had kissed before, but it didn't feel as right as this. He detaches his lips from mine a little too soon.

He breathes in. "Asp—"

"Can we do that again?"

He laughs. "Yeah. Definitely."

We kiss for a second time, warmth filling me once again. It's been a while since I've kissed anybody like this, and it feels so good. He doesn't make a move to go further like I expect him to. He doesn't show that he wants anything more. Not that I'd give it anyway. I'm nowhere near ready to take things to that stage.

"Let me take you out to dinner," he says after pulling away slowly.

"Yeah," I mumble, a wave of tiredness suddenly overtaking me. "Definitely."

"Wow," he comments. "It was really that easy."

I lie back on my pillow. "Why wouldn't it be?"

"I don't know. But I've been stressing about how to ask you all week. Turns out all I had to do was kiss you."

He's been stressing about me?

"Don't stress," I answer. "It's bad for your health."

"Okay." He chuckles. "I'll take that under advisement."

"Do you want to walk me out now?" he asks cautiously. "You know, make sure your parents don't find me here?"

"In a minute." My legs are still crossed over his as I'm lying down, and he's sitting up with his back against the wall.

"A minute?"

"Yup," I whisper.

"Okay."

"Okay."

But before I know it, I'm drifting off to sleep, far away from the world of my parents, or anyone else but the two of us.

CHAPTER
eleven

"This Is Why We Can't Have Nice Things" by Taylor Swift

November, Present

Snow falls on Rome and me as we walk downtown to Sally's Diner. Today is the very first snow of the season. Pretty soon, fall is going to end, and Fertsville will go into full Christmas mode. As a kid, the holiday lights and outdoor ice rink were my absolute favorite parts of the holidays. With Thanksgiving only days away, everything is starting to feel a bit more real.

We walk in tandem, holding cups of hot chocolate he bought for us. Rome and I agreed to go for lunch today to discuss casting after the auditions. At first, he suggested I come back to his place, but I knew that would end in disaster. The temptation would eventually become too much for us to handle, and I'd give in, therefore ruining my chances of keeping my heart intact. If that's even possible.

The smell of burger grease fills the air with childhood memories as I open the doors to the diner, which is just down the block from the church.

I've known the owner, Sally, since I began to come as a kid. I quickly became one of her most frequent customers, coming here most days after school for a burger, fries, and an Oreo milkshake. When I turned fifteen, she hired me as a waitress. It's one of the ways I saved up money for my move to LA, aside from babysitting.

"Aspen!" calls Sally as she walks out from behind the counter. "Do my eyes deceive me? Is it really you?"

She looks as she always has, her bright red hair tied into a tight bun on top of her head.

"Hi, Ms. Sally. It's great to see you."

"It's a pleasure to see you again, Aspen. And you too, Roman."

"Hey, Ms. Sally. It's always good to see you too."

"Come, right here," she says as she ushers us over to a secluded table by the back, where I typically sit. "Best seat in the house."

"Thanks so much," Rome says, sliding into the booth.

"Y'all ready to order?"

"I'll have fries and an Oreo milkshake." I look at Rome. "He'll have the same but add extra bacon on the burger. Thanks."

Rome has ordered the exact same thing for years. It doesn't take much thought to know what he wants.

She looks at me, then him, then me again, before giving us a small smirk. "Coming right up."

"Hey," Rome says as soon as Sally's gone. "What if my order had changed? What if I was in the mood for something else?"

I just laugh. "It hasn't, and you're not."

He returns my laughter.

"Okay," I say. "Back to business. We've got to cast Dad's play. Narrator?"

"I thought Joey was good, but not for Joseph like he wanted. Maybe he'd be a good narrator?"

"I agree that he's not quite right for Joseph. I think he's got the confidence and a strong voice for the narrator. Wow. This is easier than I thought. Next?"

"Joseph? It's between Ryan and Lucas for me."

"What about Nick?" I definitely liked him the best out of the three.

"You're right," he says, double-checking his notes. "He was good, too." Rome sits deep in thought for a long while.

"Okay, let's break this down," I suggest. "Ryan. What did you like about him?"

"I really believed him."

"Okay, that's always good. I liked him, but I feel like something was off in his delivery of certain lines. I can't remember specifically. I feel like I liked the others a little better."

"Yeah, that makes sense."

"How about Lucas?"

"I don't know," Rome says. "The same things, I guess. I'm not the expert at this."

"Okay. Well, I already know who I want, but I don't want to feel like I'm making all the decisions without you having any say. So, let's talk this through, and if you still have no idea after that, I'll give you my opinion."

"I don't really have too much to say on the strength of their performances. I just know I liked them all."

"Is that all you wrote down?" I ask him.

"What?"

"What did you write in your notebook?" I ask, not waiting for his response and instead taking it from him.

"Seriously?"

It's as I suspected. He only wrote character names and names of people he thought fit the part underneath in his messy, all-caps handwriting.

"What?" he asks, faking pain. "I did the best I could!"

"No, no," I cajole. "We can work with this."

We spend the next several minutes talking through why Rome wrote each boy down and why he'd make a good Joseph. Obviously, my heart's still set on Nick, but he's given me things to consider about the other two.

"Okay," I say. "I think all of that's great. Now that we've discussed it, who do you see playing the part best?"

"Nick," he replies confidently. "Or maybe Lucas...."

"No! Go with your gut."

"Yeah," he says, laughing. "*My* gut."

A server, presumably someone new, arrives at our table with the food. I've never seen him around town before, though I guess I haven't been around these past few months. By the looks of him, I'm guessing he's in high school. He doesn't look me in the eye as he sets my plate down in front of me.

"Thanks, man," says Rome as the server sets his down.

"Yeah, thanks," I say. The boy smiles at Rome but doesn't even look at me before scurrying away.

"Do I intimidate people?" I remark, only half joking.

"I don't know. Probably," he says with a smile.

"How about we cast Lucas as Gabriel?"

"That sounds good," he answers while taking a bite of his bacon.

"Great. Another lead out of the way."

I pick up my glass to take a sip of my milkshake as we're interrupted by a woman across the restaurant calling, "Aspen! Is that really you?"

At first, I smile, thinking it's just a fan or another employee of the diner who I haven't seen in a while, but I couldn't be more wrong.

Filled with dread, I start to sink into my seat.

Rina, of all people, is here, marching across the restaurant.

In this diner.

Today.

"Oh my God, Roman, I almost didn't see you there," Rina says. She places a hand on his shoulder, and my knuckles turn white due to the strength with which I'm holding my glass. "How are you? I feel like we don't hang out as much as we should."

"Hey," Rome wearily replies, breaking the tension of my prolonged silence. "I'm great, thanks."

Rina shifts her focus to me. "What a surprise to see you here! It's been so long."

And thank God for that.

I can't stand the way I act around her. I can't stand to see her goddamn face. I'm finally successful. I've finally done it. Why do I still feel the need to prove myself around her?

No matter how rich or successful or famous I become, I'll always shrink in her presence.

"Yeah," I finally manage to say, "it's been a while."

"What are you doing in Fertsville?"

I run my fingers through a lock of my hair. "Just visiting for a few weeks."

"I heard some rumors about you and Cane Dawson back in LA. A shame, really. And his girlfriend is so much uglier than you!"

I can see Rome tense up across from me.

"We never dated," I say, looking straight at Rome. "I never even kissed him."

"Oh, I find that so hard to believe. The chemistry you two had on stage was off the charts! I saw it all over the internet."

Yes. Those dreaded pictures they took of us face-to-face when I invited his band out to sing my last song with me during our closing show.

"Well, believe it. He's with Sierra. Not me."

"Things always change," she responds cheerfully, painfully oblivious to my feelings. "I wanted to come to see you guys in Philly, but your tickets sell out in minutes."

"Yeah," I repeat. "I'm really grateful to all my fans and everyone who comes to my shows."

"You know it's almost hard to believe," she throws in. "Back when we were kids, I never would have envisioned this path for you."

"Miracles happen every day," I say dryly.

Rome finally pipes in. "Your success is no miracle, Pen. You're super talented."

I look over at him. "Thanks, I appreciate that."

"Maybe one day you'll say it like you mean it," he whispers just loud enough so only I can hear.

"Well, I've got to go," chirps Rina. "I was just here to pick up my food. But we should catch up sometime!"

"Mm-hm," I mutter.

"I still work at the makeup counter downtown. You know Chanel? So you know where to find me." And with that, she's off.

"Well, she's always been a pleasure."

"I'm sorry she said that, Rome. People just took certain pictures out of context. It was nothing. I swear."

"Relax," he tells me. "You don't have anything to prove. It's not like you owe me anything."

This situation doesn't seem to bother him, but it sure as hell bothers me.

I know it's true, but I really wish he wouldn't phrase it like that. Like he doesn't care who I see. Like he doesn't want to know.

I've never once asked him who he's been with while I'm gone. But not because I didn't want to know. Because I know it would hurt me too badly to find out he has no issue moving on during the in-between, meanwhile I think about him in every guy I meet.

I haven't been able to go on normal dates or hook up with anyone in years. I tried to when I first got to LA, but I never felt the way I thought I should. The butterflies weren't there.

After Keith, I couldn't bring myself to be with anyone else. The thought of letting some guy I barely know touch me ever again scared the shit out of me.

Rome was different. He was my everything. He was *safe*. And some days, I couldn't even feel okay around him.

It was all too much to process. And it's still too much to think about.

"Next role," Rome says. "Mary."

"I think it should be Ella."

"What about Millie? You know she was really good too."

"Ella just seems more." I suck in a breath before letting it out. "Coachable."

Rome shakes his head. "You don't always get to work with people you like."

It hurts that he thinks I need to be reminded of this. "Trust me, Rome. I know that."

Working with my former TV costar Keith for so long and putting up with as much shit as I did really fucked me up. He knows this better than anyone. He saw the state I was in when I came home after everything went down.

"Of course you do," he says quickly, putting his hand on my forearm. "I was just saying—"

"No, I get it. And I hear you, but I still think we should go with Ella."

"I don't know. I think she's still got a lot to work on. She seemed too nervous. I'm not sure if she can handle the lead part, and I would never want to put her in a position where she gets too nervous on stage. I want this to be a good experience for her."

"Trust me," I plead. "We can work with her. I know she'll be amazing if we give her the chance."

I can almost see the wheels turning in his head. "If you think this is what's best."

"I do! Trust me. She's gonna be amazing."

"So where do we cast Millie?" he asks after a moment.

"Her, Evie, and Grace can all be angels. She'll still get to sing. It'll be perfect, I promise."

"Okay. But only because I trust you."

We finish casting the play over a shared piece of apple pie. Sally makes the *best* apple pie. Better even than Mom's.

Things back in Fertsville are starting to feel like how they used to be, and given my current predicament, I'm enjoying the return to my roots. But what happens when I have to leave the bubble of Fertsville and return back to my reality?

CHAPTER
twelve

"bored&blind" by Ella Jane

November, Seven Years Ago

$\mathcal{P}$en!" Roman calls from across the cafeteria as I walk in Monday morning.

I'm sure I had a goofy smile on my face—I had just been replaying our kiss from Friday night. And waking up Saturday morning to find Roman asleep on my bedroom carpet. I'd had to sneak him out through the garage…

He calls my name again. "Aspen! Come sit with us!"

I wipe the smile off. He knows damn well I won't want to sit at his lunch table. I normally sit at the table farthest to the right, away from his clique, with a nice group of girls. I'm not close to them or anything, but they've always been welcoming.

"Hey, Roman," I say as I walk over with my tray of lasagna. "What's up?" I don't make a move to sit at the crowded table. And nobody moves over to make space. Rina and her friends are tittering with one another.

"Nothing. Just want you to sit with us today." It feels like a million eyes are locked in on my face.

"No, it's okay," I say. "I should probably go back to my table."

"Yeah," says Rina. "She doesn't really have anything in common with *us* anyway. Right?"

Margo is the first to laugh, patting Rina on the shoulder as if she should be proud of the way she spoke to me. It hurts that after spending so many days over at my house, getting to know me better than anyone else had, that she could do this to me.

"It's one day, Pen," he says, ignoring Margo completely. "I'm sure they can spare you for a day." He tugs on my arm, moves his backpack, and pulls me to the bench next to him.

I try to speak, but the words stay put in my throat. I set my tray down, open my bottle of water, and chug.

"How was your weekend?" Rome asks after about a minute.

I try my best to keep my composure. His question seems normal enough. "Normal. You?"

He gives me a big smile, and it's obviously what he's about to hint at. "Pretty good. Great start to my Saturday."

Dread rises in my stomach. I really don't want him to bring this up right now. What will everyone say if they find out he spent the night at my house? Will they think something happened between us?

I try to calm myself. Only we know what he's referencing. "I can only imagine," I say dryly.

I take a bite of my lasagna. Everything about this cafeteria puts me on edge. The room's too loud. The smacking of lips, sounds of people chewing from miles away. The crappy lunch food they serve. The endless chatter. If I were allowed to eat my food in the library, I would.

"I'm thinking of throwing another party at my house this weekend," Jeff says, his mouth full. "My parents are going out of town."

"Again?" asks another one of the guys, Chase.

"Yeah, man," he says. "My mom's birthday is coming up, so he's taking her on a surprise vacation."

It's only now I learn the reason Jeff throws parties all the time. His dad is constantly out of town and asks his older cousin to come keep an eye on him for the weekend. Since his cousin is only twenty-two and has other things to worry about, he doesn't give a crap what Jeff does as long as he cleans everything up after. Plus, I heard his house is huge. He lives in the nicest part of town, so I guess that's to be expected.

Everyone hears about his parties. All of the well-known kids in our town are invited, even underclassmen. It's impossible to miss the talk of Jeff's "epic" parties in the halls.

"You should stop by this time, Aspen," he says.

"Yeah," offers Roman. "I'll swing by and pick you up."

The universe is playing a joke on me. It must be. I've never been to a real party in my life. While I don't know much about them other than what I've seen in the movies, I know they're a lot.

Drinking, dancing, loud music, smoking. I need to be eased into the social scene. Maybe I could try approaching some of the girls I sit with at lunch and ask them to hang out or something. But I can't just go to my first party with a bunch of people I'm constantly on edge around.

"I don't know," I answer in a shy tone I've hardly heard myself speak before. "I've got a big test coming up soon for AP Lang."

All the girls snicker.

"That test sounds pretty serious. Seems like you should stay home," Rina says, rolling her eyes.

"Yeah, maybe," I say, looking right at her. "Or I don't know. Maybe I'll go."

"Awesome," Rome says as if it's a done deal.

The conversation breaks into pieces. The guys are discussing their plans for getting alcohol for the party. I play with my food. Being here makes me feel so much worse than at my other table. There, I don't feel judged. Or hated.

The girls are sitting close, whispering to one another. If people don't like me, they typically ignore me. But now I'm dealing with this face-to-face.

"I don't even know why she's sitting here," I hear Laura say. They all laugh.

"Yeah," says Anna, another girl who I don't see too often. "Some people just can't take a hint."

"Guys," Rome says, "shut the fuck up. Seriously."

Everyone is shocked into silence.

My chair scrapes across the floor as I pick up my tray and leave the table.

Roman looks over to me, then back at the group, then immediately follows.

I feel disrespected on a level I haven't been before. And it hurts more than I care to admit.

"Where are you going, man?" Chase calls.

"I'll see you guys later," Roman throws over his shoulder.

He calls my name as I'm making my way over to clear my plate.

"Pen," he says. "Wait up."

I don't know what to think. Maybe I like the idea of him following me. I like that he wants to check in on me. But it's probably just pity.

"You can go back to your table, Roman. Those are your friends. I never wanted to come in between you guys. Don't worry. I'm okay."

And in a few minutes, I will be. I'll sink into one of the library couches and spend the next twenty minutes studying in peace. The best way to recharge.

But he's persistent. "I want to eat with you. I called you over because I wanted to spend time with you. Don't walk away from me because you don't like those girls. They're assholes. I like you. You like me and—"

"You think I like you?" I ask over a lump in my throat.

"Don't you?"

I pause, really considering what I'm about to say. "Why do you hang out with all those girls if you don't like them?"

"Maybe I shouldn't anymore," he replies, staring down at his sneakers. "The guys were all I had when I moved here. Football was my way to make friends. They hang out with the girls, so I hang out with them. But I'm not sure they're not the kind of people I want to be around anymore."

He empties his tray into the garbage and sets it on top of the pile.

"Something about you is different from everyone else in this town in a way I can't really explain. I like being around you. I like how you make me feel."

I have no idea how to respond to his kind words or react to the way he stuck up for me earlier. All I know is that something about him feels different from anyone I've met here too.

"I'm gonna go to the library. You want to come with me?"

He smiles. "Yeah, Pen. Of course."

It's so strange for me to be doing this. Inviting someone like him into my safe space during the time I like to keep for just me. But despite how wrong it seems on paper, it feels so right.

CHAPTER
thirteen

"New Romantics (Taylor's Version)" by Taylor Swift

November, Present

*A*lthough you might think my incident with Rina at the diner would have stopped me from going back again, it's always been a home base for me in Fertsville, so it's natural for me to come back here whenever I want to clear my head. I order a caramel latte and sink back behind the same table I sat at yesterday. My table.

The ambiance here is perfect for writing, so maybe I can write some lyrics and piece them together later. I always came here in high school to generate new ideas and do my homework, even when I wasn't working a shift that day. This diner was the birthplace of two of the songs on my first EP. I hope it helps me out of the writing slump my fallen celebrity seems to have put me in.

The lights are dim, and the soft hum of conversations from the tables makes for decent background noise. I'm staring at the same blank page I have been for the last few minutes when I'm approached by a girl who looks about my age.

Her hair is long, black and curly, her skin a deep shade of brown. She's gorgeous, I must admit, and her style is on point too. She's wearing light wash jeans and a white cashmere sweater, Prada boots on her feet.

I assume she's a fan or someone interested in knowing the dirty details about the drama going on in my life.

"Hey. Can I sit down for a second?"

I swallow my dread and shift my notebook, making room for her at my table. "Sure. What's up?"

"I'm hiding," she informs me, her tone in such a loud whisper it makes it hard to take her seriously.

"From who?" I ask, looking over at the direction she's staring in.

"My ex-boyfriend." She attempts to hide behind the napkin dispenser. "He can't know I'm in here."

I look toward the window to see a tall brunette man standing outside, taking a phone call.

She obviously has no idea who I am. If she did, she never would have chosen to hide next to me. This is wonderfully refreshing, given the current predicament I find myself in.

I point to him. "Is that the man you're talking about?"

She nods her head.

"Why can't he know you're in here?"

"He's been calling me for weeks since I moved out of our apartment. This is just my luck. The day I decide to leave my house is the day I run into him!"

I can tell she's in a great deal of emotional distress right now. If her furrowed brows and hyperventilating didn't give it away, the way she clings to my hands as she braces herself certainly does.

It's been so long since I've had someone to talk about this kind of stuff with. And for once, it might be nice to focus on problems that don't involve me.

Her ex stalks into the restaurant, scanning the room, but our table's far in the back and hidden off. Despite this, I move my chair in a little more and shield her from his gaze. I would tell her to go to the bathroom, but he's blocking the entrance. There's no escaping now unless she wants to be spotted.

The man is tall, not as tall as Rome, but maybe around six feet. His dark brown hair is slicked and combed back into a clean look. He's wearing an all-gray suit and matching loafers. I assume he works in finance or something like that. I've met his type before through agency events and all the time I've spent around my management firm and my lawyers.

Everything about him screams pretentious.

"Thank you so much for letting me join you," she replies. "You're a lifesaver."

"It's going to be okay," I reply. I take the conversation a little further, hoping I'm not being too invasive. "Why did you break up?"

"I found out he cheated on me with like twenty other girls. Obviously, I dumped his ass within the hour."

I've never understood it. How can men cheat on girls as beautiful as her or Sierra? Men who clearly never deserved them in the first place? Sure, Sierra's latest ex, Alec, was moderately attractive. But he had the personality of a door handle and never knew when to let things go. They argued all the time, but Sierra genuinely thought he loved her. Until he slept with half the city behind her back.

"Well, whatever you do, do not take him back."

"It's just so hard, you know? We run in the same circles, and our families are obsessed with each other. I mean, I moved out here from Manhattan just for him. And I really miss his cat."

"Trust me. It's not worth being with someone who doesn't value or respect you. It's not about you or anything you've done, but sometimes guys just can't appreciate what they have. Relationships are built on trust and knowing that your partner is fully there for you. Do you think you could ever trust him again?"

She sighs. "Honestly, probably not."

"So, you've got your answer right there. Don't go back to him. But don't hide, either. He can't force you to do anything. You're the one who's got the power in this situation. He wants you back, not the other way around."

I look over again and scan the restaurant, assessing whether or not her ex is still there.

"I think he's gone now."

"Thanks," she says, shooting me a wide smile. "You know, for the hiding me and everything."

"It's no problem. Anytime."

"You sound like you've got it together," she incorrectly assumes. "You got a man or woman in your life?"

"Not in the way I'd like," I reply slowly.

She could be acting for all I know. Waiting for me to drop the bomb so she can sell it to a gossip magazine. But I've felt so… lonely. For weeks.

"I've been on and off with my high school ex for a couple of years now." Her jaw drops. "I guess we never really fell out of love with each other."

"And now you want something more?"

"I just don't think our relationship would even work out long term. I live out in Cali while he's here for school. My situation is super complicated. I'm staying here for a couple of weeks now, so we've decided to keep things platonic. But I'm having a hard time not letting my imagination run wild." It feels a little wrong to imply that this was a mutual decision between us, but I think Rome and I know subconsciously that being just friends is best.

"Why couldn't you guys be something more? What's so complicated about it?"

"He won't move to LA, and I'm out there for my job."

She tucks a strand of curly hair behind her ear. "He wouldn't be willing to go to school out there to be closer to you?"

"Maybe he would. But he won't be happy there. He's said as much. I'd be all he has."

She shrugs. "He'll be in school. He'll make other friends. A fresh start can be good for everyone."

I'm not sure a new group of friends could ever make up for the caveats that come with dating a celebrity. Rome would have to give up his privacy and force himself into a life he never wanted.

"Would you ever move back here? Do something else?"

"I work in an industry that's super specific to LA. If I move, I'll put myself at a disadvantage early in my career."

"Well, I can't say that I have all the answers. As you can tell from how my love life is currently shaping up, I don't. But I think you need to assess if your relationship with this guy is worth fighting for. If you really care about each other, there's always a way to make things work."

"I'll give that some thought."

"Well, thank you," she says. "It's been really nice talking to you, but I need to head out. I was on my way to a yoga class."

This is my chance. I can put myself out there. Try to make the most of these next few weeks.

"Okay," I reply. "Maybe we should do this again sometime. More formally."

"Yes!" she squeals. "Let me get your number."

I grab my phone from my back pocket. "Wait. I just realized I never got your name?"

"Leila," she answers. "And yours?"

"Aspen," I tell her, praying this doesn't cause her to realize who I am.

"Well, it was nice to meet you, Aspen." She pulls me into a hug. "We'll make plans."

I nod. "Yes. We will."

I leave the diner shortly after she does. Leila is so new and refreshing and real, a stark contrast to many of the people I've met over these past few years in LA.

And for a short while, I finally forgot about the stupid media and what they're saying about me.

CHAPTER
fourteen

"Untouchable (Taylor's Version)" by Taylor Swift

November, Seven Years Ago

$\mathcal{I}$ didn't think I was going to go to Jeff's tonight. I told Roman I wasn't interested. That I didn't want to go. But the heart-melting expression on his face the day we kissed still remains clear in my head. Why am I letting Rina and her friends win? I'm in high school. I should be doing things like this. Going out to parties. Having fun.

I asked my mom to take me to the mall yesterday, and she happily obliged.

She curled my hair, and I put on a little more makeup than usual. I add a little eyeliner, smudging it out a bit, and nude pink lipstick instead of my usual clear lip gloss or Chapstick. For my outfit, I found a blue long-sleeve blouse and black skinny jeans.

"You look beautiful, Aspen."

"Thanks, Mom."

"So," she says, "is this boy coming to pick you up?"

We've already gone over all the details for tonight a hundred times.

"I think so. It's just Roman. I told you about him, right?"

She looks around for a few moments like she's trying to remember him. "Yes," she replies. "He lives right around the corner."

A few moments later, there's a knock at the front door.

"Alright," I say. "That's probably him."

She looks impressed. "He's coming to the door to get you. What a gentleman."

I check myself one last time in the mirror before opening the door to let him in.

He looks absolutely gorgeous in his standard loose jeans and a black tee. He stands there, taking me in for a moment, staring right at me with an expression I can't quite place. Something about seeing him like this, on my porch, in the moonlight, gives me chills.

"Wow, Pen," he says under his breath. "You look gorgeous."

"Thanks," I mutter. "You look gorgeous too." It's nerve-wracking when he's looking at me like this.

But then he gives me one of his big smiles, melting me all over again. "I'm really glad you decided to come with me tonight."

"Yeah. Me too."

My mom appears behind me in the doorway, placing her hand on my shoulder.

"Mrs. Moore," says Roman, holding out his hand for her to shake. "It's so nice to finally meet you."

"You too," she says. "Have her back by eleven thirty. Latest."

"Of course," he says, nodding.

"Thanks, Mom," I whisper.

"No problem, honey," she says. "Enjoy your night."

I give her a quick hug and kiss on the cheek, careful not to ruin my makeup.

"You about ready to go?" Roman asks.

"Yeah," I tell him. "I'm ready."

Roman opens the passenger door to his Toyota Tacoma truck, gesturing for me to get inside.

I pause. "Are you sure you want to give me a ride home later?" I don't want him to worry about restricting himself tonight. I want him to have fun.

"Yeah, of course," he replies. "Why wouldn't I?"

"I don't know," I say, getting in and shifting uncomfortably in my seat. "I thought you might want to drink and stuff."

He looks at me like I've offended him. "I obviously wouldn't get drunk and then drive you home. Jesus, Pen."

"I know. I just don't want you to feel like you're babysitting me or anything. I want you to have a good time."

"I will. If I drink anything, it'll be one drink earlier on in the night. I've got precious cargo. I need to be in full control."

"Yeah," I say, blushing slightly. "Thanks."

CHAPTER
fifteen

"The Greatest" by Sia

November, Present

Okay, everyone!" Rome calls out. "Welcome to our first day of rehearsal."

All of the children in the church auditorium erupt in whoops and cheers.

I've been awaiting our first day of rehearsal ever since we finalized the cast list. It was bound to hurt some kids' feelings. But I guess it's part of the reality of directing a show full of kids. Not everyone can play a lead. I'd sent an email with the cast list out to the parents last night with shaking hands.

I know they already think I'm a bad influence on their children. Now I might be responsible for making them upset?

Rome and I brought the kids tons of grocery store holiday cookies and a box of hot chocolate to amp up the mood.

"I know you're all super excited to get your scripts, but first, we want to talk to you all about a few things." I preface.

"We know that not all of you ended up with the parts you wanted," Rome says, "and that that might have made you sad or disappointed. But we also want you guys to know that we are so proud of each and every one of you and that we've cast you where you'll be the greatest fit. Remember, there are no small parts. Only small actors."

The very cliches I'd told myself repeatedly during the start of my career. Though they're hard to believe sometimes, I know they're true.

I nod at him. "Right. But if you have any questions or concerns about where you've been cast, please let us know."

"Alright," says Rome, grabbing the pile of scripts that sit on the table beside us. "With that being said, let's begin."

But soon, everyone is staring, not at Rome, but at a loud voice from the back of the room.

"I just don't understand!" cries Millie, her voice extremely loud. "I did everything perfectly! My school drama teacher says I'm the best kid in our grade. I should be Mary. How could this have happened?"

I could see Ella sinking into her seat as Millie cast her a scathing glance. The whole room, once filled with excitement, goes absolutely silent.

"Okay!" Rome says in an attempt to break up the awkward tension. "It's time to pass out scripts."

He passes a pile of scripts down to the first kid, Nick, who passes the scripts down the line. I do the same on the other end, along with a box of highlighters and pencils.

We briefly explain to them our rules and expectations. We obviously want them to go through their lines and familiarize themselves with the script, but there's no need for them to be memorized anytime soon.

"Remember," I add, "this is super low stress. The goal is to have fun with it."

The kids branch out into scattered conversations. I walk over to collect the now empty box from the highlighters and pencils, then sit back down next to Rome to begin the read-through.

"Okay, everyone," I say. "We're going to read the script. Don't worry too much about character work or anything now if that's going to stress you out. We just want you to have fun with this."

We spend the next few minutes going through each scene, with Rome reading the stage directions. It's beautiful to see our casting decisions coming to life and what the kids are already starting to bring to their parts.

Millie isn't excited to be playing the part of an angel: reading her lines with low energy, as if she doesn't care. At least she showed up.

Shortly after we've finished our table read and passed out snacks for the kids, a tall, lanky red-haired woman enters the auditorium and makes her way toward me. I gather she's irritated from the tense expression on her face.

"Aspen, right?" she says as she approaches me. "I'm Larissa, Millie's mom."

That would make sense. Her auburn hair is a similar shade to her daughter's, and her eyes are the same emerald green.

"Hi," I reply. "Yes, that's me."

I assume she's here to discuss her daughter's role.

"Mom!" shouts Millie, who is sitting next to her friends on the stage, clearly embarrassed. "What are you doing here?"

She ignores her daughter, focusing her attention solely on me. "Could we talk?"

"Sure. Let's go out in the hall."

Larissa marches toward the auditorium door, her heels clacking against the cement floor. I follow behind, leaving a small distance between us, sensing the anger radiating off of her.

"You cast my daughter as a secondary character," she says once the door shuts behind me. "When Millie is clearly lead-character material."

"Oh," I answer. I was prepared to have to deal with Millie…I'm not sure why I hadn't expected to deal with Millie's mom. "Your daughter's amazing, really. I just think the girl we cast fits the part."

"Well, Millie's been doing theater since she was a little girl. We came to see the show at the church last year, and I thought it would be nice to do you all a favor by bringing some *real* talent in here."

I shake my head. "We're delighted to have her talent in the show. She's an angel, meaning she will get to sing as well as have a speaking role."

"Millie doesn't deserve a *few* lines. She deserves the lead! Now, I…"

It's easy to see where Millie may have learned her negative behavior. Her mom is painfully uncaring of others' feelings. I bet she puts a lot of pressure on Millie to be better than everyone else.

"I'm sorry, Larissa, but all casting decisions are final. We've cast a wonderful actress as Ella, and I'd never want to take that away from her."

She scoffs, and the furrow between her brows deepens. "Well, I'm starting to doubt your directing abilities."

"I can assure you that Roman and I have got this under control. I've worked in the industry before. I know what I'm doing."

Larissa isn't fazed by my logic. "And we all saw how your time in the spotlight turned out. If you can't appreciate my daughter for the talent she is, then she won't be in your production after all."

I'm silent at her mention of my fall from grace.

"Mom, stop!" Millie says from the doorway, surprising me by adding, "It's fine. I want to do the show."

Her mom scoffs. "You want to stay here with these people who are treating you like second-rate talent?

She nods. "It's just for fun, Mom. Plus, Grace and Evie are in it."

"If you want to value your fifth-grade friendships more than being treated with respect, fine. Go right ahead!"

With that, she stomps out of the building, slamming the rickety door behind her, leaving her daughter with tears welling in her eyes.

Drawn by the slammed door, Rome pops his head out. "Is everything alright?"

"Yes," Millie quickly replies, anxiously wiping her eyes. "Everything is fine."

Rome nods, then shares a look with me before going back into the auditorium.

"I'm sorry about that, Millie."

She rolls her eyes and flicks her wrist as if this had no effect on her. "It's fine. I'm used to it."

"Well, you shouldn't be. You're very talented, but that doesn't always mean you can get the lead part. And no one should expect that from you all the time."

"Whatever," she replies, turning on her heel and sauntering back to the other kids.

Rome joins me as I follow the child back inside. "What happened?"

"Millie's mom is pissed about her part," I say quietly.

He puts his arm around me and pulls me in for a quick hug.

"Don't worry about it," he says. "I'm sure everything is going to be okay."

I switch topics, not wanting to think about her outburst any longer. "What are your plans for next weekend?"

I know Thanksgiving is coming up, and this time of year is rough for him since he lost his dad as a kid and then his mom six years ago. He's spent quite a few holidays with me at my parent's house, even after we broke up, so it's not like this is out of the ordinary for us.

"I don't know," he shrugs.

"Well, you're always welcome to come over to my parent's house. I'm sure they'd love to have you." And so would I.

He gives me a hug. "I know. Your dad invited me last week. But thanks, Pen. That means a lot to me."

Wow. My parents thought about inviting him before I did?

Suddenly a pang of guilt hits me in my chest for all the holidays I spent away from my family. The holidays I spent with my old group of "friends" or with Sierra.

For all the holidays I spent away from *him*.

"You're welcome," I say. "Really. It's my pleasure."

CHAPTER
sixteen

"Miss Americana and The Heartbreak Prince" by Taylor Swift

November, Seven Years Ago

As we walk inside Jeff's house, the smell of smoke and teenage intoxication hits me. I don't know how to calm the hell down. I've never drunk or smoked. The opportunity has never arisen. And now don't even know if it's something I'd ever want to try.

The only thing keeping me steady right now is Roman's hand in mine. "Do you want a drink?" he asks me.

"Uh, sure."

"*Are* you sure? You don't have to drink if you don't want to. I can get you water if you prefer."

I'm sick of being left out. I want to know how this feels.

"No. I want to try something. Maybe something." I hesitate, searching for the right word. "Light?"

He laughs. "Okay. I got you."

We walk over to the makeshift bar area before Rome hands me a can that reads White Claw on the front of it.

"Here," he says. "Try this."

"Aren't you gonna have one?"

"No. We can just share yours."

"Bold of you to assume I want to share with you."

"God, just try the drink already."

I laugh before taking a small sip.

"Wow," I say, studying the label. "That's not nearly as bad as I thought." It obviously doesn't taste as good as a soda, but it's okay.

Roman takes the drink out of my hand, sips it, and gives it back to me.

"Glad you like it. I usually go for mango, but watermelon's pretty good too."

"Torres!" calls Jeff, emerging from the crowd surrounding us. "Nice to see you guys here, finally."

Roman daps him up. "Hey, man. Good to see you too."

"We got a game of beer pong going downstairs if y'all wanna join. Most of the teams are down there right now."

"We're not planning on drinking much tonight, but it won't hurt to watch."

"Come on, man! Live a little."

The loud music fades to a comfortable volume the farther down the stairs we go. Roman grabs my hand again, reassuring me that he's here.

I scan the room. Not only are some of the guys from Roman's team here—Kevin, John, Derek, Travis, and a few others—Margo, Rina, and their friends are here too. There are a few people I don't recognize, but most I'm at least familiar with.

"Torres!" shouts Kevin.

"Hey, Kev," he replies.

"Nice to see you again, Aspen."

I smile at him. "It's nice to see you too." Most of the guys on the team have been fairly nice to me.

"Torres. You wanna be my partner?"

"I don't know," he replies warily.

"Come on! We gotta kill these losers," Kevin says, nodding to Jeff and Derek.

"I don't know, man. I can't really drink tonight."

"What if." Rina walks forward, placing a hand on his forearm. "You play, and I drink for you?"

He looks uncomfortable, which makes me feel a bit more confident. He's clearly not interested in her.

"Doesn't that defeat the whole purpose?" I ask.

"What?" she responds. "I'm sure it'll still be fun. Right, Roman?"

He looks straight at me.

"I'll do it," I blurt out. I don't even know how to play, but somehow my subconscious thought this would be a good idea.

"What?" She snorts.

"I'll drink for him. He came here with me anyways," I say, trying not to trail off on that last part. Rina scoffs as Margo and her friends snicker behind her.

"Are you sure?" he asks. "I don't think this is a good idea."

"Yeah," I say confidently. "I'm sure."

"Okay, then!" Kevin shouts. "Let's get this party started!"

Roman pulls me next to him.

Rejected, Rina walks away, which makes me so happy, I almost forgot that tonight was my first time trying alcohol. And I have no idea how much I'll be able to tolerate. Maybe I should be worried, but I'm enjoying myself too much to care.

Roman leans over to whisper in my ear. "You don't have to do this if you don't want to. I didn't think you were a big drinker."

I'm immediately on the defensive. "I'm perfectly fine. Don't worry about me."

He simply shakes his head. "I should go get you some water before we start."

I put my hand on his forearm. "Stop treating me like a child. I got this."

Roman shakes his head yet again, obviously still concerned. "I don't think you fully understand what you're getting yourself into."

"Just let me worry about myself. Okay?" If I want this to go smoothly, I need to at least pretend to feel confident.

He turns away from me, whispering, "Whatever you say," under his breath.

"Who's going first?" Derek asks.

"We'll go," says Jeff, handing him the ball and motioning for him to throw.

He throws and misses his shot, but just narrowly. I clap my hands as Roman and Kevin whoop and cheer.

"Kev, you wanna throw first?"

"You got it, man."

Roman takes his shot, and being the person he is, he makes it. "Drink up!" shouts Jeff.

As the minutes pass, I'm having more fun than I ever thought I would at a party like this. It doesn't matter that Rina and Margo are here. All I can think about is the giddy feeling I get when Roman looks over at me or pulls me close. A smile spreads across my face every time Roman celebrates a shot he's made with Kevin.

As time passes and the game continues, I drink at least five plastic cups of beer. It tastes awful in comparison to the mixed drink I had before, like sour apple juice but worse. The cups weren't full, of course, but my head is starting to hurt. I don't say anything, though. I can't. Everyone else has been drinking far more than me, and they're all fine. I know I should tap out, or at the very least pace myself somehow, but I can't. I can't risk the embarrassment. I put myself in this position anyway.

I begin to wobble as I stand next to Roman, catching myself on the side of the table. *Breathe!* I can do this.

By now, most of the cups on both sides are gone, and Kevin and Roman are winning but just narrowly.

I start to stumble backward a little, but Roman catches me.

"Pen!" he says.

I can barely hear him, though. My head is spinning too fast. I wander around aimlessly, looking for a trash can. Or a bucket. Shopping bag. Anything.

The second I open my mouth to ask where the nearest bath-room is, I let it out. All over the floor. The *carpeted* floor.

"Oh my God," I mutter, trying to keep the rest back.

"Bathroom!" shouts Roman. "She needs the bathroom."

"That way," says Kevin.

As I stare at the mess I've made, Roman grabs me by my hand and drags me over to the bathroom. But I don't have much time because I feel even more about to rush out of me.

"Let it all out," Roman says, holding my hair back.

I respond with another shameful gag, wanting nothing more than for all of this to stop. And to sink into the floor beneath me. Just as I think it's over, I hunch again, hurling into the toilet bowl.

Through all of this, Rome just holds my hair and rubs my back, telling me everything's going to be okay, even though it's not.

Finally, I'm able to sit up.

"Are you okay?" he asks and helps me as I struggle to my feet.

"Yeah," I say, wiping my mouth with my hand and heading over to the sink. I wash my hands and rinse my mouth out before sitting back down on the floor next to Roman.

"This was a mess," he says after a long beat.

"Yeah. You can say that again." My head still hurts, and my throat feels rougher than gravel.

For just a few moments, I thought I finally understood the hype of why everyone drank and came to these parties. I was happy. I was happy because I was doing what everyone else did. Because I was a high school girl out at a party, having fun with a boy she likes.

But it seems that the universe doesn't like letting good things happen to people like me.

"I shouldn't have let you drink so much. I should have been paying more attention. I brought you here knowing it wasn't really your scene, and I wasn't even watching. I'm so fucking sorry, Pen."

"Don't worry about it," I say. "I did this to myself. I knew I couldn't handle it. I don't know why I even volunteered."

"She gets under your skin," he replies, referring to Rina. "I get it."

"I feel so stupid."

"Never," he says. "You could never be stupid."

He envelopes me in a warm embrace, and we stay like this for a while. The gesture is simple, but right now, his comfort means more than he can imagine.

After he pulls away, he holds his hand out, gesturing for me to take it. "You about ready to get out of here?"

"Yeah," I tell him. "I think I am."

But it only takes a few seconds for me to eat my words. Just as we open the bathroom door and make our way into the hallway, the sound of loud voices from the other room where we were playing pong carries over. We both go completely still.

"I seriously cannot believe she's here with him. Like, what the fuck does he see in her?"

"This was supposed to be a night where he could let loose. I feel like he's babysitting," adds a guy I recognize to be Kevin.

They all laugh. "She's seventeen and can't hold her alcohol? How much did she have? One beer total?"

A female voice emerges—Laura, I think. "I can tell they're gonna crash and burn."

"How long do we think it'll last?"

"I'm surprised they even lasted a week. What could they possibly have in common?" Margo asks. Which hurts me the most.

"The sex must be really good."

Rina laughs like the little bitch she is. "I doubt it. I heard she's a...."

That's all I need to hear. I take off running, bolting past everyone and hightailing it to the front door.

"Pen!" Roman calls, charging after me. "Assholes!" I hear him call out to the group. "You're all assholes. Pen! Wait up!"

But I'm already halfway out the door.

CHAPTER
seventeen

"ivy" by Taylor Swift

November, Present

$\mathcal{M}$y mom is seldom more frantic than she is around a holiday. In her mind, Thanksgiving, the holiday all about food, is second most important to the obvious most important, Christmas. But don't even get me started on how my mother treats Christmas. She's so wild about decorations, you'd never peg her as a lapsed Christian. My mom is crazy about the holidays. So crazy, it's hard not to go insane right along with her.

Late last night, my three cousins, aunt, and grandparents on my father's side arrived at our house after a long drive from Ohio. We don't see them much other than the holidays, so it's nice for us to come together as a family, even if it's only three times a year.

While my mom's been worried about the food prep, I've been anxiously checking my phone all day, waiting to see when Rome will get back to me about coming over tonight.

I was casual when I asked him about it, but that doesn't mean I don't want him here more than anything.

The holidays are hard for him. I imagine they'd be hard for me too if I lost the two people I grew up spending them with. For some holidays like Christmas or Easter, Rome, and his parents would go back to the Dominican Republic to visit family, but since Thanksgiving is more of an American thing, he'd spend it home with them in the States.

A few minutes later, as I sit down at my desk to get ready, my phone buzzes.

> **Rome:** Hey, Pen. I'll be over around four

I smile and type out a reply before getting started on my holiday look, a sweater dress paired with black boots.

> **Aspen:** awesome!! i'm really glad you decided to come

> **Rome:** You thought I wouldn't?

I laugh.

> **Aspen:** don't worry, i knew

TIS THE DAMN SEASON

> **Rome:** Haha. See you later.

Rome arrives about when we said he would, two minutes after four o'clock.

My mom just put the turkey in and is now in a frantic state, trying to make sure the house is clean and roping my dad in to help her out. I've volunteered to grate the cheese, peel the apples for the apple pie, and the potatoes. Rome enters to see me doing just these three things at once.

He points to the block of cheddar cheese and grater in my hands. "They're putting you to work, I see."

I smile. "You know how it gets around here."

Rome is wearing black jeans today instead of his regular blue jeans, with a hunter-green crewneck sweater. The color looks amazing against his light brown skin, and the jeans fit him just right. He wears his all-white Forces on the bottom.

Rome chuckles. "You need my help?"

"My mother would kill me if I put a guest to work." And she really would. She's always hounded me about not delegating my holiday tasks.

"That's what you're calling me now? A guest?"

I suppose he has a point there. I couldn't count how many hours he's spent in this house even if I tried.

"I guess if you really want to, you can wash your hands, pull up a chair, and get started on the potatoes." I point to a pile of them sitting on the kitchen counter.

"Yes, ma'am," he says, in such a way that instantly sends a heat throughout my body that I work hard to ignore.

He has a way of doing that. Turning completely normal phrases into the most attractive statements I've ever heard.

"So," I start as he sits down across from me at the table, "how are you feeling about the way everything's looking so far with the show?" We haven't had much time to debrief since our last rehearsal four days ago.

"Good," he responds. "I feel confident that everything will come together. We still have a lot of time."

"Yeah, you're right," I agree. "I think we've got a good group of kids."

I try not to think about the cold stares Millie was giving Ella the other day.

By the time the rest of the family comes into the kitchen, we've finished both the cheese and potatoes, and we're almost done with the apples.

"Morning, Aunt Martha!" I say, giving her a big hug.

I greet my grandparents and each of my cousins: Calee, who just started her master's program; Zara, who's a college senior; and Jacob, who just turned eighteen. Even though we're not super close during the year, it was always fun to spend the holidays with them growing up, whether it was here or in Ohio.

They weren't super surprised when I moved out to LA. Zara, Calee, and I used to give concerts on the holidays, and they knew I always loved to perform. They send me pictures and videos whenever they see me on TV or hear my songs on the radio.

"Roman!" exclaims my aunt. "It's wonderful to see you again. It's been a while." They've met many times now, so everyone in my family is comfortable with him.

"It's nice to see you all again."

We both shift uncomfortably, suspecting how this is going to go. She's always been a fan of us together and never really understood why we broke up, and she makes sure we know it.

"You two seeing each other again?" asks my aunt. She's sort of like Rome in a way, always the first to ask the questions no one else wants to ask.

"No, we're just friends," I reply a little too quickly.

"Isn't that a shame," she says. "From what I've seen, you were good together."

We were, weren't we?

"You know I live in LA now," I say, sharing the surface-level reason for our split.

"You're still here in Fertsville?" my aunt asks Rome.

"Yeah. I'm trying to get my associate's degree here at Fertsville Community and then transfer to a university next year."

"Well, isn't that wonderful!" my grandma chimes in. "But aren't there universities in California?"

Aren't there?

I wait for him to respond. Wait for him to show any sign that this might be an option in his mind, but he says nothing. If anything, he looks uncomfortable. At best.

I'm only slightly disappointed. It's not like I expected anything different from Rome. I've known he's felt this way since I came home after the premier of *Soon After*. He never believed he could handle all of the criticism and the rumors and the drama. Each time I told him about it, he commended me for how well I seemed to be dealing with everything. And that he'd never want this for himself.

The sound of my mom's entrance breaks the silence in the room. "Good afternoon, everyone! Dinner's not quite ready yet. The turkey's still got about an hour left. I laid out the snacks and put the Eagles game on in the den."

Everyone makes their way there. Rome and I hold eye contact for a while, but he still says nothing. He goes back to the table and starts again on the apples without me even asking him.

I guess that's the end of that conversation.

I shouldn't feel this disappointment. But I really wish he would have said something. Anything.

We sit down for dinner a little over an hour later. We all line up around the kitchen counter to load our plates. My mom cooked a bunch of different dishes, turkey, stuffing, sweet potatoes, salad, and a blueberry pie. My grandpa goes first for his food, and the rest of us form a line behind him.

Once we've finished helping ourselves, Rome takes a seat next to me toward the end of the narrow dining table.

"You've really outdone yourself tonight, Linda," says my aunt as she takes another bite of her meal. "These sweet potatoes are wonderful."

"You're too kind. But I can't take all the credit. Aspen peeled them and watched them for me."

I laugh. "That was all Rome, actually." My mom shakes her head at me in disapproval. I shrug. "He insisted on helping."

"How sweet!" my grandmother says.

"If I didn't know better, I'd think you guys were in a relationship," says my aunt.

Not this again.

"Anyway," says Rome, immediately switching topics, "I really like this turkey."

We all fall into our separate conversations, and I take this time to catch up with Calee and Zara while Rome and Jacob talk football. The Eagles, to be specific.

"So," says Zara, "does the fact that you're not dating Roman mean you've got someone special waiting for you back in LA?"

"Nope," I answer easily. "I've been single for a while now."

"Oh," says Calee. "Good to know. I hear rumors all the time, but I'm sure most of them aren't true."

It mortifies me to think that my cousins read about me in the news. They've never treated me like I was famous or anything, but they will occasionally bring up when they hear something about me. It's become normal to me now, people knowing things about my life before I can tell them anything about it, but it's always strange coming from family.

"Almost none of them are. Trust me. Especially when it comes to my dating life." Which has been practically non-existent for years.

According to the rumors, I've had four boyfriends during my time in the spotlight. Henry Hooke, an actor I starred in a commercial with a few years back. Robert Chang, a model I hung out with at a few parties because Sierra was sleeping with his best friend. Zachary Broom, a country singer I befriended at my first MVAs. And, of course, Keith Haverton, a man whose name I wish I could never ever hear again. At the advice of my publicists, I haven't said anything about these rumors. Though untrue, they got my name out there. They didn't start them or anything, but they saw an opportunity to get people talking about me, and they took it.

"I'm sure it must be hard having all that stuff written about you then," Zara says.

"Yeah, I guess. But I try not to think about it too much if I can."

"Does Roman read what they're posting about you now? Has he asked you about…that?" asks Calee.

I wonder if she knows how much that question really bothers me.

Rome probably never looks me up. He's not up-to-date on celebrity drama, although he told me he saw the covers of the recent tabloids.

I want him to wonder what I'm up to and what I wore to dinner last night. I want him to stay up-to-date on all my recent projects and who I'm seen with. I want him to care.

When I'm here, he wants me. But what about when I'm not?

"I don't know. We've never really had the conversation before, but I assume he doesn't. He normally stays off social media."

"If I were him, I'd be googling you every day."

Zara sighs. "But then again, I guess it would get hard seeing my ex-girlfriend on the cover of every gossip site after she's had an alleged affair with her BFF's man."

"Hey!" I say, offended by her comment.

"I'm joking, Aspen! Don't worry."

They're forcing me to think about things my brain simply cannot handle at this current moment. Or ever.

"So," I begin. "Zara, how's your master's program going?

Despite my resolution to go out more, I don't do much the following days. I do decide to shoot Leila a text, though.

> **Aspen:** hey, it's aspen from the diner! let me know if you want to hang out soon :))

It's about ten o'clock when I get a call from my manager, Dean. I can already tell why he's calling. It's like him to call over the holidays, and I know for a fact he still means business. We've only spoken a few times by text in the past two weeks, so I've been expecting to hear from him.

"Hi," I say into the phone as I pick up.

"Hey, Aspen. How are you doing?" Dean sounds cheery. A little too cheery. He's either got great news, or really bad news.

"Good, good. It's nice to be back home. How are you? How's Olivia?" I ask about his wife in an attempt to delay whatever he's about to tell me.

"She's good. I'm good. Listen, I've been meaning to talk to you about your next project."

Anxiety rises in my stomach. "Mm-hm."

I signed a three-record deal with the major label, Dayton Records, about a year and a half ago, just after I finished my last season on *Soon After*. I wanted to break into music, and out of the box, I felt the show had cast me in, and at the time, Dayton seemed like the best fit. I wasn't the two-faced, iron-hearted sorority girl I played on TV. I was Aspen Moore, and I wanted people to know that.

"Dayton's got big things lined up for your new album," Dean says, unable to contain his excitement. "They're looking to have you collaborate with some bigger artists. They need to know when you'll be ready to lock things down. Get back in the studio. A new project would be a great way to make a comeback."

"Yeah, I know."

My first EP, *dreamer*, came out about a year and a half ago, then my debut album, *wallflower*, followed.

Getting signed hadn't been as hard as I thought, considering the buzz I'd already generated from the show, not to mention the relationship rumors circulating about Keith and me. As much as they disgusted me, they helped. We played two of the world's favorite characters. The ones they loved to hate. Putting out music when I did turned out to be half the battle.

But ever since my tour ended, I've known an inevitable topic of conversation would be waiting for me, whether I was in LA or not.

My next album.

Though it's only been a short time since my last project, my name's been in the press a lot recently. My label's been telling me for a while I need to get back in the studio. Despite their encouragement, I haven't felt like throwing myself into a project I wasn't completely sure about yet.

But the industry's all about timing, whether you're ready for it or not.

"You have good news for me? Have you been working on anything recently?"

"Um, yeah. I've got something going on," I lie.

Though I've had some brief melodies floating around my head, I don't have anything good enough to bring to fruition. My writing recently has been so *different*. I've been writing more at my piano instead of upbeat pop on my guitar. It's definitely not anything Dean would be interested in hearing about. A complete change in sound would not be good for branding right now.

I can practically hear him smile. "Perfect. You might wanna have a song or two to start with."

"Yeah, I've been meaning to talk to you guys about that, actually," I say, seeing an in to discuss the renegotiation of my contract.

"One more thing first. They want you to work with Rob Falista on this album. He's super pumped about it."

There goes that plan.

I suck in a breath. "You know, that's sort of what I wanted to talk about."

Well, not exactly.

Rob was the main producer I worked with on my first two projects. Sure, he's nice and all, and I enjoyed our time in the studio creating my EP, but he doesn't exactly capture what I'm looking for. His expertise is bubblegum pop, which is exactly what my label wants me to do. But I'm ready to step out of this box they've put me in. He is the polar opposite of what I want for this record.

I want to break out of my comfort zone by going a more alternative route. I want to sing the songs that mean something to me, and I feel like my pop music lately hasn't been encapsulating the person I've become since I moved to LA.

But I'm not quick enough to object.

"Perfect!" Dean says. "So glad we're on the same page about this."

I can tell there's no point in arguing with him right now. Anything I say will go in one ear and out the other.

Dean's not a bad guy. He's always wanted what's best for me. But what he thinks is best for me, and what I want? They don't always align.

"Hey, I've gotta run. But let's catch up later, yeah?"

There's definitely a lot we need to catch up on. "Yeah. Thanks, Dean."

"Of course. You have a wonderful day now. Keep writing!" and with that, the call goes silent.

I thought that by leaving LA, I could escape at least most of my problems, but clearly, that's not the case. I know it's a shot in the dark, but I decide to try writing something now. Inspiration could strike when I least expect it.

After grabbing one of my old guitars and a notepad, I strum my favorite chord progression, thinking of something I want to say. I find my best songs always come from nowhere. When it's just me. Low stakes.

Somehow, no matter how hard I try to think of someone else, Rome always filters into my songwriting process. Even as the years have gone by, I can always remember how I felt the day I boarded that first plane to California. Or the day he told me he could no longer be with me. Or the months of dealing with the aftermath. Or how it felt to leave him. Again and Again.

What can I say? I guess I have my muse.

Close enough to see,
Too far to reach
You're in my head
Like a symphony

It's not the same
Everyday
Why did things
Have to change
Hit me like the sea
On my knees
I'm into the deep
It's killing me

I picture his face as I think about who I used to be. How I was when I first began in this industry.

It never stops

I'm impressed with how quickly I was able to write a song I'm mostly happy with. I sing through it a few more times, getting a feel for how it sits in my voice. A smile spreads across my face as

I come to the realization I like this song. It's got this flow to it that satisfies me. With a little more legwork, it could be something.

That's if I'm allowed to put it out.

CHAPTER
eighteen

"Ribs" by Lorde

November, Seven Years Ago

$\mathcal{I}$t doesn't take long for Rome to catch up to me as I run out of Jeff's house. I can feel his presence several feet away.

"I'm so—"

"Stop!" I turn around. "Stop apologizing for things you didn't do. You didn't do this. They did. It's not your fault."

"I shouldn't have—"

"If you didn't want me here, why the hell did you bring me?"

"Aspen, stop walking!"

I still at his use of my real name.

"I'm awful at this. I have no idea what to say. But I really am sorry. No one usually cares about these things. People mind their own business. I'm sorry you felt like you had to drink to prove yourself. I'm sorry that you threw up. I'm sorry that the people I used to call friends are fucking shitheads. And I'm especially sorry that I'm ruining us before we even have a chance to begin."

I almost can't believe he's saying these words to me.

"You haven't ruined anything, Roman. Not at all."

"Rome," he murmurs.

He wants my nickname. It feels so personal. Something special for just us.

"I'll call you whatever you want me to," I reply.

"What about your boyfriend?"

My mouth hangs open as I stare at him. "You want me to be your girlfriend?"

"Of course I do. What did you think this was?"

"I don't know. I thought we were just hanging out."

I hardly know myself. I shut my thoughts down every time I dare to wonder. All I know is that I like the way he makes me feel. I like the way I get butterflies around him. I like the way he treats me.

"Would you ever want to do more than that?"

"Yes!" I say a little too quickly. "Yes. I'll be your girlfriend."

I've never had a real boyfriend in my life, but if it's anything like how I imagine... Chasing this feeling. Spending more time with Rome. I think it's something worth exploring.

"Good. I'm glad," he says, laughing. "You had me worried there for a second."

"You thought I was going to say no?"

"Sometimes you can be a real wild card, Pen."

CHAPTER
nineteen

"Chasing Cars" by Snow Patrol

November, Present

$\mathcal{I}$ spent much of my childhood behind the gray walls of my dad's auto shop. It was here that he taught me all kinds of important things. How to change a flat tire. How to change my own oil. Though I was never interested in cars or taking over for him later in life as much as he wanted me to, it was always one of my favorite places to be.

This is why I decide to stop by this afternoon, two coffees in hand. After my call with Dean, I need to clear my mind. And the smell of old tires and cheap air fresheners never really grows old.

I check my phone quickly and reply to a message from Leila regarding plans we've just set up.

> **Aspen:** cool! see you soon !!

We've been texting back and forth for about two days now and have decided to go for lunch on Tuesday.

I just hope she hasn't figured out who I am.

When I enter the shop, Rome is standing behind the front desk. "Pen?"

"Hey, Rome!"

I walk over and lean across to give him a hug. He looks good in his uniform. I mean, he naturally looks amazing, but especially right now. His jumpsuit is showing off his muscles just right.

Rome looks down at the coffee in my hand. "What brings you in today?"

"Just came to see if my dad has time for a break. Speaking of my dad, is he in the back, or…?"

"Yup. Hold on one second."

I place the coffee on the table in front of me while I wait.

A few minutes later, the men emerge from the back room.

"Hey, Penny," Dad says.

"Hi, Dad." I walk over to give him a quick hug.

"Heard you were looking for me?"

I nod. "Yeah, I was wondering if you wanted to go out to lunch?

Dad looks down at his watch. "Sure. Let me get a few things sorted out in the office. I'll be out in twenty."

"Okay."

"Need my help with anything?" Rome asks him.

"No, son, it's okay. You've done more than enough."

Whoa.

It's so weird hearing him say that. Back when we were dating, this endearment would have absolutely thrilled me. But I don't know how I feel about it now. In a way, it kind of makes me sad.

"How did that nickname come about?" I ask the moment Dad shuts the back office door.

"What?"

"Him calling you *son*?"

"I don't know. Over the months, I guess."

"You've worked here for *months*?"

"Yes."

I've called my dad at least a hundred times over the past few months.

I brush it off the best I can, though it still seems strange to me that he'd take this job in the first place.

"What happened to your job over at the grocery store? Or assistant coaching?" He absolutely loved doing that.

"Obviously, this job is much better than the one at the grocery store. And I only assistant coached for one season."

"Would you ever go back? I thought you really liked it."

"Maybe if they paid me."

That's right. My dad told me about the budget cuts the school had made two years ago. I wish I could do something about this. I want him to be able to do whatever makes him happy, even if it doesn't pay very well.

An awkward tension lingers between us.

It annoys him to no end when I bring up financials, but sometimes these things need to be brought up. "You know I would help you out, Rome."

"I know you would, but I don't want you to do that."

"Why not? I swear it won't hurt me." I have more money in the bank than I think I'll ever spend in a lifetime.

He scoffs and looks away from me, beginning to reorganize a few of the messy piles of papers on the desk. "You don't even have an apartment anymore, and you're asking to give me thousands of dollars?"

"I don't have an apartment because I don't want to sign a lease somewhere else. I want something more permanent, just not right now. Trust me. I can afford it."

Did he forget that I was on three seasons of one of the most popular shows on the American Television Network? Not to mention I was the main character.

I wish he'd let me pay for his college tuition. He could have gone to a larger school for all four years. Had the experience. I wish, at the very least, he'd let me help him out of his shithole apartment.

He didn't accept the offer I made to support him when he first told me he was considering re-enrolling in classes at Fertsville Community. Or when I offered to help him get a new apartment when I first saw the one he's been living in. I never expect a yes, but I try.

"Aspen, drop it. I don't want your money."

"Rome," I whisper, wanting him to understand that this is nothing to be embarrassed about. I'd never judge him. Especially not over this.

I'm not his girlfriend. I know I won't ever be again. But even though we've ended things romantically, I won't stop caring about him. I can't. And if it takes lending him some cash for a little while to help get him to where he wants to go, I don't mind.

"Stop," he says firmly.

Over the years, I've learned his different tones like the back of my hand.

"Fine. But if you ever change your mind…"

"Call you. Yeah, I know," he says shortly.

Just as the air grows thick and we realize we've been staring at each other for far too long, my dad returns from his office.

"Ready to go?" he asks.

"Yup. Bye, Rome," I say, my tone softening.

My dad and I settle on eating at a relatively new restaurant about three blocks down. It's a standard American place with burgers, pizza, mac and cheese, milkshakes… All the typical delicacies.

"So," Dad begins, "how've things been since you came home? I know we haven't had much time to talk."

"Yeah, things have been busy. But I kind of like it this way. It's nice having something to keep me distracted."

When Dad's at work, I'm normally home. But when he's home, I'm normally at rehearsal. It does frustrate me a little bit that we don't see each other much, but I like the structure the show has given me.

We schedule our rehearsals in longer blocks after school rather than every day for an hour like my dad used to do. Most times, this overlaps with the nights my dad is working, but we surveyed the parents and found four to seven on Mondays and Thursdays work best for everyone involved.

"You never did tell me your version of what all went down back in LA," Dad says.

I suck in a deep breath. As much as it's been on my mind, when the whole world hates you and your career is imploding, it's not something you want to talk about with anyone. Not even your loving father.

"Just friendship drama, that's all. I needed to get away for a while. Get out of that apartment."

"Yeah, John Davis came into the shop and mentioned this business with Cane. And your roommate believed him, huh? Some friend. I hope this won't hurt the career you've worked so hard at."

I take a sip of the Oreo milkshake I ordered. "One can only hope."

He nods his head like he understands and doesn't push for details. "What's your plan for the new year? Will you go back?"

"Hopefully, I'll buy a house."

"That's awesome, Penny. I'm so happy for you."

"Thanks, Dad, but I haven't bought it yet." To be quite honest, house hunting isn't even something I want to think about. Way too stressful.

We chat for a little while about the areas I've been thinking I want to settle down in. I was considering Beverly Hills, but now I'm starting to think a place in Malibu might suit me a little better.

"Well, how are things going with Roman and the Christmas show?"

"Good, good," I reply. "He's easy to work with. We've had some drama with a parent, but overall, I think we've got a great cast."

"Drama?" he asks.

I shrug. "You know how entitled some parents can be sometimes."

"Yeah, I suppose. It just hasn't been long since rehearsals started."

I switch the subject. "How have things been for you? With business and all?"

He's always excited to talk about work. "They've been good. More of the same old, same old."

"Mm-hm. I just hope you're not tiring yourself out." Even though he's got around seven other employees on the schedule, he still seems to be handling the most.

He shakes his head and rests his hand over mine. "You've got absolutely nothing to worry about."

"Okay," I say, dropping the subject. I know he'd tell me if something was wrong. "How's Rome doing?"

He stares at me. "You were just talking to him, weren't you?"

"I mean in terms of working with him."

He nods. "He's good. That boy can do anything he sets his mind to. Why do you ask?"

"No reason. I'm just curious. That's all."

For a while after, the conversation flows smoothly. We both order the lobster mac and cheese.

Once he's had a few bites of his food, Dad asks, "Have you been writing recently?"

I nod. "A little bit."

"I haven't heard your guitar as much recently," Dad says.

"You know how it is when things become work."

"You enjoy it less?"

"No. I just feel like the idea of having to actually finish things and get them done clogs my creativity." Not to mention I've had a massive lack of it lately.

"You used to be so passionate about writing."

"I still am. It's just different now. But I'm renegotiating my contract, getting some things in order."

"You'll tell me if you need to talk or anything, right?"

"Yeah, of course. I'll always come to you when it counts." I hope he recognizes that.

"Okay," he says. "It wouldn't hurt to talk to Rome either."

"Dad, what's this about?"

He scoots his seat forward slightly. "It's just that he used to be such a great support for you. I know you don't call him much while you're in LA."

"It's not like that. I—"

"I'm not judging you, sweetheart. I'm just saying it wouldn't hurt to give him a call. Lean on him a bit."

"I do. But I can't get too attached. I can't let myself—"

"I get it. Trust me. We don't have to talk about him anymore."

I, more than anyone, wish I could lean on Rome.

"Okay," I say, glad we got this out of the way.

"Okay," he says.

CHAPTER
twenty

"Feels Like" by Gracie Abrams

February, Six Years Ago

$\mathcal{Y}$ou ready?" I ask Rome as I hold his hand at the front door to my house.

"I'm sweating balls over here, Pen."

"Rome!" I hit him lightly on the chest. "That is *not* what you're supposed to say."

Rome and I have stayed together over the past few months. We've been hanging out almost every day, after school and over the weekend, so I think it's about time he formally meets my parents.

My mom is home most of the time, so she's seen him around a lot. But my dad works at his shop all day, and they haven't had a chance to meet.

We're having dinner tonight. I'm a little nervous about bringing him home, seeing as I've never introduced anyone to my parents, but I'm not nearly as nervous as Rome. He's wearing his Sunday best and is smoothing his hands down his jacket nervously. He'd even sent me pictures this morning debating which button-down he should wear. I told him he wouldn't need one, my parents are definitely cool with casual, but he didn't listen.

"Don't stress, baby," I say. "You're going to be perfectly fine. My dad loves me, so he'll love you, and my mom already adores you. It's fine. You're gonna be fine."

She's liked him ever since he came to the front door to pick me up for Kevin's party.

"I know," he says, breathing heavily. "I know. I just want to make a good impression. These are your parents, and…"

"Just take a few breaths, calm down, and remember, it'll all be fine. Okay?"

"Okay."

"I'm going to open the door now," I say slowly. He just nods his head.

Though my mom is still working on dinner in the kitchen when we walk through the door, I see my dad as soon as we enter.

"Hey, Dad!" I say, giving him a little wave. "This is Rome."

"Roman Torres," he corrects me, shaking Dad's hand. "It's nice to meet you, sir."

"Nice to meet you too," he replies curtly. I give him a stern look, urging him to be kinder, but he just brushes me off.

My mom breaks the tension as she waltzes in from the kitchen. "Roman! It's so nice to see you again.

"Hi, Mrs. Moore. It's nice to see you too."

"I keep telling you, call me Linda."

Roman doesn't say anything, but he blushes.

"Come!" she says as she ushers us into the kitchen. "I've already set the table."

My dad, who usually lets me take the head seat, sits down at the very end of our six-person table. I roll my eyes and sit down beside him, pulling Rome to the next seat over.

"So," I say, unsure how to make this any less awkward. "What did you make for dinner, Mom?"

I've been with Rome all afternoon, so I have no idea.

"Steak and potatoes," she calls as she runs to the kitchen to get the food.

"You need any help with that?" asks Rome.

"No!"

She returns a few minutes later with the steak on a platter. She sets it down quickly on the table before returning for the potatoes.

I take Rome's hand under the table, feeling his nerves from my seat. He rubs it, tossing a soft smile at me.

My mom kisses my dad's cheek and whispers something in his ear before she sits. Probably telling him to calm down and be nice. "Okay. Are we ready to dig in?"

We all nod and start to eat.

"Wow," Rome says. "This is really good, Mrs. Moore."

"Yeah, Mom," I tack on. "Good job."

"Thank you, kids. I—"

"So," Dad interrupts, "you live around here?"

"Yes, sir," Rome replies. "I live on Rosewood."

He nods. "You're in the same grade?"

"Yes, sir."

"He's on the football team," I add.

Dad loves talking football whenever he gets the chance. Mom and I understand next to nothing about the game, so it's not like we talk about this often.

But Dad takes things in another direction. "So, he's one of those?"

"Dad!"

He's not normally like this, but I give him the benefit of the doubt. Sometimes, he can be protective of me. I understand his qualms about me having a boyfriend. Much less one of the guys on the football team I've complained about finding obnoxious in the past.

"No, it's okay," says Rome, rubbing my hand under the table. "I'm proud of being on the team."

Dad doesn't apologize or say anything else, so we eat in silence. This really isn't going the way I wanted it to.

Rome points to a splatter painting we have hanging on the wall above our kitchen table. "I really like this painting," he says. "Where did you guys get it?"

My dad replies shortly, "The flea market."

My mom finally breaks the silence. "So, Roman. What do your parents do?"

"My mom is a paralegal. And my dad…." He pauses. "He… uh…passed away a few years back."

I gasp, guilt surging through me. Why had he never told me this?

We haven't exactly done a deep dive into each other's pasts, but we've talked about enough. I told him about all my struggles making and keeping friends, and I've played more music for him than I've played anyone. He told me about how hard it was adapting to the culture at Fertsville Middle when he moved and how football has always been such a big part of his life.

My mom looks at him sympathetically. "How? If you don't mind me asking. I'm sure this must be hard for you."

"He was in the military."

"Oh my God, Rome," I say on an exhale. Really, how had this never come up in conversation?

"I'm so sorry, Roman," says my dad solemnly.

"It's okay," he says. "I appreciate your condolences."

For the next few minutes, Rome's father is the only thing on my mind. I want to ask more questions. How did he die? Where was he stationed? How old was he when it happened? But I know none of these are appropriate in this setting.

Mom begins to ramble about a recent book she read in one of her book-club meetings and talks about a new book she wants to read next week. My dad gives her the attentiveness he always does, pretending to be interested in something he's not.

Eventually, my dad finds a way to weave the Eagles into the conversation, which gives Rome an in.

They end up spending most of the night discussing their favorite players using a lot of random sports terminology I don't even try to understand.

I'm starting to think the night hasn't gone half as bad as it could have.

CHAPTER
twenty-one

"Brave" by Sara Bareilles

November, Present

The first day of rehearsal goes about as well as can be expected. Some kids have memorized their lines. Some kids have even gone as far as to memorize *all* the lines and have made it their mission to correct anyone who says anything wrong.

On the other hand, a lot of kids haven't even read through the script and are starting from ground zero.

"Okay," says Rome. "Let's take it from the second scene. Mary, Gabriel, Joseph?"

All three kids stand in a line on stage.

"Lucas, let's have you right…" I guide him to stage left. "Here."

"Ella and Nick, let's have you guys over here on stage right. Ella, are you able to go down on your knees?" She does. "And Nick, let's have you standing next to her."

"Perfect," says Rome before whispering to me, "Why don't we run through it before doing any more staging?"

"We're going to run the scene all the way through. Do you guys want to go grab your scripts?"

"No!" says Nick immediately. "I've got it memorized."

"Me too," proclaims Lucas. "I don't need it."

"Ella?"

"I'm okay," she says slowly. I can tell she's stressed out of her mind.

"Are you guys sure? You don't have to have it memorized now. If you want them just in case, that's totally fine."

All three kids still nod. There's nothing I can do about this without singling her out, so I leave it be.

"Okay." Rome shrugs before cuing them to start the scene.

The scene seems to be going well at first. Lucas and Nick actually know their lines, and Ella is extremely good at telling a story with just her face. But when it comes time for her to start speaking...

Well, that's where our problem lies.

Now all we can read in her expression is fear of messing up. I definitely think she needs her script.

"That's wrong!" Nick says as she stumbles on another word. "That's not the line."

"Yeah," Lucas chimes in. "You said so much wrong."

"I'm sorry," she says, her voice breaking. She looks at Rome. "Can we start again? Please?"

He looks at me. I nod, though I'm starting to think it's a bad idea. "Sure. Go ahead."

I want to tell her to go grab her script, but I don't want to embarrass her in front of the other kids.

She tries again, but she's not much better this time. The scene barely moves past where they made it before.

"She's doing it again!" Lucas says.

"Did she even practice?" Nick asks.

"Stop," I say to both of them. "Ella, do you want to come outside with me?"

I hear Millie's voice as we walk toward the hallway. "Special treatment, like, always. First, she gets the lead, and now she doesn't have to practice. My mom was totally right."

I look at Rome, who immediately jumps into action. "Millie. Don't talk about your fellow castmates like that. Ella's just practicing, and she's doing a great job."

"Seriously?" She laughs. "I'm just speaking the truth."

"Come on." I pull Ella out of the room. "Ella, you don't have to be off-book right now. No one expected that of you—"

"But they all knew their lines. Everyone. You don't understand!"

"Of course, I understand. I've been in that place before. Not knowing your lines perfectly on the first day is completely acceptable. Don't let others pressure you into not doing your best. You're a wonderful actress, and you deserve to be able to perform in this scene without anything holding you back from putting your best foot forward."

"Okay," she mumbles weakly, a tear falling. "I'm sorry."

Shit.

Maybe I should have just handed her the script. Saved her the embarrassment of being called out by her peers?

"Don't be sorry," I say, leaning in for a hug. "It's not all your fault. People can get under your skin. We've all experienced it before. But you can't let them affect you like that, okay?"

"Okay," she tells me. "I won't let them bother me. I promise."

"Let's get back in there, pick up your script, and give the best performance you can right now. That sound good to you?"

"Yes," Ella says, wiping her eyes. "I can do that."

CHAPTER
twenty-two

"400 Lux" by Lorde

February, Six Years Ago

There's nothing quite like driving around town with your boy-friend until ten o'clock at night. Rome and I have been doing that a lot lately. If we want alone time, we spend it driving around in his dad's old Toyota Tacoma until my curfew. Right now, we're parked on the end of my street, spending a few precious moments together until I have to go inside.

Rome's lips are on mine as I run my fingers through his curly hair. We've obviously made out many times before, but something about what we're doing right now feels more passionate than it's ever been. I climb over to the driver's side so that I'm sitting on his lap and shift upwards to get closer to him. But I stop this motion as I feel him grow stiff underneath me.

"I'm sorry," he says, clearly uncomfortable. "I don't mean to—"

"No, it's fine," I say, climbing off of him and back onto the passenger seat. "Really."

Something about what just occurred between us doesn't feel strange or uncomfortable at all. It feels exciting. Flattering. Like something I want to explore.

"I don't mean to pressure you into anything you're not ready for. I just got—"

"Yup. I know," I reply, thinking back to what I felt beneath me. "Besides, you're not pressuring me into anything. Maybe I don't mind. Maybe that's something I'd like to explore with you one day."

Rome makes me feel safe. Comfortable. He helped me unlock a version of myself I didn't even know was hidden inside of me. If I were going to feel that close with anyone, I'd want it to be him.

He blushes. "Okay. Whenever you're ready, Pen. No rush. No pressure. I'd like to experience everything with you, but only if that's what you want."

"Soon," I answer. "That's what I want too."

CHAPTER
twenty-three

"Pompeii" by Bastille

December, Present

$\mathcal{L}$eila and I meet at the diner the day after rehearsal, and I called ahead to reserve the same table. They don't typically take reservations, like most other restaurants in town, but since I used to work there, I have some pull with Sally. Because this table's farther in the back and closed off from public view, it's perfect for our first official hangout.

"Hey!" I say, standing to give her a hug. "It's so nice to see you again."

"Yes," she says. "It's great to see you. There's so much more we need to chat about!"

First, we get our coffee. I stick with my usual caramel latte, and she goes for an espresso.

"So," I begin, "what's been going on in your life?"

She shrugs. "I was thinking about moving back to New York, given there's not much left for me here anymore, but I got into a huge fight with my parents, so I'm thinking I should stay about as far away from them as I can get."

"Oh my God. What happened?" I can tell by the look on her face that this wasn't just some petty fight. She seems really bothered by it.

"In their eyes, my break-up from Martin was completely my fault. They've known him for years and adored him. They couldn't believe he'd do something like this."

I can't believe anyone could make that assumption about their daughter. From what she's told me, Leila's got proof for days that Martin's a piece of shit. It's hard for me to believe that parents would treat their own child that way. Sure, my parents and I have had our ups and downs, but I trust and care for them as they do me. They know I'd never lie to them, and they'd never lie to me.

Despite how much my dad loves Rome, I know that if I never wanted to speak to the guy again, my parents would support me in that decision.

"It's really that important to them that you guys stay together?"

"That's just how it is back home. And like, I know that things could be worse obviously, and not trying to make my circumstances sound bad or anything…."

"No, it's okay. Keep going."

"But growing up with parents like mine was hard. My mom always goes on and on about marrying the right person, money, public appearances, and all this superficial stuff. It just feels like I have no say in my own life anymore. She finds out my boyfriend is a cheating piece of shit, and all she can think about is how much it will impact my dad's company?"

The fact that Leila comes from such wealth surprises me. I knew she had money, given how she dresses, but she seemed so down-to-earth, I never pegged her as the uber-rich type.

"It's whatever, though. I'm living my own life, even if it means they're cutting me off."

"Wow. I'm so sorry, Leila."

"No, it's okay. I just need time to cool off. My brother's got a friend out here, so he's gonna give me a job."

"Doing what?"

"It's a waitressing position at a bar he owns. It's not the best use of my skills, I have a degree from NJU in advertising, but until I can get another job, it's the best I can do."

I wish there was more I could do for her, but it's not like I know any advertising firms in the Fertsville area. "Have you tried to apply for anything in Allentown? Or maybe even Philadelphia?"

Philly's about an hour away, depending on where in the city you're going to, but if she takes the train from Allentown, it won't be so bad.

"Yeah, I've been thinking about it. I'm just trying to get all my shit in order so I can apply. Maybe some time away from the city is what I need. That's enough about me. How have you been?"

"It's…complicated," I reply.

"How so?"

She's giving me an in. A way to tell her about my complicated life as a celebrity.

"Have you ever heard of the show *Soon After*? It ran for a couple of seasons on ATN."

"Oh, yeah!" she says. "My best friend, Katie, used to be obsessed with the lead guy on that. I never watched it, though. Soap operas aren't really my thing. Why?"

Her mention of Keith makes my heart drop to my stomach. I hate remembering him. It's like no matter how many years go by, the memory of what he did will forever be burned into my mind.

"I'm an actress. I was the lead on the show."

Her eyes practically bulge out of her head. "Oh my God! I'm so sorry. I didn't mean it like that. Now that you mention the show, I do recognize you a bit."

"Can you promise you won't tell a soul?"

"I swear. You've got nothing to worry about."

"So, I'm a singer too. I was on tour for my first album last summer. I had a band opening for me called *The Disasters*. The lead singer, Cane, is dating my best...my *former* best friend, Sierra. But she couldn't come on tour because it conflicted with New York Fashion Week. Before our last show, an article came out saying we were sleeping together. She was obviously super pissed and took his side over mine when he said I came onto him, which I didn't. I never touched him."

"Sierra Wong?" Leila asks. "I think one of my old friends from New York is friends with her. How long had they been dating?"

"Four months. Two and a half years less than we'd been best friends."

Her eyes go wide. "Holy shit. That's bad."

I nod.

"You miss her?

"Yeah, I really do. I miss the person she used to be."

It was such a sudden shift. One day, we were best friends like we'd always been. The next, she was infatuated with her new boyfriend and willing to forget all about me and believe him.

"Is that why you're in Fertsville right now?"

I nod. "I grew up here, but Sierra and I were roommates back in LA."

We spend the next hour talking about a bunch of things. Her life back home and her controlling parents. How I got started in the industry. My time on the show.

When we've paid the check, and it's time to leave, I find myself not really wanting to go.

"It was nice chatting with you today, Aspen."

"Yeah, agreed."

"Let's do it again sometime. I'll text you."

"Sounds good. Have a great rest of your day."

She blows me an air kiss. "You, too!"

I've been sitting on my bed, wracking my brain all afternoon, desperate to come up with a verse for my new song. I've fallen in love with the chorus already, and I'm itching to get it done. There's something so calming about sitting with a guitar and strumming out a chord progression I love or a song I've just written. It gives me that giddy feeling similar to nailing a performance on stage.

I tried this last night, but I kept getting stuck and ended up just repeating the chorus to myself a bunch of times. I'm in a more creative mood today, though, so hopefully, things go a bit better.

I mumble a simple melody to myself, trying to find the right words. This normally helps me the most.

Close enough to see,
Too far to reach
You're in my head
Like a symphony

It's not the same
Everyday
Why did things
Have to change

Hit me like the sea
On my knees
I'm into the deep
It's killing me

It never stops
It never stops
The pain won't stop

It's hard to move away
When you're in my dreams
I see you as I fall asleep

It's not the same every day
Why did things have to change

I sing the last part over and over again, trying to come up with what's next.

No matter what I say
No matter what you say

Can't erase the scars
Won't erase the pain

Don't say my name
Not in vain
I'll take the blame
Just for today

I try not to think too hard about what this song means to me or who I'm writing it about. It's hard to write a song when I'm back in my hometown. It's hard to pick up my guitar and have all of my thoughts shift back to the one person I know I can never have.

The one person I've only ever really wanted to have anyway.

A loud knock on my door takes me out of my thoughts.

"Good afternoon, honey," says my mom as she opens my door.

"Hey, Mom."

Unlike my dad and me, Mom's totally a night owl. While Dad and I can be found enjoying our coffees together at seven in the morning, Mom is sleeping for about as long as humanly possible.

"I heard the guitar. I was just coming in to see what you were up to." It feels like the old days all over again. Mom coming into my room, asking me to play something for her.

I've always been super appreciative of how supportive she is. Moving to LA would not have been possible without her support and help in convincing my dad.

"I've been working on a new song."

"That's wonderful, honey! Would you want to play for me?"

It's been well over eight months since I've had anything new to play her.

"But just know it's not done yet, and there's still a lot to be worked out. I only have the chorus and half a verse."

I like it so far, but it's so different from anything I've ever done, so I'm not sure how others are going to take it.

"Of course. I would never judge you," Mom says.

My hands find their way to the position of the first chord as I begin to play an intro to the song. I close my eyes as I sing, trying my best to let go of all the emotions I've kept pent up under the surface.

I finish what I have so far, and Mom wraps me in a gentle embrace. "That was beautiful, Aspen. So beautiful."

"Thanks, Mom."

CHAPTER
twenty-four

"Young Volcanoes" by Fall Out Boy

April, Six Years Ago

I never thought I could turn my dreams into reality. No one, with the exception of my parents, had ever told me I had the potential to make this possible. But lately, I've been feeling more and more empowered to take control of my life.

I've never been more shocked than when I got my acceptance letter to the University of Pennsylvania last weekend. My parents were so thrilled, especially my mom. They were so happy I'd worked so hard and gained acceptance into such a highly ranked school, plus it's only an hour away. But after the initial shock and happiness wore off, I was left with nothing but dread.

The idea of a four-year-long university program doesn't really interest me. I knew I didn't stand much of a chance to apply for music or acting, so I decided to apply for English. It's my best subject in school, and I thought maybe one day I could teach it. My mom has been encouraging me to go to school for teaching, so I could go into education like her. But now, the idea of spending all this money—tuition is still a lot even after financial aid—to get a degree I don't really want is crazy.

"How long have you been thinking about moving?" my mother asks me once I've told her my master plan.

"Years, probably."

I want to move to LA. I want to chase my dreams of finally doing what I love and becoming a star because of it. I know that I'll work for this harder than I've ever worked for anything. I just need a chance to prove it.

I can't remember a time when I didn't want to sing. Melodies have been spinning around my head from the moment I could speak. I'd always thought I wanted to sing, but it was never something I actually thought I could do. Not until recently. Rome has empowered me to believe in myself more than he can ever know.

Even after the way Rina and Margo treated me. The way I became the laughingstock of everyone at that party, he assured me that nothing they thought mattered. That I deserved a part in that show and that I had the talent to back it up. So I worked up the courage to audition for the musical. And much to my surprise, I got the lead.

Now that I've done it before, I felt so much more confident when it came time to audition for a community theater production nearby. And luckily, the cast list just came out, informing me that I'll be playing the lead once again.

My dad sighs. "I suppose we can save up some money for a few months' rent at a place in California. We'd have to check the prices."

"I've got some money saved up from the diner already. And I'll find a support job while I'm up there so that I can work while auditioning and writing new music."

I never thought I could act until I joined drama last year, but recently it's become even more of a passion of mine. Actors transition into the music industry all the time nowadays. I'm thinking this is the perfect way to get my foot in the door.

"How are you planning to find these auditions?" asks Mom.

I turn my laptop screen to show her. "See. I found this website that shows you auditions to attend in whatever area you're in. And it also has agents and managers who are looking for new clients."

My parents are silent for a while. Then my dad is the first to speak up. "It seems like you've got everything all worked out."

"Yeah, I really want to do this, Dad." And I mean this more than anything.

I know it's far. I know it's not the path they expected me to take. But I have to give this a shot. I owe it to myself.

I can tell my dad's a little upset. "LA's a long way away from Fertsville, Penny. And I know it might not be as beautiful or glamorous, but it is home."

He doesn't understand why I need to leave Pennsylvania when I have perfectly good prospects here. I'm his only child, so he's probably struggling to let me go. But at some point, he's going to have to.

"But are there opportunities for me here?" I ask.

My mom seems slightly more comfortable with the idea of me moving so far away. "We know there aren't, honey," she says. "And we're going to support you in everything you do. Right, Mark?"

"What about school?" Dad asks. "Don't you want to further your education? You've taken all those AP classes, haven't you?"

"Yes," I reply. "And I've enjoyed them. But nowhere near as much as I enjoy performing. And I'm not sure I have the credits or time to apply for a performing arts school. I have to do this now, Dad. I have to see this through for myself."

He's silent for a while longer. "I love you, Penny."

"I love you too, Dad."

He nods. "You're sure this is what you want?"

I nod. "I'm sure."

Mom takes my hand from across the kitchen table. "How about you defer your admission to UPenn? Give this LA thing a shot for the next year. If you make it, you live your dreams out there. If not, you come back and finish your education."

I wrap my arms around her. "Thank you, Mom. That's an amazing idea. I promise you won't regret this."

"What about your boyfriend? Isn't he looking at schools on the East Coast?"

I don't even want to think about this right now. There are a few reasons I haven't yet told Rome about my plan to move to LA. It feels selfish to consider moving when most of his applications were in by the time we got together, so it's not like he could change anything anyway. I know he's added a few West Coast schools to his list as safeties, but he'd likely never choose to attend any of them.

His mind has been set on Temple University since he was a kid. His dad went there, and they'd always go to games as a family.

I'll have to talk to him about it at some point, but I just don't know how. It's not like we can change things anyway. Maybe it's worth waiting to see how everything plays out… I don't want to end things with him. I'd never want that. But maybe I'll have to adjust my plans a little, depending on the school he picks.

"He's applying to one in California, actually. CSU LA." Maybe if he ends up committing, we can get an apartment near campus.

"So, you guys have talked about this?"

"Not in depth," I say vaguely.

"Well," my mother says, "I'm so proud of you, honey."

I run over to the other side of the table and give both her and Dad a hug. "I love you guys so much."

"We love you too," says Dad.

Though I can't help but feel that leaving this town might be a little harder than I expected.

CHAPTER
twenty-five

"Battle Scars" by Lupe Fiasco and Guy Sebastian

December, Present

*R*ehearsals have been going great. In just a week, we've managed to stage the first few scenes. I've come to appreciate directing more than I ever could have known. It's strange being in charge of a whole production, especially with a cast of young, impressionable kids, many of whom seek nothing but our validation. But I'm getting into the swing of things. And I'm enjoying it.

Our new rehearsal schedule has been working great for us so far. By having longer rehearsals fewer times a week, we find we can get a lot done and have time for vocal warm-ups and fun theater games.

"Let's take our places for scene eight," I say.

Hopefully, Millie is at least semi-excited for this one. She's been less than enthused with how things have been shaping up. Her friends seem to be enjoying their roles as they didn't want a lead in the first place, but Millie has the ability to quash their excitement in a matter of seconds.

The three girls, Millie, Evie, and Grace, make their way to center stage.

"Okay," Rome begins, "you guys did really well with this last time. I think the most important thing to work on is cheating out to the audience. You want to make sure that your back is never—"

"Can we just get this over with?" Millie asks. "We've heard enough of your talking."

His mouth falls agape. Not even her friends can stand behind Millie at this point. Every kid in the room looks over at her.

"Millie!" I exclaim. "Apologize to Roman right now. That was extremely rude."

"I'm not apologizing to anyone. I'm only here to annoy my mom."

"Millie," Rome says surprisingly calmly, "if you need to take a second to cool off, take a second. But I'm not going to allow you to disrespect me like this and still continue to be in this production."

If she wasn't angry then, she's absolutely fuming now. "You're kicking me out now? Can you even do that?"

She has got to be kidding me.

"If you continue this disrespectful behavior," I say, "we'll have no choice. If you're incapable of being kind to your peers and taking direction, then maybe you don't deserve to be a part of this cast."

The words come out harsher than I intended, but I've been putting up with her attitude for a while now, and I'm fed up. I look over at Rome, but his expression remains neutral.

"I quit!" she shouts as she dramatically stomps out of the room.

Her friends don't follow her, but Rome does.

I organize a game of communication chain for the kids to play while we wait for their parents to get here and try to take their minds off of what just occurred. I first learned this game in my senior year of high school when I joined the musical. It's fun to pass something like this on to the kids.

They stand in a straight line, facing the same direction, one behind the other. The one on the end picks an action and demonstrates it to the kid in front of them. This chain continues until the person at the front of the line has to guess what the action is. A broken telephone of sorts.

When Rome returns, he's by himself.

"Hey," I say. "Where's Millie?"

"We called her dad. He's picking her up now."

I nod. "It's about that time anyway. What did you say to her?"

"Don't worry. I didn't kick her out of the show. We had a heart-to-heart," he replies.

I smile. "That's great."

"She's going through a lot right now at home. I think she just needs to know someone cares about her, even when it comes with a bit of tough love."

"Well, I'm glad you're giving her that. I feel bad for her. Her mom seems like a bit of a nightmare."

He nods. "Yeah. Me too. I think everything's going to be okay."

Rome and I head into town for ice cream after a long day of rehearsals. Though ice cream in the winter is borderline psychotic, the Fertsville Frosty Ice Cream Shoppe has special flavors this time of year, my absolute favorite being gingerbread.

It's been hard for me to teeter this line between friendship and whatever we were before, but I can't bear to shut him out. No matter what he makes me feel when we're together. It's hard to control myself around him. But I have to.

We sit down at the farthest table away from the cashier after getting large gingerbread ice creams.

"How has school been going this semester?" I ask him. I know he's on break, but that's about it.

"It's fine," he replies. "Busy. I still need to take a lot of credits to transfer."

Transfer?

As selfish as it sounds, I never imagined he'd move away from this town. I never wanted him to move on. I wanted a reason to come back to him. But now, I'm not even sure what I want.

I want him to be happy.

"Do you have anywhere specific you're looking to apply?" I ask. In my head, I'm hoping he applies to at least one California school.

"I don't know," he says, shrugging. "I was thinking about Lehigh. Maybe Penn State if I can't get it in. I still have a little while to decide."

Lehigh, it's close enough. But Penn State?

I can't help myself. "Penn State. That's pretty far from here."

I know how I sound. Why should he have to stay in this town when I up and left the moment I could? It's selfish, I know, but I want him to be here when I am.

I want an excuse to run into him at the grocery store and show up at his place unannounced. I want to see him in town and have an excuse to invite him home with me. I want to find him working the morning shift at my dad's shop and take him for lunch on his break.

And none of that will happen if he moves across the state.

"Aspen," he says, sounding serious.

Oh God. "I shouldn't have—"

"No," he says. "You shouldn't have."

It seems like no matter my intentions. I always say the wrong thing.

"You moved to LA, for God's sake, and you're complaining because I'm thinking about moving to the other side of the state?"

Maybe he has a bit of a point, but we'd planned that we'd move out to LA together so I could give my career a shot. The moment I found out about his mom, I told him I'd stay home with him.

"Why do you wanna keep me here so badly, Pen? So I can be your booty call whenever you come home? Just so you can go on pretending like nothing happened two weeks later?"

"If I remember correctly, you came onto me, not the other way around. And I'd never consider you my booty call. Don't treat me like I'm some slut you fuck occasionally whenever I come into town. Don't cheapen what we had."

"Pen, I—"

"God only knows how many other girls you were with. I can barely let anyone else touch me without thinking of you!" *Or Keith.*

"Aspen," he says, much softer. "I never asked you to do that. I didn't want this for you. I want you to be happy with someone. Even if that's not me."

I feel the same way about him. But hearing him say it, well, that stings.

"I care about you. I'm here until New Year's. Let's just enjoy the time we have together. Even if it's as friends."

At some point in the new year, I'll have to go home and face the music. But we can be how we are until then.

Rome puts his hand over mine. "I'm sorry that I made you feel like less than what you mean to me. I would never do that intentionally."

We sit there silent for a while before my body relaxes into him as he pulls me into his arms. I meant what I said earlier. I want to enjoy the time I have left with him.

"So," I say. "After you finish school?"

"Teaching, hopefully. Maybe coaching too."

The image appears in my head again.

Rome with a small group of little boys, teaching them to play football, a sport he once ate, slept, and breathed.

"I hope you know that I want that for you, Rome. I want you to be happy."

"I know, *mi cielo.* That's all I've ever wanted for you too."

CHAPTER
twenty-six

"Die Alone" by Ingrid Michaelson

April, Six Years Ago

It's been years since I last came to this park. Sitting on the light blue swings brings up all sorts of nostalgia. It was Rome's suggestion we come here since it's just down the street from his house, and we wanted a quiet place to eat our ice cream, Cookies & Cream from the Fertsville Ice Cream Shoppe.

But he's been silent since we got here. I hope it's not something I said.

"Are you okay?" I ask him.

"What?" He shakes his head. "Yeah. I'm good."

"You've been off since we drove here. I don't want to have to guess how you're feeling. It's fine if you don't want to talk about it, but can you at least tell me what's wrong?"

He speaks in an irritated tone he's never once taken with me. "I'm not mad at you, Pen. Can we just leave it at that?"

"You're obviously upset, and I just—"

"Do you ever leave well enough alone?"

I put my cup on the ground beneath us and give him my full attention. "Aren't you supposed to be my boyfriend?"

My inquisition just angers him further. "I'm not 'supposed' to be. I am."

"Then why are you acting like this?"

"Couples fight," Rome huffs.

"Yeah, but they also support each other. What are we even fighting about? If I did something to upset you, tell me. Don't get an attitude and get all pissy when I try to fix it."

"Goddamnit," he says in a hushed tone. "I already told you. I'm not mad at you."

I sense that this might be something serious.

"Okay then. If I'm your girlfriend, you're gonna have to learn to lean on me. Tell me what's wrong."

He's silent for a moment.

"Come on," he says, taking my hand and bringing me over to the playground. We sit down just above the slide, our legs dangling below us.

"I haven't been totally honest with you," Rome says.

Lately, I have been feeling like he knows way more about me than I know about him, but I've been trying not to pressure him about it. Ever since I found out about his dad a few weeks ago, I've known there was more he wasn't telling me. But I also know that losing a parent must have been incredibly difficult, so I didn't push.

"Honest about what?"

He lets out a deep exhale. "It's my mom," he says. "She's not doing so well right now."

I can't say I know Rome's mom super well; I've only seen her a couple of times in passing.

"What do you mean?" I ask him.

"She's got cancer, Pen. Stage three."

"Oh my God, Rome. I'm so sorry."

As hard as I try, I can't imagine how he feels right now. On the verge of losing the only parent he has left. I don't know what words are appropriate or what I could possibly do to make him feel any better.

I pull him towards me, and he lays his head on my shoulder, his body on mine. We're silent for a few seconds, but before I know it, his body shudders as he cries.

I thread my fingers through his brown hair and rub his back. All I can do is be here for him in his pain. There's nothing I can say to make it better. He pulls away and wipes his eyes after a little while.

"I'm sorry for pushing you," I apologize. "If I would have known the severity of your situation, I never would have—"

"Stop," he says gently, cupping my face with one of his hands. "You had no idea. Besides, I was being an asshole. And you were right—I needed to get it off my chest."

"You can always talk to me," I say. "Always. Even about the heavy stuff. The depressing stuff. The things you'd never tell anyone. You can tell me. And I'll do whatever I can to comfort you."

"But you've got enough going on, Pen. Sometimes it's easier not to bother you. I—"

"You never bother me. What bothers me is when you hide things from me. You can always come to me. How can I make you understand that?"

"I do understand. And I'll try."

"Good. And I'm sorry. I don't mean to lecture you right now. I just care about you, and I want to make you happy."

"Thanks, Pen. But you're okay."

I softly kiss his cheek. "Okay."

"She wants to meet you, you know."

"You told her about us?"

"Of course I have. I see you every day. She knows where I go."

"Oh," I say, taking a moment to collect my thoughts. "Well, I'd love to meet her whenever you're ready."

"Soon." He promises. "Soon."

We head back to his car. It's almost ten o'clock, and I told my parents I'd be back by nine-thirty, so we hurry home. Luckily, it's only a two-minute drive.

I give him a quick kiss before getting out of the truck.

"Night, Rome."

"Good night, Pen."

CHAPTER
twenty-seven

"Otro Atardecer" by Bad Bunny & The Marías

December, Present

$\mathcal{L}$eila called me later yesterday evening and invited me to her new job in order to scope it out before she starts. Bars aren't my scene unless I have to be there for a business obligation or networking, but they can be fun. Since I don't drink, it's hard to be around people who need to get shit-faced to have a good time. But I doubt that would be Leila.

When we arrive at the bar the following night, it's just as I expected. The place has got a small-town feel, filled to the brim with local college kids, most of whom are probably underage. Since it just opened last year, I've never been. Not that I have any reason to visit bars when I come home anyway.

The man tending the bar is a tall blonde. He seems nice and charming, obviously, but I assume that's a requirement of the job.

"Good afternoon, ladies," he greets us, his voice coated in sugar. "What can I get for you?"

Leila smiles and leans into the bar. "I'll have a lemon drop."

"I'll take a sprite."

I haven't had alcohol in the years since Keith ruined drinking for me, and I honestly don't mind that. Drinking reminds me of what can happen again if I ever let myself lose control.

"Coming right up," he replies, his voice raspy and deep. He winks at Leila before turning to start making our drinks.

"He definitely likes you," I tell her the moment he's out of earshot.

"Don't be ridiculous, Aspen. He does not."

"Yes, he does! Martin's been with other people. You could be with someone else too."

Not that I'm in any position to give dating advice, but I think being with someone else could be good for her. She's so gorgeous I'm sure any guy would be more than thrilled to take her out on a date and show her what being with a good guy is like.

We've just received our drinks when a tall, muscular man approaches us. I can practically feel Leila go still next to me. And I can definitely see why.

The man is attractive. I'll give him that. He's got on blue jeans and a simple black Henley. His hair is dark brown, and his eyes are green. He's certainly not my type, but it doesn't take a genius to know that he's Leila's. She's eyeing him down with a look I've seen before.

Attraction mixed with an "I want to kill you" expression.

"Boss," the bartender says, flashing the man a smile.

"Carson," he replies, but he says it like it's a bad taste in his mouth.

It's obvious who he came over to speak to.

"Leila," he says, his tone sharp. "I wasn't expecting you here until Monday."

"I just wanted to check the place out," she tells him before looking over at me. "Aaron, this is my friend Aspen. Aspen, this is my new boss, Aaron."

"I know who she is," he replies shortly. "Hey."

Jesus. Who spat in his coffee this morning? "Hi."

"You sure about taking this job?"

"What?" she asks. "You don't think I can handle it?"

The way these two banter, I'd guess they've been doing it for years. They seem to know the exact thing to say to piss the other off. As much as he's being rude, I don't think his words are coming from a place of malice.

"It's not just that," Aaron answers her.

She scoffs before taking a sip of her drink. "Wow. You used to be much nicer to me, you know?"

I didn't think his tone could get any colder, but apparently, it can.

"That was when I used to go to your house every day. I couldn't piss off one of the people actually living there."

Maybe I was wrong about him not having bad intentions.

I can tell his words cut her to the core. "Whatever. I just wanted to check out the place before I started the job."

"Any thoughts?"

"No. Not yet."

The two have an intense stand-off, staring at each other without uttering a single word. Now there's no doubt in my mind that he feels something for her. But it no longer seems like hate.

More like lust.

Anger. Sadness.

Finally, he says, "Well, enjoy your evening, ladies. Let me know if you need a ride home."

"We're good, but thanks," Leila says.

He stalks over to the other side of the bar.

"Oh my God, I cannot believe that man! After all this time, I really thought he'd changed."

"So, I assume he's always gotten under your skin?"

"I guess you could say that," she replies. "It's embarrassing to admit what I'm about to say, so promise not to judge me.

"Of course."

She runs her hand along the edge of her top. "I used to be totally in love with him."

Well, *duh*.

"Used to be?"

"Yeah, in high school. He was in the same grade as my brother, who's two years older than me."

"Did you guys date?"

"Not really," she hesitantly replies.

"I feel like there's a story there."

"We made out one night when I was visiting my brother at college, but that was it. He's been avoiding me ever since."

"You haven't seen him since then?"

"No, I have. He just acts like this every time I do."

"Come on," I say, sensing she needs to get her mind off things.

"Let's get out of here. I can call us a car. We can be at this cool club in Philly in less than fifty-five minutes."

Clubs are fun for me. I get to dance to upbeat music, watch people let their guards down, and have real connections with them.

"I am so down!"

But before I can call a car, I see an incoming call from Rome appear on my screen.

"Who's that?" Leila asks.

"Just Rome," I say, declining the call and opening the Uber app. "I'll answer him later."

"No!" she overdramatically cries. "Invite him out with us."

"You want me to do that?"

"You talk about him all the time. It'll be fun to finally meet him in real life. Besides, If I'm going to take your advice and try to get laid tonight, I don't want to leave you all alone when I go home with someone."

"Well, you should have led with that," I reply. "I'll text him now."

> **Aspen:** wanna meet me and a new friend of mine at a club in Philly?

> **Roman:** New friend of yours? A club?

> **Aspen:** apparently I go to those now LOL. i'll send you the address. meet us there!

Roman: Sounds good.

The car comes within ten minutes, and the ride doesn't feel near-ly as long as it should. Since I've been here before and the staff knows me, I'm able to get us in without having to wait in the long line, which practically wraps around the back of the building.

I almost forgot what this feels like. The vibrant colored strobe lights, the loud pounding of the jumbo speakers, the sweat in the air from what seems like hundreds of bodies danc-ing pressed up against each other. It's been a while since I've been to a club. The last time I went to a club was with Sierra in Miami about a year ago.

She helped me face my fears and feel comfortable in places like this again. Being here without her now feels strange, to say the least.

Leila and I are both a little underdressed for the occasion. Though all of the other girls here are in short dresses or mini-skirts in contrast to our blue jeans, it's not like we care too much.

Rome arrives about ten minutes after we do. I see him walking toward me and immediately drag Leila along to introduce her.

"Hey," I say, wrapping my arms around him in a quick em-brace. "This is Leila. Leila, this is Roman."

"It's so nice to meet you," Leila shouts over the loud techno music. "I've heard so much about you over the weeks."

Rome looks over at me and smiles. "All good things, I hope."

Leila nods. "Only the best."

"So, tell me more," says Rome. "How did you guys meet?"

"It's a funny story, actually," Leila replies. "I came into the diner a few weeks ago, trying to avoid my liar ex-boyfriend. I came up to Aspen's table, begging her to hide me."

"Then I hid her until he left and had her tell me all about the breakup."

"And we've been friends ever since."

"Wow. I wouldn't have guessed," he remarks before looking around. "Let's head over to the bar. It only feels right to buy you guys drinks after you so graciously invited me to hang out with you."

Leila and Rome both get tequila shots, while I stick with a virgin mojito. Eventually, a lanky blonde catches Leila's eye from across the bar, and she's off to flirt.

Rome smiles at me. "She seems nice."

"Yeah. I'm glad you like her."

"Come on," he says, putting down his glass and taking my hand. "Let's dance."

I smile as we walk over to the crowded dance floor. The DJ is now playing a bunch of pop remixes, the perfect music for dancing.

I've never danced with a guy at a club before, which might be surprising to some. But after my first few experiences going out with Keith during season one of *Soon After*, I always felt out of place in situations like these.

But with Rome, I feel bold enough to try things I never thought I'd feel comfortable enough to do with anyone.

I wrap my arms around him as he pulls me in close, and we grind to the beat of the music. I feel him pressed against me as we move in tandem, staring into each other's eyes.

It's only a short while before I see the cameras pop out, and people start to realize that Aspen Moore is dancing in their midst. I can't believe it's been so long since I left the Fertsville bubble that I hadn't even considered this. A year ago, few people cared about me unless they'd watched the show. But things are different now, which is something I seem to have forgotten.

"Rome," I whisper into his ear. "We should probably head out before people start posting pictures of us."

"Shit, really?"

He scans the crowd before nodding and grabbing my hand as we leave the dance floor. As we approach the bar, Leila is still in deep conversation with the blond from earlier.

I get close to Leila's ear and tell her, "Hey, I think I'm gonna head out. I saw people taking pictures of me earlier, and I don't want the paparazzi to show."

"Oh, okay," she says, nodding. "I'll come with."

"You sure?" I say in her ear, nodding over to the man scrolling on his phone next to her. "Things aren't going well with this guy?"

"Nah," she replies. "I wasn't really that into him anyway."

"If you're sure."

I open the app and call a car, which is luckily only three minutes away.

"Sorry to cut our night short, guys," I say once we're in the car. "I feel awful."

"Don't stress about it, *mi cielo*. I understand."

"Yeah, don't worry," Leila adds. "It's not your fault. Plus, these heels were starting to hurt my feet anyway."

I look down at her black stilettos and then down at my wedge boots. "Why you would willingly wear those deathtraps tonight, only God knows."

"Beauty is pain, Aspen. I knew there was a chance I could run into Aaron."

"Gotta make him regret all his terrible choices."

When it comes to my career of late, I've been all over the place. It's been a whole day since I've checked my inbox, and in my world, it may as well have been a year.

A large reason I've been so nervous to check my inbox or contact my team is the event I know they'll want to talk about.

The Blitz Ball.

The Blitz is the most exclusive industry event of the year, hosted in New York City by none other than the fashion icon of the century, Beatrice Dubois. Only the most influential celebrities and designers are invited, and it's seen as one of the biggest honors in the industry.

I'll never forget the day I got my first invite to the Blitz. When I accepted my role on *Soon After*, I never thought it would lead to this. I, Aspen Moore, landed an invitation to the most exclusive party of the year. People spend months designing their outfits. Attending alongside Sierra last year was an absolute dream come true.

Though I like it in Fertsville, I somewhat miss the normalcy of my daily life in California. I miss when things weren't so complicated, and the weight of my imploding image wasn't hanging above me. But I cannot bear the thought of going back and seeing Sierra and Cane again so soon. I can only imagine the way she's bound to rip into me. And Cane will let her do it.

She's a love skeptic. Under that hard exterior she works so diligently to uphold, there's a sensitive, deeply vulnerable, and distrusting person.

I trusted Cane. He was my friend. Nothing more than that. I trusted him enough to tell him how I felt about LA. Tell him how rough it was being thrust into the spotlight so quickly without a clue what I was doing. He even brought me endless crackers and ginger ale after I got food poisoning from that awful shrimp I ate when we played a show in Atlanta.

I just don't understand how he could do this to me. What did he stand to gain from lying about me?

I walk downstairs and into the kitchen as the smell of fresh pancakes and sweet syrup hits my nose. "Morning, Dad."

"Morning, Penny."

"Turns out I might have to leave sooner than expected."

His face falls.

"I don't mean permanently," I rush to add. "I just have to go to New York for a little while. The Blitz Ball is in two weeks."

"Oh, really!" he exclaims. "That's wonderful."

I wish I could say I felt the same.

I want to tell my dad about what's been happening. I used to tell him everything. But as I've gotten older, I feel myself holding back more and more.

And even now, it's the same person I'd rather call. The same guy I know who could make me feel better. Feel like me again.

If I gave him the chance.

"Yeah, I guess. I had my final fitting for my dress in New York just before my last show."

"When do you have to leave?"

"I'll probably fly out in a couple of days. I don't know. I want at least a night to settle in."

I've been to NYC a few times, mostly for tours or press junkets. But this trip is ten times more stress-inducing. Every news outlet, fashion blogger, or celebrity critic in the country reviews outfits from the Blitz Ball. This is my chance to get my name out there again in a positive way and really impress people, yet my mind has been somewhere else.

I've worked with the designer Mauro on my dress for the evening. I've been wearing his designs ever since my first red carpet, and they're always stunning. Interestingly enough, this year's theme is American glamour, so we decided to go for a classic twenties-inspired look with a modern twist.

"Well, that's exciting, Penny," Dad says with a small smile. "I know things were rocky for you when you left LA, but maybe this will be fun."

"I don't know," I say, exasperated. "We haven't even finished staging the first act of the show, and some of the kids still have to learn their lines." I guess Rome could do it without me, but I feel like it might be unfair to ask that of him.

"Breathe, Penny. It's all going to be okay. You're going to talk to him, figure this out and make a plan. I know you guys will work everything out."

Rehearsal goes about as well as can be expected.

Millie doesn't seem thrilled about her decision to be a part of the production, and Nick and Lucas have dubbed themselves the line police, but all in all, we're making progress.

"Hey, Rome!" I say as I walk over to him after rehearsal. "Can I talk to you for a minute?"

"Yeah, of course," he says. "What did you want to talk about?"

"There's something I forgot to tell you…"

It's so strange talking to him about my career. About things that to him may seem like a distant world away. But this is my real life, and it's scary bringing him into this part of it.

"And I know to you it might sound stupid—"

"I promise it won't."

The nerves are rising yet again. "And I know it's a little late, but—"

"Pen! Just tell me. You're starting to scare me."

"I'm going to the Blitz Ball next weekend."

"The what?"

"Rome!"

He now looks surprised. "What?"

"Are you kidding me?" I ask, not convinced he's serious. I mean, this is seriously the biggest event of the year.

"Seriously, what is it, Pen?" he asks, still uber-confused.

"Only the biggest celebrity event of the year! It's, like, one of the biggest honors of my career to be invited again."

I can't believe how out of touch I've become by surrounding myself solely with others in the spotlight. I thought everyone in the world knew what the Blitz was.

I run my hand over my face. "What are we gonna do about the show? We've got less than a month left."

"I know. But we'll get it done. If we need to add more rehearsal time, then we will."

It's a lot harder than he's making it out to be. We have to coordinate with the parents, pick new rehearsal times, and make sure they fit within everyone's schedule. If even one kid is missing, it throws off the scene.

"Okay," I say. "But it's not just about the rehearsal times. It's everything."

Rome runs a hand through his curls. "When is this ball?"

"Next Thursday.

"When are you thinking of heading out?"

I ponder this for a second. "After rehearsal on Monday."

"I can figure something out for the rest of the week. It'll be hard with—"

I can't help but associate the Blitz with dread in my mind. I don't want to see my ex-best friend and her awful boyfriend, who's sent my career up in flames. I don't want to be judged by other celebs who pity or dislike me because the world hates me right now. People who would have wanted to take pictures with me and hang out before the scandal likely won't even want to speak to me anymore. I don't want to smile as I do interviews, knowing the clips are going to be dissected on the internet in the morning.

Rome represents everything I miss about my life in Fertsville. And he feels like home. He always has.

"Will you go with me?" I ask.

I can see the surprise in Rome's expression.

But he doesn't look horrified. He looks … happy.

"Yeah," he says quickly. "Yeah, of course, I'll go with you, Pen. Of course."

"Great," I respond, starting to get all flustered from the raspy sound of his voice. "I mean, you can't walk the carpet or anything, obviously, but there will be somewhere you can wait for me inside. I know it's not ideal, but—"

"Calm down, *mi cielo*. It's fine. I'm happy to be there with you no matter what. I don't want you to stress about this."

This is the first time he's ever gone to an event with me. At the start of my career, before Sierra and I met, I went to these things alone. Ever since I met Sierra at my premier of *Soon After*, I've gone with her.

And it makes me wonder. What would things have been like if he had come with me? Before I was famous or there were any other complications regarding LA life. If he let me wait a few years and we'd gone together. I probably wouldn't have booked *Soon After*. Maybe my career wouldn't have taken off. Maybe it would have. But I'd have him. And I can't help but ask myself, would that have been better?

"Thank you so much," I say. "I don't know why I'm so lucky to have someone like you in my life."

He tucks a strand of loose hair behind my ear, his eyes staring into the depths of my soul. "No need to thank me. I'm lucky to have you."

CHAPTER
twenty-eight

"Wake Me Up" by Avicii

April, Six Years Ago

𝒥 finally understand what Rome was feeling before having dinner with my parents. Standing outside his front door, waiting to meet his mom for the first time, I'm so nervous I can hardly breathe.

Rome and I have been spending less time together these past few weeks as he's been spending more time with his mom. He helps her get to doctor's appointments and hangs out with her on the weekends sometimes. I'm glad he's spending more time with her.

Rome says the doctors are hopeful she can recover from this, which is great news. He tells me the chemo will be hard on her, but hopefully, it means she can make a full recovery.

"Hey, Pen," he says, looking me up and down. "You look gorgeous."

"Thanks," I reply, peeking down at my blue floral dress and white boots and then up at him. "So do you."

He takes my breath away, even in simple blue jeans and a black tee.

"Come inside," he says, ushering me through the door. "Mom's in the kitchen getting started on dinner."

"You're not helping?"

He just laughs. "You're crazy if you'd think she'd ever let me help in the kitchen. Every time I try to make something, she complains about how I haven't done it right."

This surprises me. Over these past few months, Rome has cooked for my family and me a bunch. He makes the best Dominican food, including my favorites, *tostones* and *arepas*.

"Don't stress," he says, putting a hand on my shoulder. "You're the best person I've ever met. She's going to love you."

My heart melts. I stand on my tiptoes and plant a kiss on his cheek. "I don't know how I got so lucky with you. I really don't."

We walk into Rome's kitchen to find his mom, a short, brown-skinned woman with her hair tied in a knot on her head.

She seems to be finishing scraping something into a bowl on the counter.

"Hi," I say. "I'm Aspen. It's nice to meet you, Mrs. Torres."

Rosa puts the bowl down and wipes her hands on a nearby napkin. She throws her arms around me. "Aspen, yes!" she says. "I've heard so much about you. Please, call me Rosa."

Most of my nerves begin to dissipate once I realize how excited she seems to meet me.

"Oh, okay," I reply with a smile before looking back toward the unfinished meal. "What are you making?"

"*Empanadas y arroz con pollo.*"

"It smells really good." I look at the filling on the counter. "I'd love to help you make them if you'd like to show me how."

Rosa's already got the filling and shells laid out on the table. There's a bowl of shrimp and another of beef.

"What a wonderful idea," she says, waving over at me. "*Ven aquí.*"

We sit together at the kitchen table as Rome brings the fillings and shells over.

"Like this." Rosa demonstrates, taking the meat and placing it in the middle of the dough before folding it in half and creasing the edges with a fork. "Then we fry them."

Our food is done within thirty minutes, and we all sit down at the table. It's only now that they're sitting next to each other that I take in how physically similar Rome and his mom are. They share the same beautiful smile and dark eyes.

"This is wonderful, Mom," says Rome as he swallows his first bite of empanada. "I didn't know you were such a good cook, Pen."

"Oh, stop it," I say. "I helped your mom stuff them, that's all."

"Aspen, you should come over again," Rosa says, swatting Rome on the shoulder. "Roman's going to need someone to cook for him when he moves out."

CHAPTER
twenty-nine

"The Lucky One (Taylor's Version)" by Taylor Swift

December, Present

𝒥t's four days later when Rome and I go to a menswear store downtown so he can pick an outfit for the Blitz Ball.

My team has everything set up for our arrival. A reservation at one of the most popular celebrity-frequented hotels. A security team and driver to get us to and from the museum and after-party. And Rome and I have decided to move rehearsals every weekday next week to offset the ones we're going to miss while we're in New York.

He had previously assured me that he already had something to wear, but after seeing him try on an old suit this morning, I knew we needed to go shopping.

"I hate everything in here," Rome says for about the hundredth time.

"Rome, stop! You need to be serious about this."

"Alright, alright, I will." He pulls me tight to his chest.

"Isn't there something in this store you like?"

Rome's brows rise as he shrugs. "I never wanted to wear a suit in the first place. But I'll do it for you.

I still for a moment, a heat rising in my chest. He always does this just when I'm starting to feel okay about the distance between us. I shake my head and rub my hands over my jeans, forcing myself back into reality.

"Do you want me to pick something for you?" I ask, still looking around at the wide variety of options on the rack in front of me. "How come you haven't bought a suit recently? What do you have against them?"

He shrugs. "It's not like I need to wear them in my normal life. Plus–I don't know. They remind me of funerals, I guess."

My heart drops.

"I'm so sorry, Rome," I say quickly. "I didn't even think about that. I'm sorry."

I take a few steps toward him and wrap him in an embrace.

"It's okay," he says, squeezing me tight. "Don't feel sorry for me."

"I just care about you."

It was hard on him when Rosa died, and there wasn't much I could do besides send him texts that often went unanswered. I could only get five days off filming to attend her funeral, and Rome was still in pieces long after I left.

"We don't have to do this," I add as he untangles himself from my arms. "You can wear whatever you want. Or you could stay home. I–"

"You've always been there for me. So, if you need me to be there for you, then I will."

Rome has always been the kind of person to protect those he loves. I guess that's to be expected when your dad passes away when you're only twelve, and you're left to pick up the pieces while your mom grieves.

"You're always there for me, too," I remind him. "In more ways than I could ever expect you to be."

"I like being there for you, Pen. Now help me find a suit."

I end up picking him a classic black suit, white button-down, and fuchsia tie that will match my fuchsia ensemble perfectly without being too matchy.

"Rome!" I say as he sits, observing me from the couch outside the dressing rooms. "Come try this on for me."

He takes the small pile of clothing from my hands.

"Pen!" Rome calls out from inside the changing room. "You wanna come help me do these buttons?"

I know he's perfectly capable of doing it himself.

"Coming."

I pop his collar before grasping the first button. "You can never do anything on your own," I comment, but I say it with a smile.

"What can I say? I need you."

"You can't say things like that," I mutter.

"Why not?"

"Because. You can't."

Rome laughs at me. "Whatever you say, *mi cielo*."

The nicknames.

Pen, he calls me. *Mi cielo*, he says. He is quite literally pulling at my self-control over and over again. Purposely.

"Pen," he says. "The buttons."

Oh my God. I realize I've been staring for way too long and have yet to move past the second button.

I finish up as fast as humanly possible. "There. You're all set," I tell him, dusting him off.

"Thanks."

I back away from him, realizing we're far too close. "No problem."

I help him slide his jacket on and straighten it out. "You look great, Rome. Really really great."

He leans in, his breath hot on my face, waiting for a second before pressing a soft kiss to my cheek.

Rome ends up buying the suit before we pile back into Rome's truck and go to my house to pick up my bags. It's the same one he's always had, a black Toyota Tacoma that always reminds me of high school.

The simpler days.

At least when it came to our relationship.

I begged him to let me cover the cost of the suit since I was the one who invited him to come with me to the Blitz, but he refused.

I didn't pack much, but I made sure to try on every outfit before loading them into my suitcase. The paparazzi can be relentless, especially in NYC. It's not nearly as bad as LA, but I'll be photographed a lot. I'm not what one would consider "a style icon" known for my street-style looks, but I'll have to put something decent together just in case.

I can't control much about how people perceive me, but I can control what I wear.

I decide on a few pairs of mom jeans, an-all white long-sleeved bodysuit, a Chanel sweater, a puffer jacket, and my favorite Doc Martens boots.

There's so much of me that's not up to par with how I usually present myself. My lighter brown highlights are in dire need of a touch-up. I've missed several appointments at my weekly salon, and it's showing. I plaster on a smile whenever possible so I don't come off as rude. But being home for so long has caused that false brightness to dim slightly.

It's not long before we park outside my house. "I'll run up and grab your suitcases while you say your goodbyes," says Rome.

I can't help it. I plant a gentle kiss on his cheek. "You're the best. Thank you."

We walk inside, and I find my parents sitting at our kitchen table.

"Bye, Mom! Bye, Dad!" I say, running up to my parents and hugging them both.

"We'll be watching the photo op from home!" Mom says. "I love you, honey!"

"I love you too,"

"I'm glad you're taking Rome with you," Dad says. "Gives me some peace of mind, you know?"

"Okay, Dad. Well, we should probably head out, but I'll call you guys as soon as we make it there."

Rome walks in just a few seconds later, my suitcase in hand. He gives my dad a quick hug and my mom a kiss on the cheek. "See you guys soon."

"Bye, Roman," Mom says. "Keep her safe."

"Mom." I roll my eyes.

Driving to New York takes three or four hours, depending on how bad the traffic is. We have the pop radio station playing quietly. I try not to think about who I'll see once we get there or the thought of having cameras constantly in my face again.

We drive for about two hours, listening to music and singing until our lungs give out. Though he plays a lot of songs in Spanish, so I don't really know the words, I fake it the best I can. Rome's not much of a singer, but he can carry a tune. I obnoxiously harmonize with each song, which he surprisingly doesn't mind.

We stop at a restaurant in Jersey City for dinner. It's a small place on a busy street, but I like Chinese food, so I think it'll be good.

We look through the menu for a bit before ordering. I get the shrimp lo mein while Rome gets the orange chicken and fried rice.

A fan approaches me a few moments after our food arrives. She's about my height, with short black hair that frames her face. I assume she's around my age, in her early twenties, or a little older.

"Hi, OMG," she says. "I'm like the biggest *Soon After* fan. Can I please get a picture with you?"

I flash her a bright smile and nod my head. "Of course! That means a lot."

Without people like her who loved *Soon After*, I wouldn't have the career I do today.

It is tiresome having people approach me constantly, wanting nothing more than a picture to prove they interacted with me, but I understand. I generally don't mind taking pictures with fans as long as they're respectful. Sometimes I wish more of them came up to me for conversations, not just for a photo op.

The girl pulls out her phone and snaps a few selfies of us. I pose with my arm draped around her shoulder as if we've known each other for longer than just a few seconds.

She's still beaming as she says, "This is so crazy that I ran into you today of all days! I was just reading about your scandal with Sierra Wong and Cane Dawson."

My smile freezes. Rome's gaze shifts to me as I sink back into my seat.

It's been a while since I've had anyone approach me this way.

Reporters are usually the most upfront when asking about my personal life. Their job seems to be to make celebrities uncomfortable. But when it's coming from a supposed fan, someone who seemed to like me, I'm taken aback.

"Don't worry," she continues. "I like totally support you! Cane is hot as fuck. Obviously, you'd want to sleep with him."

Her words are like a sucker punch to my gut. I'm not the kind of person who sleeps around, not that that's a bad thing. But I'm also not the kind of person who would betray her best friend over a guy.

It's one thing to have people writing Twitter posts telling me how much of a slut I am. It's a different thing entirely when someone is bold enough to say it to my face.

"I didn't come onto him," I respond slowly. "I would never do that to her. She was my best friend."

"You can cut the shit," the so-called fan exclaims. "I was just trying to be supportive. There's no need to lie to me. We've all seen the way you look at him."

"If she said she didn't do it, she didn't," Rome says for me. "Now, if you'd let us get back to our food."

"Wow!" she says. "You know I really used to support you, Aspen. I can't believe you're treating me like this. Who is this anyway? Your new man?"

I don't dignify her with a response. She knows she's in the wrong. And she's not privy to any more details about my personal life.

"Please," I say as calmly as I can. "We'd like to get back to our food now."

The girl storms over to her table where a man, I presume her father, sits.

"That happen to you often?" Rome asks.

I nod. "Before the scandal, people were nicer. But they'd ask for pictures, yes."

"Is it always so annoying? I mean, it feels weird that we never really talk about this stuff. This seems like such a big part of your life now."

"It can feel like a different world sometimes," I reply simply. "It's not annoying, I understand. I just wish people would be nicer about it."

"She had no right to talk to you like that, Pen. I'm so sorry."

"It's okay. I'm used to it."

"I'm sure you are." Rome adjusts the knife and fork in front of him. "But I commend you for having the ability to deal with shitty people like that all day and still put a smile on your face. I could never do it."

And therein lies the reason Rome and I can't be together.

I'm not willing to give up everything I've worked so hard for. And he's not willing to put up with the shit that comes with it.

Back when we were still together, I couldn't imagine being okay with him ending up with someone else. Never in my wildest dreams. But if someday that's something he truly wants, I'll at least pretend to be happy about it.

Suddenly, I get the feeling that someone is watching me. I glance over at the fan's table just as she pulls out her phone again and snaps a candid picture of us together. I know what this means. She's sending my location to her friends or social media. Or worse.

The press.

If they think we're on a date, a million paparazzi will be all over us in a second.

"Let's get the check. I'm not hungry anymore."

"You barely ate anything. You don't like it?" Rome asks. He tries to pass me a piece of chicken. "Here, try mine."

"No, it's not that," I reply. "But thank you."

I nod over at the fan, who's now in deep conversation with her father. "She took a picture of us together."

Rome looks at me like I'm being ridiculous. "No, Pen." He turns back to his plate and forks up some rice. "We are not letting her ruin your day any more than she already has."

"Don't you understand? She took a picture of us!" I crumple my napkin and toss it onto the scarred wood table. "We need to leave before the paparazzi and half of the town show up to catch a glimpse of me with my mysterious new boyfriend."

He wipes his hands on his napkin before looking up at me with a small grimace. "Okay. We'll get the check." Rome gestures to our waitress.

I reach for my wallet to pay, but he doesn't let me, and I don't have the energy to protest. The restaurant is fairly short on staff, so it takes a few minutes.

The paparazzi are outside with their cameras the moment we exit. The car is parked about a block away, meaning we will have to endure their harassment until we make it to safety.

"Aspen!" they all shout, inching closer toward us, their flashes blinding me as I walk.

"Are you still friends with Sierra?" one man asks.

"Are you guys working things out?" shouts another.

"They can't be serious," whispers Rome.

I'm filled with nerves as I think about what they're currently capturing. What stories they could potentially spin about this interaction.

They're going to want pictures of Rome. Not only his picture but his name, his relationship with me, our story.

"Aspen!" another calls out. "Look over here."

Another shouts at me, but this one is much closer. "Aspen, why did you sleep with Cane?"

Rome stops dead, and I can't get him to keep walking.

"Is this your new boyfriend, Aspen?" shouts a guy I actually recognize, the Daily Reporter.

"Is he replacing Cane?" another asks.

The questions all begin to blur together.

"Is this your new rebound?"

"What's his name?"

It feels like the air is closing in on me. I'm usually better protected by two bodyguards when I go out, but now all I can think about is how close they're getting to me. How the flashing lights of their cameras are in my face. How hard it's getting to breathe.

"Back off, dude!" shouts Rome to one of the paparazzi closest to me.

He just laughs. "She's famous. You don't expect people to take pictures?"

"We're entitled to some goddamn privacy," Rome spits, now facing the group of them while I start to walk again. I have to get to the car. "So back. The fuck. Off."

"Aspen!" the guy continues shouting. "Aspen, are you over, Cane? Is this your rebound?"

"What did you just say?"

"Stop!" I turn back and grab Rome's arm. "They're filming, Rome!" Tears of pure frustration well in my eyes. He can't argue with them. It'll only make things worse.

I can tell he wants to argue with me, but he sees my teary eyes and just nods his head.

We walk the rest of the way without speaking as I try my best to block out all the noise. I think about how things will feel when I finally make it back to my hotel room and shower this whole day off me. I think about myself floating above this situation, pretending none of this happened.

Our hotel is only twenty minutes away. Rome puts his key in the ignition and pulls off. "It sucks you have to deal with that, Pen. I—"

"It's fine," I whisper. "It's fine. I don't want to talk about it."

I don't know whether I'm angrier at the paparazzi or myself for causing my worlds to collide. For bringing Rome here.

"It's obviously not fine, Pen. What is with you never wanting to talk about anything?"

"This is what the paparazzi do! What did you think this was gonna be?"

I should have warned him what to do if this happened, but I was worried I would scare him off.

"I could see the look on your face, Pen. You looked like you were drowning."

"I know you care, and that's why you tried to fight back, but this is just how things are, and I've learned to be okay with that. They can say whatever they want about me. They're just trying to get a response. It's no different than what people are saying on the internet."

"The people on the internet don't know you. Not like I do. If they did, they wouldn't be attacking you like this."

I throw my hands over my face. "I know. And I don't even begin to deserve the way you're fighting for me. To you, this might all seem irrational, but it's a part of my job. This is what I do."

We pull into the valet parking lot of the hotel, and Rome hands them his car key. It takes us about ten minutes to check into the room my team set up under a fake name. There are a ton of celebrities staying here this weekend because of the Blitz, so this hotel is used to celebrities needing privacy and security.

We thank the porter but handle our own bags as we make our way upstairs, not saying much.

"Back in high school," Rome finally says when we're alone on the elevator, "you showed all of them that they were wrong about you. You can do that again. Show all these people that you're not the person they say you are. They just don't know you, Pen."

"This is all my fault. I never should have—"

"Shhhh." He tucks a strand of hair behind my ears. "It's okay, *mi cielo*."

I take comfort in Rome's kind words.

He makes me feel fearless.

So much so that I might be able to face the publicity that will arise at the Blitz tomorrow if he's standing beside me.

We walk down a long way hallway and make it to our hotel room. There's a living room when you first enter, a small kitchen attached, and a door to what I presume is the bedroom.

"Take a shower, then get some sleep, yeah?"

"Okay," I mutter. I could use some rest after today.

We quickly realize after moving from the living room of our suite to the bedroom that there's only one bed. My team must have forgotten to book a double.

"I'll take the couch," says Rome.

"No, it's okay," I respond a little too quickly. "We can handle sleeping in the same bed together without sleeping with each other, right? I mean, it's a king bed."

"Yeah, of course."

Though I have an ulterior motive behind wanting him in the bed with me. I need his calm tonight. I need him there to reassure me that everything's fine. To keep me from spiraling.

I shower first, and Rome follows. We're in bed by ten, earlier than usual for me, but we could both use the sleep after the long day we've had.

"Good night, Rome," I say.

"Night, Pen."

CHAPTER *thirty*

"coney island" by Taylor Swift

April, Six Years Ago

$\mathcal{R}$ome and I were having a good couple of weeks. We hadn't argued. He hadn't been hiding things from me since that night at the park when he told me his mom was sick. When he was having a bad night, he'd tell me about it. When he was panicking or depressed, he'd let me know, and we'd deal with it together. Even if that meant he needed some space.

But it's been four days since he last texted me. And five since he's answered one of my calls. We've been on spring break for the past few days, so I haven't even gotten to see him around school. I've been debating going over to his house since last night. And as much as I wish he would come to me, I know I have to do this.

Because now he's starting to scare me.

By the time I arrive at his place, it's nine o'clock in the evening. His street is pretty quiet, so there aren't a ton of people walking around or cars passing by. Just as I'm about to knock on his door, I see his truck pull into the driveway.

He stumbles out of the front seat, clearly drunk.

"Oh my God!"

Rome's never been much of a drinker. He's never been the type to get drunk by himself on a random Tuesday night.

On top of that, he's never been so utterly careless. I can't believe he would be so reckless to risk his life behind the wheel.

"Pen!" he says, steadying himself against the truck. "What are you doing here?"

"Are you serious right now? Where have you been? Drinking and driving? Is that really what we're doing now?"

"Relax." He stumbles over to me. "I just drove back from the park. I'm perfectly fine."

"No, you're not. You're slurring your words, and you can't even walk to me in a straight line. What the hell is wrong with you?"

"What's wrong with me?"

"Yes! I want to help you work through this, but you've been ignoring me all week. What's going on?"

"You know what's going on, Aspen! You made me tell you."

"I didn't *make* you do anything. Don't blame me because you opened up, and now you wanna take it back."

"Of course, how could I forget? You're just so perfect. You know everything, don't you?"

He's making it seem like I'm the most obnoxious person in the world when all I've tried to do is love and care for him.

"Where is this coming from?" I ask.

"Can you never just leave shit alone? Why do you always have to bother me?"

I think back to the night he told me about his mom. I never wanted to hurt him. I didn't mean to force him into opening up when he was going through a rough patch. He has a right to feel how he feels. I don't know what I would do if I were in his place. But I thought we were past this.

I just don't want to live in fear that his emotions could cause him to do something reckless like this again.

"Please, I just want to make sure you're okay."

"I don't need you checking in on me!"

"This is being in a relationship—at least, it's what I want a relationship to be." I hesitate. "And...if you don't want that, then... maybe we shouldn't be together."

He runs his hands over his face, then through his hair.

"So, you're breaking up with me? Right now?"

"You're the one who refuses to speak to me!"

"I haven't been refusing shit. I've been busy."

"With what? Getting drunk by yourself at the park?"

"So fucking what, Aspen? I'm going through a rough time right now. This is what people do. Grow the fuck up. It's not my fault you didn't have a life before you met me."

More tears begin to well in my eyes.

"We're over!" I say. "Done!"

"Pen!" he calls after me as I begin to run as fast as I can down his street. "Stop it! I didn't mean that. Aspen!"

Out of the corner of my eye, I see him make his way back to his car and presume he's about to follow me in it.

"Roman Torres, I swear if you get into that car, I'm gonna make you regret it." My voice is shaking as tears stream down my face, but I'm deadly serious.

"How? You've already broken up with me."

"Just stop!" I shout. "We can talk about this in the morning."

"You can't break up with me," he says. "I love you, Pen. Please. Don't break up with me." A single tear rolls down his cheek.

This is how he decides to tell me he loves me? When he's drunk off his ass, and I've just broken up with him. I want to kill him and kiss him all at the same time, and it's all too much for me to handle.

"Go inside," I tell him. "Go inside and sleep off all the alcohol. When you get up, call me."

"Does this mean—"

"It means you should call me in the morning when you're sober."

I walk back toward my house. "Pen?"

"What?" I toss over my shoulder.

"I'm sorry."

I know.

CHAPTER
thirty-one

"Bad Liar" by Selena Gomez

December, Present

$\mathcal{I}$ wake wrapped in Rome's arms. I can hear his heartbeat as I lay with my head on his chest. It's not the first time we've woken up together like this, but this time it's supposed to be different. I'm not supposed to want to touch him or plant a kiss on his lips. I'm not supposed to feel for him anymore.

Some days it seems like everything has changed between us. But most of the time, it feels like nothing has happened at all.

"Morning," I murmur, trying to sit up to check the time, but he pulls me back toward him, still half asleep.

"Morning."

The curtains are closed, so it's not too bright in our hotel room, but the sun is peeking through, bringing some light into the space.

"I have to get up," I say, pulling away. "It's already seven thirty."

"Why?" He groans. "It's still early. There's time for TV in bed."

"You clearly have no idea how long it takes to prepare for these things."

"It starts in thirteen hours, Pen. You can take twenty more minutes."

I curl into his chest and feel the warmth of his body spreading to mine.

I feel his gaze on me, so I turn to face him. We stare into each other's eyes for what feels like an eternity.

I miss when we were together. I missed the way things used to be. I want to kiss you right now.

Rome shifts under the covers, moving his body on top of mine. He looks at me and tucks a strand of brown hair behind my ear, coming in closer to me.

And I can only think about one thing.

Fuck the rules.

Fuck protecting our feelings when we part ways once again.

All I can think about is the way he used to take away every worry that I had by simply being here with me.

My phone rings on my nightstand, and Rome rolls off me as I reach for it. The call is from Murray, the head of my PR agency.

He only calls when there's something serious.

If I had to guess, I'd assume that this something serious is new rumors about me in the press based on the paparazzi debacle last night.

"Aspen," Murray says in an even tone. If I wasn't already on edge, he makes no attempt to reassure me.

"Yes?"

"Have you gotten a chance to google yourself today?"

I prepare myself for the absolute worst. "No. Why, is every-thing okay?"

"I don't know, Aspen. Does everything look okay?"

I frantically type my name into the search bar, struggling to hit the right keys. I almost can't believe I allowed myself to wake up in such a state of calm this morning. Wake up in the comfort of Rome's arms, knowing that the events of last night were likely out in the world.

Shit.

The pictures of Rome and our walk to our hotel have been plas-tered on every single news outlet, gossip account, and magazine. It's clear people are scrambling to find his identity, but it's hard for them to do considering he isn't on social media and isn't famous.

According to the media, I've had five boyfriends in the past two years, none of whom I've actually dated. People talked about us being together, but they never created crazy rumors.

Now people are scrutinizing every single thing he said, cling-ing on to any reason they can find to prove I'm an ungrateful bitch who is unworthy of her following.

"Pen, are you okay?" Rome says, sitting up next to me. "Who are you talking to?"

"I assume that's the man you were seen with last night?"

I hate the disdain with which he mentions Rome. It's not his fault I can't seem to please anyone lately.

"What do we do?" I ask, ignoring Rome's question and Mur-ray's snide remarks.

"For now, there's nothing to do other than keep yourself un-der the radar. This isn't the kind of thing you can apologize for, but a fight with the paparazzi is *not* what you needed after you were accused of being a homewrecker."

"I already know what the media thinks of me. I do *not* need my own head of PR regurgitating it back to me. Treating me like this awful person I'm not."

There's a long silence. I wait him out.

"You're giving people more reasons not to like you, Aspen. Do you want to book another project? Do you want your next album to be a success?"

"Of course I do! Stop being condescending."

"Then put on a smile, go to the Blitz tonight, pose for the cameras, be nice to your interviewers, and do not get involved in drama! I don't care who you see there or what they say. You *cannot* afford another scandal."

This career means so much to me. It's why I moved away from my hometown seven years ago, leaving behind the guy I love the most. It's what gave me happiness and showed me that after years of feeling like I was nothing, I finally belonged and had a gift worth sharing with the world.

I cannot let them take this away from me.

Not over something this utterly stupid.

I nod though he can't see me. "Okay, okay. No more drama. I promise."

"Good. We'll set up a meeting after the holidays to discuss rebuilding your image."

He hangs up.

Rome's frustration radiates off him as I flop backward on the bed. "Who the hell was he to talk to you like that?"

"It's fine. He's on my PR team. He just wants the best for me."

"What happened last night obviously wasn't your fault. Anyone can see that."

I didn't ask for those photographers to be there, and I didn't tell Rome to engage with them. But I've also had media training. Plus, I should have warned him.

"I should know better. It's okay."

"That was not okay. None of this is okay!"

I probably would have thought the same way if a situation like this was my first introduction to what it's like being in the spotlight.

I take his hand in mine. "We just have to stay off the drama tonight, and hopefully, this will all blow over by the time the holidays are finished."

Phones aren't allowed out during the event, so it's not like anyone would be taking pictures or videos.

I don't waste any extra time before brushing my teeth and doing my skincare, which is extremely important for today, seeing as I'll have ten pounds of makeup on.

Leila sends me a text saying she heard about everything and wants to talk, but I don't have the energy right now. I'll shoot her a response when I get back into town.

I quickly answer a text from my group chat with Dean and the rest of the team about my seating arrangements and who I'll be doing interviews with tonight. Thank God Dean was able to get us seated as far away from Sierra and Cane as possible.

Our staggered arrival time is in the middle, not too early or late, which I'm extremely grateful for. Last year, Sierra and I were some of the first to arrive, so we had way less time to get ready.

"Are you hungry?" I ask Rome, sitting on the bed after changing into sweatpants and a tee.

"Sort of."

"We should probably order something to eat. My stomach is already feeling uneasy, and it's barely eight a.m."

"Okay. Bagels?" he asks, pulling out his phone to search for the nearest restaurant. He's never been to NYC before, and I've only been a few times. But after the drama of last night, I can definitely go for a hot meal.

I groan, curling into him.

"If you want. I'll order one from room service."

I turn over and snatch the hotel phone, dialing the number for food. I order a bagel and an assortment of different breakfast foods because I can't decide what I want as Rome stares at me.

"I thought you said your stomach hurts?"

"It does."

"So why did you order enough food for a football team?"

"So I can pick at everything throughout the day. The food is good at the ball, but no one ever eats it."

This earns a chuckle from Rome. "What time are you going to start getting ready?"

I grab my phone off the nightstand and pull up today's schedule. "Probably around nine. So we have about an hour to have breakfast before my team arrives."

I end up having just enough time to quickly eat a pancake and a piece of sausage before the stylists arrive. Some are new, but others I've been working with for a while, so we fall into an easy conversation.

My head makeup artist, Karina, has been doing my makeup since my first red carpet, the season one premiere of *Soon After*. She also worked on my tour, so it's super nice to see her again and catch up.

"How are the kids?" I ask her as she starts on my foundation. She has two daughters, Sam, who is eight, and Leonora, ten.

"They're good," she says. "Nora's nervous to start at her new school next year since most of her friends are switching to private schools for middle school. She wants to apply, and I'm letting her, but I had to be realistic with her about our situation. I may not be able to afford tuition, even on a half scholarship."

My heart breaks for her. Karina is one of the best parents I know, and she does everything for her kids. Things have been rough for her since she left her piece of shit husband, but I know things will be better in the long run, even if she's struggling now.

"I can always help you guys if you need me," I offer. "I'm just a phone call away."

She sighs. "I could never ask that of you, Aspen. You've already helped us enough."

I know she's referring to the fact that I helped set them up in a place a few years ago when she first left Dylan, but I'm long over that by now.

"I would do it over again in a heartbeat. It's not like I need the extra money."

"I know you would, but that doesn't mean you should."

"That's not true. Besides, you've been my lifesaver for the past few years." In more ways than she's even aware of.

"I can't take more of your money, Aspen. The apartment. This job. It's all enough. The school by us is fine. Far better than her old school district."

"Please," I beg her. "Let me know how the applications go. If she gets in and you realize you can't afford it, I can give you a loan. We can even set up a proper plan for you to pay me back. You can do a couple of free sessions for me."

Obviously, I'm still going to pay her for her time, but she doesn't need to know that right now.

She's silent as she works on my eye shadow. "Maybe," she finally says. "Anyway, let's focus on your makeup."

By the time we're done with my face and getting started on my hair, the nerves have really set in.

I couldn't care less if people hate my outfit or think I don't fit the theme. I don't care if I look bad in pictures, even though I know they'll haunt me for the rest of my career.

I care about having to see Sierra and Cane again for the first time since I left LA. I care about watching them shove their PDAs down my throat as Cane whispers dirty lies in her ear about what a bitch I am. I care that I have to finally grapple with the fact that my best and only friend was ripped away from me and that there's absolutely nothing I can do about it.

"Rome!" I call out once I'm changed and have my hair done. "If you want to come in now, I'm ready."

Butterflies take flight in my stomach. As much as I shouldn't care, I want him to think I'm pretty, and I want him to love my look.

But I sort of forget about that once I get a look at him in his tux.

Rome looks great. My hair stylist helped him with his curly hair, so it's falling perfectly into place. The suit we bought looks like it was made for him. I can't help but admire the way the sleeves cling to his muscles or how nicely the white shirt looks against his brown skin.

Seeing how nice his suit looks makes me want to rip it off him even more.

We both stare at each other for a long while before Rome finally breaks the tense silence.

"Wow, Pen," he says. "You look great."

"Thanks," I respond. "But you look even better."

That's not to say I don't love my dress. I'm wearing a gorgeous fuchsia flapper-inspired number that comes just below my knees; my brown hair is half up, half down with a bun that sits on top of my head. My makeup features a dramatic smokey eye with purple and pink glittery shadows, with a grayish black cat's-eye liner.

Rome crosses the room and kisses me on the forehead, careful not to ruin my makeup. "Not possible."

I don't realize now that the room of stylists who had been packing up are all staring at us now.

"Thanks," I whisper.

Soon enough, my security team ushers us out to the car. There are dozens of paparazzi taking pictures of us as we leave our hotel, but luckily Rome isn't as phased by them as he was last night. We have a large security team, so they maintain their distance.

Rome opens the car door and helps me in, blocking me from the cameras with his body. I can tell he's still uncomfortable around them, but he's trying. He's keeping his composure, and that's really all that matters.

Once he's in the car, he turns to me and takes my hand. "You ready?" he asks.

"As I'll ever be."

CHAPTER
thirty-two

"The Other Side of the Door (Taylor's Version)" by Taylor Swift

April, Six Years Ago

$\mathcal{R}$ome doesn't call me until about one o'clock that next afternoon. I assume he's hungover, but a small, insecure part of my mind has been thinking that maybe he just didn't want to talk to me.

"Aspen?" Rome says, his voice a bit raspy. He sounds tired. As if he just woke up.

"Hi."

"Can I come over?" he asks. "I have so much I want to say to you. But I don't want to say it all over the phone."

I sigh. "I'm not sure that's a good idea right now."

This situation is complicated. He's already going through a lot, and I don't want to say the wrong thing.

"Please just give me a few minutes."

I want nothing more than to make everything alright and be close to him again.

"Okay," I say. "You can come over."

"Good. I'm outside."

I should've known he wouldn't take no for an answer.

"I'm coming," I say, hanging up. I throw on an oversized hoodie before heading to the door.

It's impossible not to want to see him now when the best person I've ever known is waiting on the other side of the door.

I open it to find Rome standing on my covered porch as rain pounds down on the roof. The air is cold, sending chills throughout my body. He looks tired, like he hasn't slept in days.

Rome doesn't even give me a moment to get a word in before he dives into his apology. "I'm sorry about last night. I should have never been reckless. It was stupid. I'm sorry I scared you. I'm embarrassed and pissed at myself that I was mean to you. I was sad and mad, and I was taking that out on you. Obviously, that's no excuse for what I said and did. If one of us didn't have a life before we got together, it was me. My life hadn't begun until I met you. I just didn't know it yet."

His words hit me so deeply, I almost don't know what to make of them. He sounds so honest, so sincere.

"Rome," I whisper.

He steps forward and takes my hands. "I meant what I said yesterday. I love you. I'm so in love with you that I couldn't wait twenty minutes after I woke up this morning to talk to you. I'm so in love with you that I get distracted in practice because I can't stop thinking about you. I'm so in love with you that I would give up anything to make things right with you. There's no one quite like you. I've known since that day I saw you perform in the talent show that you were special. Real. I know you better than I know anyone else on the planet. I want to keep discovering new parts of you for as long as you'll let me. Please. I love you, Pen. You have to believe me."

I love him so much it hurts. All I wanted was for him to reassure me that I mean as much to him as he means to me.

I take his face in my hands and plant a soft kiss on his lips, but he instantly deepens the kiss, wrapping his arms around me.

"I love you too, Rome. I don't care about what you said to me. I can tell you're hurting. I can tell you weren't mad at me. I care that you didn't talk to me. I care that you were drunk driving. You could have hurt someone else. You could have hurt yourself. I care because I love you."

His face is immediately painted in regret. "And I'm—"

"You really scared me last night." I look down at my slippers.

He holds me tight in the warmest embrace I've ever known, which nicely contrasts the brisk April air. "And I'll never make you feel that way again. I promise you, *mi cielo*."

I smile against his chest. "*Mi cielo*?"

"A Spanish endearment. It signifies how much you mean to me."

I can't stand to think anymore. All I know is that I never want to feel the way I did this morning. I never want to know what it's like to lose him. Never again.

"You want to come inside now?"

He presses another soft peck on my lips. "Of course. You've got something to sing for me?" Rome's been wanting to hear me sing more and more lately. And I've been happy to oblige.

I've been writing a lot of songs lately, most of them about him. I haven't played him a lot of the real emotional, I love you songs quite yet, but maybe I'll change that today.

"I've been working on a couple of things."

He kisses my cheek. "I'm thinking I need to hear your voice right now. I've been way too emotional this early in the morning."

I couldn't agree more. "You do realize it's one in the afternoon, right?"

"Yes," he says. "But I couldn't sleep last night. It feels like eight in the morning."

"I never want to think about last night again. I'll never break up with you again."

"And I'll never give you a reason to."

CHAPTER
thirty-three

"Elastic Heart" by Sia

December, Present

$\mathcal{B}$y the time I get into the car, my anxiety is at an all-time high. My chest is on fire, and my stomach is tossing and turning. I'm on edge, and there's absolutely nothing I can do about it. Most people would drink to ease their anxiety, but I, more than anyone, know the dangers of drinking to numb my emotions. I refuse to put myself in that situation. Even if it means sitting with these awful feelings.

Rome can sense the tension in the air as we sit side by side. "Relax, *mi cielo*. You're gonna be okay. You can't let things like this freak you out so much."

I wish I could take his advice, but he has no idea how stress-inducing these events are. Last year, my only concern was the media outlets that would be picking me apart all night. Criticizing my look and how I responded to the interviews. But now, I'm worried about everything.

Getting freaked out by all the cameras in my face. Having to answer invasive questions on the carpet. And most of all, seeing Sierra and Cane.

Mystique magazine is making a YouTube video documenting Sierra and Cane's Blitz Ball experience. They haven't done any interviews in these past few weeks, thank God, but I assume they'll be doing a bunch tonight. Not to mention they've been posting Instagram stories together all morning like they have been for the last couple of weeks.

This would never have bothered me before. I would have been happy for them. They were my friends. But now, all I feel is anger. I'm angry that she believed him over me. Angry that there was even something to believe in the first place. Angry at the goddamn paparazzi and the media for being so invasive and ruining the one good thing I had in LA.

"I'm not stressed," I say, knowing Rome can see right through me. He's always had that ability.

"Whatever helps you catch your breath."

I pick up my headphones and turn on my destress playlist, but the racing thoughts never subside.

I'm wound ten times tighter by the time we reach the venue, if that's even possible. It physically hurts to keep breathing, but I know I have to try.

"Aspen," says Rome, "please take a deep breath."

"I think I'm going to throw up."

He shakes his head. "I don't know how you manage to do these things all the time if they stress you out so badly." He curls me into him. "Do you need some water?"

I nod, and he passes me one of the bottles the driver keeps in his car. I take a sip which helps a little bit.

"How do you feel?" asks Rome.

"Okay," I reply weakly, not wanting to discuss this. "I'm gonna walk the carpet, but you can stand and wait for me, if that's okay. I'll probably do a few interviews too."

"Sounds good to me," he replies. I detect no stress or hostility in his tone. I wonder what it would be like to feel as calm as he is right now.

Okay. I can do this.

First, I have to pose for pictures on the carpet. It can be stressful to have so many people screaming your name, asking you to look at them, but I manage. It's not the first time I've done this, and it certainly won't be the last.

But the lights flashing in my eyes…the click of the many cameras…it all becomes too much extremely quickly. I can hardly catch my breath as photographers call my name and tell me to look at them. I don't want to pose for any more pictures. I don't really want to be here at all.

My first interview is with *Mystique*, which, surprisingly, I'm least nervous about. Their interviewers are trained to be respectful, and they mostly ask about your outfit and designer. *Mystique* wouldn't ask invasive questions like some of the others would.

Interviewing on the carpet tonight is Melody Russ, an influencer who has interviewed with them on the red carpet a few times before. She and my ex-friend Aubrey have gone to two or three events together and posted on their socials about it.

"Aspen!" she says, hugging me. "It's nice to see you. You look gorgeous!"

I hug her back before brushing my hair out of my face and smoothing my dress. "Thank you so much, Melody. You look wonderful too."

"Tell us a bit about your look today. How did you and your stylist interpret the theme?"

"We took the theme in a more old-fashioned direction. To me, the twenties were the epitome of American Glamour. Mauro designed this gorgeous dress, and I knew it was perfect."

"That's awesome!" she says. "I absolutely love it. Fuchsia is so your color."

I smile. "I appreciate that."

"Now tell us about you. Is there anything you can share about any of your upcoming projects?"

I don't let the smile on my face dim. I'd love to say I have as much going on as the other stars on this carpet, but I don't have a new show premiering or a movie coming out. I haven't been working on my next album or doing any brand campaigns. I've just been hiding from the world in Fertsville, Pennsylvania.

"No, not really," I reply with as much enthusiasm as I can muster. "But you guys will find out soon. I've got a lot on the horizon."

Melody smiles and puts a hand on my forearm. "I love that for you! I know we're all excited to see what's coming next."

"Thanks so much! Likewise."

"Well, I'll see you in there. Have a great rest of your night."

My next and final interview is with *LA Today*, a standard gossip magazine that makes money writing about and criticizing the lives of celebs. I haven't had any good experiences with them on other carpets.

I can't complain too much about the subject matter, though. Last year I did four interviews, but given my current circumstances, Dean was only able to negotiate two for me.

"Aspen!" the interviewer, a pretty blonde I don't recognize, calls. "It's sooo nice to see you. How are you doing today?"

I flash her a bright smile. "Good. Good. No complaints. And you?"

"That's wonderful!" she replies. "I'm doing well. Tell us about your look tonight…?"

I give her just about the same spiel I gave Melody.

"Wow!" she says, acting as though I've impressed her. "Well, you look gorgeous. I might need to hit up Mauro for my next red carpet."

"I definitely recommend him."

"Okay, for those of you who haven't been keeping up with the news, Aspen's been in some hot water recently with her ex-best friend, supermodel Sierra Wong. Aspen, you want to shed some light on any of the rumors going around recently?"

My breath catches as I struggle to say the response my PR team has schooled me to come back with. But the words don't come out. I expected her to be blunt, but I wasn't truly prepared for it. Especially not in front of so many cameras.

"Um," I struggle to say, "No, not particularly."

I was specifically advised by Murray in our group chat today not to answer any questions about this. So…now what?

I'm a deer in the headlights.

She looks surprised that I declined. "Are you sure? Because we heard that–"

I can't do this anymore.

I flash her a small smile. "Thank you so much, Lana. Have a great rest of your night."

I can't get out of there fast enough. By the time I get off the carpet, I'm itching to go inside. Get back to Rome.

"Hi," I breathe, wrapping my arms around him.

"You were awesome out there, *mi cielo*," he tells me. "You look so gorgeous. I'm sorry she–"

"It's okay. I really just want to head inside."

Rome plants a kiss on top of my head. "It doesn't matter what people say, Pen. I know you. You know you. No one else matters."

I squeeze his hand, grateful…wondering what it could be like to have him with me all the time.

Walking through the museum where the ball is hosted is like walking through America over the centuries. The exhibits are gorgeous, and each covers a period of American history. We spend about an hour walking through the various rooms, each filled with memorabilia from a different decade.

We spend most of our time in the '90s era, as Rome is obsessed with many of the artists from that decade. There's a collection of records dedicated to different popular '90s styles. It's fascinating. Many of the celebs don't pay much attention to the exhibits, though, mainly talking to themselves or brushing right through to the dining room.

When we finally arrive at our table a little while later, sitting to the left of us is Evelyn White, an Emmy-award-winning actress

I used to fangirl over as a kid, and her husband, Paul Ritch, an R&B singer. Evelyn starred as a badass female firefighter in one of my favorite soap operas. I've met her several times at events, and she's always been really kind. I know Rome is a huge fan of the show too. When I first met her and told him about it, he almost didn't believe me.

Another couple is sitting across from us. They're social media influencers who gained a big following this past year. The pair seem nice enough, but don't make much attempt at conversation.

Rome leans over and whispers in my ear as discreetly as possible, "Aspen, look who's sitting next to us."

"I didn't want to tell you she'd be here when I got the finalized seating chart this morning. I knew you would have freaked out."

"Seriously, Pen?" he says. "What do you think I'm doing now?"

I turn to face Evelyn and Paul. "Evelyn, Paul, hey. How are you?"

"Aspen!" Evelyn says. "It's great to see you again." She reaches out to shake my hand, and Paul does the same.

"And who's this?" Paul asks in a friendly tone.

I push Rome forward a bit. "This is my friend, Roman Torres. He's a big fan of your show, Evelyn."

He shakes both of their hands. "It's so nice to meet you."

"It's nice to meet you too!" Evelyn says. "Are you in the industry as well?"

Rome shakes his head. "Oh no, I'm from Pennsylvania, actually. I work at an auto shop."

I take note of the confidence with which he says this. Most guys in LA who aren't famous with millions of followers or don't have jobs that might impress people shrink in the presence of people who do. Everyone cares so much about status that they shut amazing people out just for not being notable in the eyes of these shallow people. Rome's used to Fertsville, Pennsylvania, where people wouldn't care if he worked at an auto shop or a law firm.

But even if he had encountered those kinds of shallow people, I don't think he'd pay them any mind.

"You know each other from back home, then?" Paul asks.

I nod. "Yup. Known him forever." Which is mostly true. It's hard to remember a time when he and I didn't know each other better than we knew ourselves.

"You know, the two of us got together when we were around your age."

I smile. "You guys are so good together."

It's rare to see an industry couple that lasts more than a few years, even married. It's so refreshing to see a couple whose love for each other is so evident, even after all these years.

"Well, I'm glad we got to sit next to you two," says Evelyn. "And Aspen, keep your head up. I've always thought there was something special about your talent ever since I watched the first episode of *Soon After*. You deserve to do what you love and be appreciated for that."

"Thank you. That means so much to me."

Evelyn and Paul go off to mingle while Rome and I end up making small talk with a few of the others at our table. Rachel Carter, an actress on another ATN show, came without a date, so we ended up chatting for a bit.

We all return to our seats to watch this year's performers.

Rome and I don't plan to stay long, though. I have no desire to run the risk of seeing Sierra and Cane later on the dance floor.

Because of the after-parties following the ball, the actual event ends fairly early. Celebrities need a good amount of time to change.

Rome and I head to our hotel, where my team is meeting us to help me get into my second outfit.

It's a shorter, form-fitting version of the dress I wore for the ball. We decided to put my hair into a bun on the top of my head as opposed to a half up, half down, and add some strappy heels.

Dozens of photographers wait outside the venue to get our picture. Rome is even calmer than he was this morning as we walk hand in hand.

This gives me an ounce of faith that maybe, one day, he could handle the media attention. I won't always be in the midst of scandal.

Unfortunately, it seems like the media attention won't be dying down any time soon. Sierra and Cane approach us about halfway through the party, clearly very intoxicated and ready to start a fight.

My stomach drops. I'd been told they weren't going to attend.

"I'm surprised you actually came," says Sierra, marching toward me. Cane is at her side, all smug.

I quickly down the rest of my water before responding. "It's nice to see you again, Sierra. I wish you would have answered my calls."

She scrunches up her face, clearly disgusted at the thought. "Why the fuck would I do that? You tried to sleep with my boyfriend."

I didn't intend for our first real conversation since she dropped me as a friend to be a confrontation at an afterparty full of hundreds of other celebs, but I suppose I have no other choice than to have this conversation now.

"Whatever he told you, he's lying. It's a shame you'd believe this about your best friend, but hey. Who am I to judge your choices?"

"Yeah," she spits. "Who the hell are you? You're a bitch, and the whole world knows it. You couldn't define loyalty if I hit you in the head with a goddamn dictionary."

My jaw drops. "How can you say that? I've been nothing but loyal to you for three years, and you know that."

"You don't get to talk to her like that," Rome says, walking around the side of our standing table and coming next to me.

Sierra rolls her eyes. "And who are you again?"

Cane puts a protective arm around her, not that he would be great at defending her if she needed it. Rome has at least four or five inches on Cane and a muscular build in contrast to Cane's lankiness.

"She asked a question, dude."

Rome's tone sharpens. "And I'm not fucking answering."

I've had enough.

"Cane," I say, "you're an asshole for letting everyone believe a lie about me. I'm not sure what you did that you need to cover it up using me as an excuse, but it's bullshit."

Cane steps closer to me. "You came onto me, bitch. No one asked you to do that. If anyone's bullshit, it's—"

"If I were you." Rome gets into Cane's face. "I'd choose your next words very fucking carefully."

"Or what?" he scoffs.

The music at the party is still loud enough that most of the crowd hasn't caught on to our argument, but small groups of nearby people have begun to stare.

"I'm not from around here. And I'll do what I have to in order to protect my girl."

His girl?

"So, the rumors are true?" Sierra cuts in. "He is your *violent* psychopathic new boyfriend. And you brought him to the Blitz Ball? Classy."

I look over at Rome. "He's not new, Sierra. And if you paid enough attention to anyone but your goddamn self for more than two seconds during our friendship, you'd know I've been in love with him since I was seventeen."

I'm taken aback by my own words.

Rome knows I love him. I don't think I could ever stop. But it's an entirely different feeling to admit this out loud.

"And yet you still had to go for my boyfriend! Nothing is ever fucking good enough for you, Aspen. Clearly, not him. Not our friendship. I mean, look at how things unfolded with Keith. I should've known back then you were a fucking liar."

"Wow," I reply, struggling to cope with the fact that Sierra would stoop that low.

It's hard to believe she would bring up the one thing I trusted she would never tell a single soul. Fear courses through my veins as I wonder if this will end up on the internet in the morning.

Keith Haverton has haunted me for the past two years. He's kept me awake at night, left me tossing and turning, wondering when I'd finally get him out of my head. Sierra was one of the only people I trusted to keep my secret. And she was the one who helped me realize it was time to leave *Soon After*, to leave the show that was causing my mental health to plummet.

But I don't recognize the woman standing in front of me.

My gaze flicks to Rome, begging him not to do anything. His jaw is clenched, brows in a deep crease. I know it's taking everything he has in him not to say anything right now. But he restrains himself, and for that, I'm grateful.

"Let's go, Sierra." Cane sneers. "Why waste another moment of our time with this cunt? Maybe what Keith's been saying is right. A slut like her is only good for one thing. I heard all about how she–"

Rome punches Cane squarely in the nose, causing him to fall back toward a table.

I don't know whether to be angry or flattered.

"Help!" Sierra calls. "I think he broke his nose! We need a doctor."

A group of staff rushes to help as the music lowers and the other guests back away. I only know one thing for sure.

We need to go. Now.

This event is full of A-listers, so many people that matter. A rush of embarrassment fills me, but there's nothing I can do about it now.

"We have to leave before they kick us out," I say to Rome.

Once we exit the main ballroom, I shoot a text to our driver.

Photographers are waiting outside of the event, catching pictures of Rome and me as we exit. But I pay them and their words no mind. I can't even seem to think right now.

It's only after we slide into the car that I can finally breathe. That could not have gone any worse.

"Pen, I am so sorry. I don't know what came over me like that."

"I know what came over you. Cane's an asshole."

I try to stay as calm as possible. I can't blame this whole thing on Rome because I know he didn't mean to make things worse. But I also know that there's a violent media storm awaiting me tomorrow.

And it makes me sick to my stomach.

It was likely my recklessness in inviting him that caused this mega shitstorm. But I don't know what I would have done without him here.

Rome reaches out for my hand. "I know it's bad. I know."

I put my head on his shoulder. "There's nothing we can do about it now."

Nothing except wait out the storm.

"Are you okay?" he asks quietly.

I suck in a sharp breath. "I'm fine. Everything's fine."

"Even about Keith? I mean, I know you'll never be truly fine in—"

"I'm fine, Rome. I just don't want to think about any of this anymore. I want to go back to Fertsville and pretend none of this ever happened."

He nods. "Okay. Whatever you want."

CHAPTER
thirty-four

"Run (Taylor's Version) (From The Vault)
[Feat. Ed Sheeran]" - Taylor Swift

April, Six Years Ago

$\mathcal{D}$ad, Rome, and I are all sitting in the kitchen eating pizza after volunteering at his church. Dad's pastor decided to hold an activity day for all the elementary-age kids, and Dad asked us to help with face paint. Neither of us is super religious, but it means a lot to him, so we pitched in. Plus, we got to hang out with a bunch of cute kids.

Rosa's been doing a lot better recently and has been up to going out more than she has since she was diagnosed. I know Rome's trying not to get his hopes up, but by the looks of it, she has a really good chance at recovering from this.

Rome is beaming as he looks up from his phone. "Oh my God, look!"

"What?" I ask. The smile on his face still sends butterflies through my stomach, even after six months.

"I got into Temple!" he shouts with an excitement I've only heard from him a few times before.

"Oh my God!" I throw my arms around him. "Congratulations!"

Truthfully, I have mixed emotions about this. I wanted him to get in. I really did. But had he not, this situation would have worked out a lot easier for me. He could have gone to CSU by default and not given up on his dream school to be close to me. CSU wouldn't be the worst option out of all the schools he applied to.

Now, everything will be complicated. What if he can't handle the distance? I thought our twenty-four-hour breakup was bad. I don't know what I'll do if we have to end things for longer than a day.

"Congrats, Roman," says Dad. "I knew you could do it."

"Yeah," Rome says. "I had hope, but, wow. I can't believe this is actually happening."

"So, you guys are going long distance then?"

I can't believe Dad's bringing this up right now. Rome is so happy, and now I have to be the one to take that away.

Rome looks confused. "UPenn is only a short drive, and I've got my truck, so—"

My dad's gaze darts to me. "You haven't told him?"

"Told me what?" Rome asks, now looking at me too.

My dad looks stricken. "I'm sorry, Penny. I didn't realize. Never mind."

I ask Dad to give us a moment alone.

"What is he talking about?" Rome asks the moment we're by ourselves.

This is what I've been fearing since I made this decision. Rome has been dreaming of going to Temple since he was a kid. It was his dad's alma mater. I know that he might consider Cal State if I told him my plans, but I can't let him make this decision solely based on me.

Not to mention that he wants to be close to his mom. I could never live with myself if she needed him, and he was too far away. LA is several hours away by plane instead of just an hour by car.

But I have to tell him now. Dad was right. I've waited far too long.

"I'm thinking of moving to LA after graduation. I want to pursue a career in acting and music, and California will be the best place to do it."

Rome sits back in his chair. "And you were planning to tell me this when?"

"I don't know," I say. "When it came up."

"You knew I was probably going to Temple, and you didn't think you should tell me you're moving across the country?"

Rome has every right to be upset with me, but that doesn't make his anger any easier to bear.

"I didn't want you to pick a school because of me."

"Of *course*, I'd do that." His voice is so loud I'm sure my dad can hear it from the other room. "Because I love you. And I want to be with you. What don't you understand about that?"

"What can I do to make this better?"

He takes a deep breath before composing himself. "Do you want to do this or not?"

"Do what?"

"Be with me."

"Yes," I say, overcome with so much emotion, I can hardly get the words out. "Of course. There's nothing I want more, Rome."

"Then you'll let me make this choice myself. Let me follow you to LA if I want to."

"Yes," I say, swallowing back every feeling I have about this situation. "Of course I will. But don't go making a rush decision because—"

"You act like I have all the time in the world! I don't. I have to choose within the next two weeks."

I bury my head in my hands. "I know."

"When did you decide you weren't going to UPenn?"

"I mean, I haven't officially yet," I tell him. "I was waiting to talk to you."

"But you're sure about this LA thing?"

"I mean, I think so. But—"

"No," he says firmly. "I'm not trying to talk you out of this. You want to go, you should. You have the talent to make it in this industry. I support you completely. I want this for you. If anyone deserves to follow their dreams, it's you."

Even when he's pissed, he still wants the best for me.

"That's not true," I say. "You deserve what you want just as much as I do. You want to go to Temple. I want you to have everything you want."

He's silent for a long while as we sit facing each other at the table. I fiddle with the hem of my top as I wait for him to say something.

Anything.

"I'll go with you."

"Rome—"

"I want to be with you more than I want to go to any school in any city. You mean more to me than that."

"But your dad—"

"Is dead. And it sucks to say that, but I'm not going to enjoy any school if you're not there with me. Sure, I wanted to follow in his footsteps, but it's not like I'm going to enlist either."

"Will your mom be okay with this?" I ask, considering Rosa's need for someone to drive her to appointments.

He nods. "I can set something up for her. She just wants me to be happy, too. She won't be upset if going to CSU is what's going to make me happiest."

"I need you to be sure," I say. "I'm sorry I put this off for so long, Rome."

"What were you going to do if I decided on Temple?"

"I was going to tell you before then. Or maybe wait. I don't know. I didn't have a plan, really."

"Okay," he says huskily. "It's in the past. That doesn't mean I'm not still pissed at you for keeping this from me, but I get where you were coming from."

"Thank you for being so forgiving."

"Come here," he says, pulling me into him and kissing my forehead.

"I love you," I tell him, meaning it now more than ever.

"I love you too."

I don't know why I was so worried to tell him before.

Rome genuinely loves and cares about me and wants to protect our relationship.

"I wish I would have told you sooner."

"Yeah, me too."

We're both silent for a while until Rome asks, "So where are we going to live?"

I smile at the way Rome immediately knows I want to move in with him.

A bit presumptuous?

Sure. But obviously, I wouldn't want us to be apart.

"Let's head up to my room. I can show you a few apartments I found on my computer."

Once we make it to my desk, I pull up the document I started with apartment listings.

"You really had this all figured out, huh?"

"I'm sorry! It's just that—"

He puts a hand on my shoulder. "It's in the past."

"Look," I say, directing my gaze back at my laptop. "These are slightly out of my budget, especially given I'll probably only be able to get a minimum wage job, but my parents offered to help cover what I'll have to pay up-front."

I was trying my best to find something I could afford by myself, but LA is expensive, and I didn't know anyone who I'd be comfortable rooming with—aside from Rome.

"That's not too bad. Besides, I'll get a job and help too."

"Thanks, Rome. That means a lot. Besides, it's not like we're looking at something fancy. Hopefully just a studio in a nicer area."

"We don't need fancy. We have each other."

CHAPTER
thirty-five

"Nothing New (Taylor's Version) (From The Vault)
[Feat. Phoebe Bridgers]" by Taylor Swift

December, Present

*L*ast night was a shitshow. I never expected Sierra to confront me like that or treat me like the villain. At least not to my face.

I feel like an idiot for having trusted her.

It's not even noon, and Sierra, who'd previously blocked me, has already gone on an insane Instagram rant, twisting the events of last night to make it seem like we provoked her.

It's like I don't even know who she is anymore.

I've been tagged about a million times. Everyone is making videos dissecting the situation and commenting #teamSierra. The world is calling me a terrible friend. An awful person. Rome is simply my nameless, violent new rebound who's not famous or important, so he bends to my will, no matter what I ask.

Somehow this hurts way worse than when they were just calling me a slut.

"Pen," says Rome, still lying beside me. "What's wrong?"

"Check your phone!" I tell him a little too harshly.

He scrambles out from under the covers and grabs his cell off his nightstand. "What am I supposed to be looking for?"

"Google me."

I know he sees it. Everyone in the universe has. I don't know what could be more humiliating.

"Holy shit, Pen. I can't believe her. None of this is fucking true."

I look down at the post, but my eyes are blurred, and I have to blink to re-read it.

As many of u know, I was betrayed by my best friend, Aspen Moore, when she tried to sleep with Cane Dawson. My boyfriend. This has been super rough to work through especially considering she was living with me at the time! Hot yoga & green juice have really helped decrease my stress levels (check links in bio). But last night at the Blitz Ball, Aspen, and her new boyfriend assaulted me & Cane. Her cruel words toward me took me by complete surprise, considering I was the one who had been wronged in this situation, not her. Her boyfriend, whom she's been on & off with for years, nearly broke Cane's nose! This is the person Aspen is and the kind of guy who'll hook up with her. Despite all of this, we are not pursuing legal action...so far. I just thought it was important to let you all know the situation. I hope you'll all be patient with me as I struggle through this incredibly hard time.

Thanks for all your love and support,

Sierra

Bile rises in my throat. "Whether it's true or not isn't the point. She's good at this. Everyone's eating it up."

Especially since *Mystique*'s interview with Cane and Sierra came out, where they were all loving-it-up while getting ready together. They're the perfect couple, and I'm the woman who tried to come between them.

Not to mention I can almost guarantee I'll be banned from future Blitz Ball events.

"Well, what are you gonna do?" he asks me, clearly still pissed.

"What can I do?" I've already been silent for weeks now.

"I don't know, put out your own statement?" he says. "Make it clear that she's not telling the truth?"

"What proof do I have? Who will vouch for me other than you? A narrative's already been told. People believe it. There's no changing that now."

He looks at me like he doesn't understand. "So, you're not going to try?"

It's not that I'm not trying. Trying simply isn't worth it at this point. The media cycle has to run its course. Trying to fight it only digs you deeper into the hole.

"I'm sure my PR team will come up with something. Until then, I'll lay low."

As low as I can in Fertsville. I just hope Cane doesn't release a statement.

Murray calls a moment later. I already know what to expect from him. Another lecture about how everything is going wrong.

I pick up the phone. "Hey, Murray."

"Aspen," he replies flatly. "I thought we agreed on no drama?"

"They were provoking us. Cane went so below the belt it's like he wanted Rome to hit him."

He sucks in an audible breath. "He probably did. And you fell for it. I suppose there's nothing we can do about this now. What's done is done. All we can do is improve your image in the aftermath."

"I know. I know."

"We'll get you started with some interviews—you'll do an apology tour. We're going to figure this out. In the meantime, I have an interview you might want to look at. It's set to release in a few minutes."

"An interview?"

"It's with a woman who claims to be your friend from high school— a woman named Rina?"

Shit.

"I've just sent you the link now. I have another meeting in a few minutes, but we'll talk later, yeah?"

"Yes, that's fine. Thank you. I'll talk to you later." I quickly hang up the phone.

My phone buzzes with Murray's text. "Rome," I say, my throat barely letting me speak. "Rome, look at this."

I turn my phone horizontally, and we watch it together.

Rina's in full makeup, including a dramatic purple eyeshadow to match her blouse. She's got a huge smile on her face as she crosses her legs and greets the interviewer. "Hi, Brenda. It's so nice to sit down with you today!"

The interviewer returns her smile. "Likewise, Rina. So, tell us, you say you have information on Aspen Moore and her new mystery man?"

"Well, he's not much of a mystery to me. Aspen and I grew up in the same hometown. She and Roman dated in high school."

The interviewer acts as if this is the most entertaining information she's heard all morning. "Interesting. So, this guy, Roman, isn't new? She's reconnecting with an old flame?"

"Yes, I think that's what's happening. I saw them together the other week. I know she must be really struggling right now, and he always seemed to have a soft spot for her for whatever reason."

The disgust with which she adds that last part is not lost on me.

"Well, you heard it here, folks, Aspen Moore's new mystery man is not much of a mystery anymore."

"Glad I could enlighten you all," says Rina, obnoxiously waving at the cameras.

It's nice to know that Rina is treating blowing up my life like her personal five seconds of fame. Suddenly, it feels like things are just as they were in high school. Me, lonely and struggling, and her, finding a way to kick me while I'm down. I turn off my phone and toss it onto the nightstand.

"What the actual hell?" Rome says. "I can't believe she would do this to me."

"She's never really cared about other people's feelings."

"I don't even post on social media. I value my privacy. I can't believe this is happening to me."

"This is happening to us, Rome. I get that you're upset, but this will all blow over eventually. People will move on. Find something else to entertain themselves with."

"This stuff doesn't just disappear. It's going to follow me on the internet forever. Shit, what if I can't get a job because of it?"

"Well, then maybe you should have thought about that before assaulting someone at the biggest event of the year."

"O-kay," he says slowly.

"Where are you going?" I ask as he puts on his sneakers and walks toward the door.

"Breakfast," is all he says.

There's no point in continuing this argument, so I let him go. We can smooth things over when the situation isn't so fresh.

I spend the next twenty minutes after he's gone packing my clothes and making sure I haven't left any of my stuff lying around. After this, I sink back into the covers of our bed and nap.

I haven't spoken to Rome since he dropped me off at my house yesterday. I know it's not really his fault that everything's gone down this way, but I've needed someone to blame other than myself.

Besides, I've been a shitty friend.

Leila's calls have gone unanswered for days now, and though I know she just wants to check in with me, I never pick up the phone. I'll have to get out of bed eventually. But a huge part of me just wants to lie here forever.

I'm still tucked under the covers at noon when my mom knocks on my door. "Aspen?"

"Come in."

"Hey, honey," she says gently. "How was your trip?"

"It was fine."

She gives me a look. "Do you want to talk about it?"

I almost do. I want to let it out. But I really can't relive the experience again. "Not particularly."

"I won't push, but I want you to know you can talk to me."

"I know," I say, sitting up.

She takes my hands and sits down on the edge of the bed. "You're a good person, Aspen. Don't let other people's opinions affect you."

But it feels like my life is burning to the ground, and I have to watch it go up in flames. Soon enough, I'll just be the has-been who hardly ever was.

"This will all blow over eventually. You're talented, and you've worked hard for what you have. Your fans won't forget that because of a few untrue scandals. Sierra isn't worthy of your friendship. And I know for certain that Roman will forgive you eventually."

I shake my head. "You didn't see the look on his face last night. He looked like I'd really let him down."

I can handle disappointing my fans. And though it may be hard, I can handle disappointing Sierra. But I can't handle disappointing Rome.

"That boy has been in love with you since you were seventeen."

He *was* in love with me. Now, I'm not so sure.

He ended things with me all those years ago. And it's always been easier for him to walk away from me when I had to return back to the real world—out of the paradise we created for ourselves every time I returned home.

Now I've gotten him in a scandal that threatens to damage the future he's working so hard to build by applying to schools.

"I urge you to take some time this weekend to think about what you want. Not what Roman or anyone else wants."

"I will."

She's now about to close my door. "Mom?"

"Yeah?" she says, pausing in place.

"Thank you.

CHAPTER
thirty-six

"Let Somebody Go" by Coldplay & Selena Gomez

June, Six Years Ago

J'm sitting on my bed a few weeks since Rome and I decided we were moving to LA, studying the California apartments we've narrowed it down to. Out of the blue, Rome texts me that he's outside. I run downstairs and open the door, immediately sensing something is wrong.

"Rome?" I say apprehensively. "Are you okay?"

He just kisses me softly on my lips. I wrap my hands around his neck, pulling him closer. He deepens the kiss.

It's not a soft kiss, but it's not wanting or desperate either. It's a kiss with the kind of urgency that makes me think he doesn't know when he'll get to kiss me again.

We pull away after a while, breathing heavily. "Rome?"

"Let's go inside, please."

"Okay."

We go upstairs and sit on my bed.

He sits on the very edge as if he might bolt. "I have something to tell you."

All the possibilities run through my head.

"Please, just say it. You're starting to scare me."

I've never seen him this nervous. Not even when he had to tell me he accidentally ruined my favorite sweatshirt by spilling juice all over it.

"I can't move to LA with you."

"Wha-at?" I say, my voice breaking. "Did you change your mind about Temple?"

"No, no. I'd never do this if I didn't have to."

"Then what's going on?"

"It's my mom."

Of course.

I haven't known her for long, but in the short time I have, she's been so kind to me. She's taught me how to cook Dominican food, gushed about how she loves seeing me with her son, and treated me like I was a real part of their family.

But I hate to see her like this. Treatment is sucking the vibrance out of her, as much as she tries to put on a brave face. I hate that I have to get to know her under these circumstances, while she's hurting so badly. Most of all, I hate that it's hurting Rome too.

"What happened?" I ask him.

"She's terminal," he tells me. "She's not getting better."

I immediately feel sick to my stomach. "Oh my God."

Tears begin to stream down his face as I hold him in my arms. "It's gonna be okay, Rome. It's gonna be okay."

"What about this is going to be fucking okay? She's dying. It's been just me and Mom for half of my life, and now she's gonna be dead."

He's right. He's losing a parent, the woman who's taken care of him for the past eighteen years. But he's not losing everyone. He still has me.

Not that that means very much in this situation.

"I'm so sorry, Rome. But you're not going to be alone. She's your mom, and no one else can fill that void, but you'll always have me. For whatever I'm good for."

"Pen," he says, the word clearly loaded.

"What's the plan?" I ask.

He lets out a deep breath. "I'm staying home with her."

I guessed about as much. I wouldn't expect anything less from him. Rome needs to spend however much time Rosa has left here with her in Fertsville. Nothing is more important than that.

"Okay," I say, feeling powerless. "I'll keep my job at the diner, see if I can switch to full-time. I can—"

"No. You're not staying here. I am."

"You don't want me to stay with you?"

"You're going to LA and achieving your dreams."

I'm in shock. "My dreams?"

"Yes, your dreams. You're going to be a household name, Pen. The world's waiting for you."

I shake my head. "What do my dreams matter if I'm not achieving them next to you?"

"Don't say that," he commands.

"Say what?" I ask him. "That I love you? That I want to be with you?"

"Yes! Don't say any of that." He runs his hands over his face. "You're making this so hard on me, Pen."

I'm still in disbelief that this is even happening right now. What happened to the guy from a few weeks ago?

"I have to stay. And you have to go."

At times like these, I would normally do anything he asks. But I can't do this. Not when it's this bad for him.

"I won't leave you, Rome. Not when you need me."

He lets out a deep exhale. "I don't know if you can be my girlfriend anymore."

It takes me a moment to process what he's just told me. "You're breaking up with me?"

"No," he says. "Yes. I just can't do this anymore."

"Just because things are hard now doesn't mean–"

"You think the past few months weren't hard? You think I wasn't losing my shit? I was. And I am. I don't know how the hell I'm going to live without you, and it cuts me every time I think about the fact that you're going to be thousands of miles away. But I have to do this. You'll make me miserable if you stay here."

How can he possibly believe I would make him miserable?

"What happens when I'm working long hours trying to pay the mortgage on my house—Mom's house—and I'm spending every hour by my mom's side? When you're bored out of your mind working a waitress job at the Fertsville Diner, knowing you're destined for so much greater? You could be at an Ivy

League. Or kicking ass out in LA. And I refuse to live with the bitter woman I know you'll become. She's not the one I want."

I don't understand how he could say that.

"You were willing to give up your dreams of going to Temple for me. Obviously, I'm willing to put chasing mine on hold to support you right now. Why would I want to do anything else? How could that make me bitter?"

"Aspen—"

"I can't," I cry. "I can't let you do this alone. Who's going to be here to pick you up when you fall? All of your friends are going to be in college. You need someone."

"But that someone can't be you."

"I'm not going."

"Yes, you are. Even if I have to put you on that goddamn plane myself."

Rome doesn't want me with him in Fertsville, no matter how much I want that for myself.

I don't know how to argue with him. How to convince him that I want to be with him, despite what it might mean to my career.

"Please," I beg him, "stay with me tonight?"

"Of course," he says, sounding as emotionally drained as I feel. "Of course."

CHAPTER
thirty-seven

"gold rush" by Taylor Swift

December, Present

$\mathcal{I}$ don't text Rome that night, opting to give him time to cool down. We were both running so high on emotions the last time we spoke, but I know that we can get past this.

We can go back to the way things were.

He can stay out of the spotlight in Fertsville and continue his life in however much peace he can. I'll eventually go back to LA when this blows over and hopefully continue my career as a musician.

But then I'll come home for Easter or next Thanksgiving, see him again, and we'll create our own little bubble until I have to go home again. And the cycle will continue until it can't anymore.

If that's the way things have to be, I'm okay with that. Even if that means sacrificing a real future with him.

'Tis the damn season, I suppose.

"Rome!" I call out as he gets out of his truck. "Hey."

"Hey, Pen," he says. "How've you been doing?"

"I'm okay," I reply. "Worried about you. I'm sorry I blew up at you like that."

He shrugs his shoulders. "Don't apologize. I knew what I was doing when I came with you to that event. And I was the one who punched that asshole anyway. If anyone's to blame for what's being said about me on the internet now, it's me."

"It's just a situation. A terrible, frustrating situation. I should have prepared you better."

He puts a hand on my shoulder. "Well, I'll work through this. I have at least two years before I'll be applying for positions anyway."

"I'm always here for you. Whenever you need me."

Today is the very first time I'll get to work with Ella on "O Come Little Children." I knew there was so much potential in her from the day she sang in her audition, so I'm ecstatic that I'll finally get to start coaching her in a one-on-one setting.

We ended rehearsals for the other kids about an hour earlier than usual. We only called a few people for special scenes, so things weren't as hectic as they normally are. While Rome stays downstairs with everyone else, Ella and I head upstairs to work on her song.

I've decided to use the practice room in the church, as opposed to the auditorium. The piano here is a little nicer, and I like the cozy atmosphere.

"You ready, Ella?" I say in my most cheerful voice.

"Yeah," she replies. "I think so."

"Are you a little nervous to be working with me one on one?"

She looks down at her shoes. "A little."

I sit down behind the piano and pull out my music. "Is there anything we can do to make you feel a little more comfortable?"

"No, I'm okay," she says.

I'm really proud of how far Ella has come during this production. She's a lot more confident, and she's been making friends with a few of the other kids in the cast.

"Let's get started then, shall we?"

We start with a series of vocal warmups, most of which I typically use on tour. I play each note on the piano, sing it for her, then she repeats it back to me. We continue up the scale until she's hitting her break.

We work on diction as well, singing another of my favorite warmups from when I was a kid: "Mommy made me mash my M&Ms." By the fifteen-minute mark, I feel like we're about ready to sing.

"Do you want to take this slow, section by section, or do you know it well enough to try it yourself?"

"Um, maybe I can try."

"Remember, there's no pressure. Let's take it from the top."

Off the bat, she sounds gorgeous. The song sits in her head-voice, the highest part of her range, and sounds breathy and beautiful. Though her vowel placement on the "o" is slightly off, so I stop her there.

"Watch the shape of your mouth on those 'o' sounds you're making." I point to the mirror. "Here, look in the mirror and check the shape of your mouth."

She looks to her side to see the small mirror. "What about it?"

"You need to round out your lips a bit to get a clearer vowel sound." I demonstrate for her.

"Okay," she says. "That makes sense."

She tries it out for herself and sounds ten times better.

"Awesome, Ella. That was really great. Let's take it from the top again, shall we?"

She starts the song again, putting my correction into place. I don't stop her again until she makes her way to the chorus.

"Pause for a second there," I tell her. "I think we need to work on taking low belly breaths. You're running out of air, and it's affecting your sound as you go through the song."

"How do I fix it?"

"I'll show you," I say. "Do you mind putting your hands on my belly?"

"Sure," she responds.

"I'm going to take a few breaths from my belly and then normally. I want you to see if you can feel the difference."

She places her hand on my stomach.

"Feel the difference?" I ask.

"Yeah!" she exclaims. "It feels so weird."

"You think you can try doing it yourself?"

"Yup!"

"Okay. Why don't we take it from the top? From there, we can work on where you need to make sure you're taking a low belly breath."

"Sounds good," she says before doing exactly as I've asked, executing it almost perfectly.

Throughout the rest of the rehearsal, we work on her breathing and a few other small notes I make for her. Ella's diligent, marking notations in her music and paying close attention to detail. I appreciate the amount of focus she has for someone her age.

Rome smiles as he comes up from the basement and watches her sing. I know he wasn't sold on choosing Ella for Mary, but now I can tell he's sure.

"You were amazing today, Ella," I say as we finish up. "Really, you were wonderful."

"Thank you so much! That means so much to me. You are my favorite singer *ever!*"

I lean in for a hug. "Thank *you*."

Considering everything that people have been saying about me in the media lately, it can often feel like there's no one left that supports me.

But it's amazing to know that there's at least one kid out there I'm inspiring. It makes all of the drama seem worth it.

"Maybe one day, if I work super hard, I can be as good as you? And make my own music!"

"Of course you can, Ella. You can do anything you set your mind to."

CHAPTER
thirty-eight

"Never Forget You" by Zara Larsson and MNEK

August, Six Years Ago

$\mathcal{J}$'ve been crying all morning. The fact that Rome and I are breaking up is finally hitting me. And it's really hard to take.

These past few months have felt like waiting for a bomb to go off. We spent as much time together as possible, but the inevitable was forever bearing down on us.

My parents are dropping me off at the airport, and he's coming with us. I wanted it this way, but I don't know what's worse. Getting on that plane and having to see his face or leaving without him there to send me off.

Though it's only five in the morning and my flight is at ten, Rome makes it over to my house bright and early.

"Hey," I say.

He pulls me into his arms. "Hi."

"I know I woke you up early," he says. "Do you want to go get some more sleep?"

"No," I tell him. I honestly don't think it's possible for me to sleep right now. "But I would like to lie with you for a while."

I'm already dressed and packed.

Rome kisses my forehead. "Okay. We can head upstairs."

He lies on the mattress, and I settle myself slightly on top of him, wanting nothing more than for him to hold me.

We don't say much. We don't need words in a moment like this.

My silent tears spill onto his shirt, but he doesn't care, not bothering to move me or make note of it.

Now that I know what it feels like, how am I supposed to live without someone who cares about me so deeply, who gets me, who knows me better than I know myself? How am I supposed to survive when I'm across the country in a studio apartment without my parents or Rome? I want this so bad, but....

But I have to do this. I have to give it my best shot. Because if I don't, Rome will blame himself. Blame himself for being the reason I'm staying home, the reason I'm not out doing what I love to do.

He rubs my arm and his breathing quickens. I know he's feeling this too. The realness of our situation kicking in.

I don't know what to say as Rome eventually peels himself off me. "We should probably get going. You don't want to miss your flight."

But I do. I do want to miss that plane.

The ride to the airport is a somber one. Rome and I don't speak. Neither do my parents. The only thing we hear is the gentle hum of the morning radio filtering through the speakers.

My mom gets out of the car with us and gives me a big hug. "I love you so much, honey."

I squeeze her tighter, determined not to cry. "I love you too, Mom."

She rubs her hand gently across my arm. "You'll call me as soon as you land?"

I nod. "I will."

"Send pictures of your apartment," she reminds me for what feels like the hundredth time.

I kiss her once on the cheek. "Don't worry, Mom. I won't forget."

I hug my dad in the driver's seat of his car. "Goodbye, Dad. I love you so much."

"I love you too, Penny. So much."

I plant a kiss on his cheek before walking back toward the entrance. Rome's already grabbed my two suitcases from the trunk.

"Bye!" I say, waving to my parents.

"I'll help you get your bags inside."

"Are you sure? Don't you have to—"

"I'll help you with your bags."

I roll my carry-on suitcase and duffle bag while Rome has my two suitcases. While it seems like I packed a lot, I'm going to be living away for the next year.

By the time we get my bags checked, I feel sick to my stomach.

We look at each other for a while, neither of us knowing quite what to say.

So I wrap my arms around him, working desperately hard not to cry. "I love you so much."

"I love you too."

We stay like this for a while, but eventually, we have to pull apart.

He leans in for a kiss.

Our last kiss.

I never thought I'd utter those words.

"You're going to do amazing things, Pen. Soon you'll forget all about me."

"Never," I say firmly. "I will never forget about you."

CHAPTER
thirty-nine

"Christmas Tree Farm" by Taylor Swift

December, Present

*R*ehearsal begins around four the next afternoon. I spent the morning attempting to write, but the creative juices weren't flowing how I'd hoped.

Today is the first time Ella is doing her solo for the rest of the cast.

She is extremely nervous, but I have no doubt that she'll be amazing. She's been killing it during our one-on-one sessions. It'll be good for her to have the experience of working through her stress and anxiety. I wouldn't want her to experience that for the first time closer to the show.

I rush out of my car and into the church, feeling a little guilty that I slept in so late today. I took a nap after I got home, thinking I was just going to doze off for a second, but I ended up sleeping for a couple of hours. I woke up with just enough time to make it here.

"Hey, everyone," I say as I enter the auditorium. "Sorry, I'm late."

"You're good," Rome tells me. "We haven't started yet."

I nod. "Okay. Thanks."

"We were thinking of running through scenes eight and nine and then going right into Ella's solo?"

"Sounds good to me," I reply. "Places, everyone!"

The first two scenes go by quickly. Joey is a great narrator and is always consistent. When scenes are based around him, I know they'll be okay. He always knows his line and cues anyone who needs it.

We've yet to stage the song yet, so that's what we start with next.

"Joey, can we get you farther stage, right?" I ask, pointing to where I want him. When he makes it over there, I take a step back and look at the larger picture.

"Evie, Millie, and Grace, can we have you guys standing off to stage left?" They make their way over, and I take a look at them standing in a line. "Grace, why don't you come slightly downstage? You two can back her."

A little dimension is better than a straight line.

"Nick, let's have you slightly off-center." I point to the star on the floor that marks it. "And Ella, let's have you next to him."

I take another step back to look at everyone's spacing. With the lightning I have in mind, this is going to look amazing.

"When you guys are performing this, we're going to have a spotlight on Ella, but we're not going to have that until dress rehearsal," I inform them. I look over at Rome. "I think we're ready to start the song."

He nods. "Ella, you're good to go?"

"Yes," she says, but her voice is small. "I'm ready."

"You got this," Rome encourages her.

So far, her improvements have been massive, and we've still got time left.

Ella makes it through about half the song without stopping, but when she gets to the second verse, she can't seem to remember the words. She starts to mumble, and I can see the anxiety spreading across her face. My heart aches for her. I know she wanted to nail it while everyone watched for the first time, but sometimes that's just not how things happen.

But what surprises me is Millie.

Millie starts singing softly to help Ella out with the words.

My mouth falls agape as I look over at her, and Rome's does too. The smile he's sporting is a mile wide. He's proud of her. And so am I.

She jumps in to help with the first two lines and then stops, but it gives Ella the confidence she needs to continue the rest of the song.

"Wow, Ella!" I say. "That was amazing. And thank you, Millie for stepping in. That was very kind of you."

She shrugs.

I look toward Rome, who's been checking in with Millie at the end of every rehearsal for the past few weeks. "I don't know what you've been doing," I whisper, "but whatever it is, keep doing it."

Rome insists on playing holiday music the entire way down to the Christmas tree farm.

My dad asked us if we wanted to get the tree this year instead of doing it as a family, which surprised me at first. But he's been trying to push us together a lot lately, so I guess I should've expected it. Plus, Rome seemed so excited about the prospect, I found it impossible to say no.

"I don't understand how you can genuinely enjoy listening to the same song so many times in a row."

He chuckles and places a hand on my thigh. "Baby, it's Mariah Carey. Who doesn't love Mariah Carey?"

I roll my eyes. "I never said I didn't like her. She's nice."

I met her last year at the Music Video Awards. She congratulated me after I won Video of The Year and told me how much she loved my new album.

"Wow," he says. "You know, for a while, I almost forgot you were famous. But you had to go and say something like that."

"I can introduce you if you want."

He smirks at me. "If we're ever in the same room, I'll hold you to that."

I can imagine it now. Rome and I, together at another industry party. Next time, I'll ensure Cane and Sierra are *not* on the invite list.

The next song that comes on is one of my personal holiday favorites. "Rockin' Around The Christmas Tree" by Brenda Lee. This song fits perfectly between overplayed and just enough.

I sing along with her, adding my own harmonies whenever the music calls me to. "Rome! You have to sing with me," I say before the first chorus.

"No," he says firmly.

"You're really not going to sing?" I ask, baiting him with my tone. Can't he just indulge me this one time?

He simply smiles at me. "No, Pen, I'm not."

"Okay." I continue to sing the song myself, as obnoxiously as possible. I like this kind of singing. The kind where it's low stakes, and I can just feel the music and be myself. He looks over at me every couple of seconds, taking in my performance. I even add in my own little dance in the passenger seat.

"Wow, Pen," he says. "I'd pay good money to see you do that in concert."

Maybe he would. But definitely not anyone else in the world. "Ha-ha, very funny," I say. "Maybe I'll do it on my next tour."

My sets aren't typically super choreographed. It's mainly just me with my guitar or on the piano, following some light blocking given to me by my tour directors.

We soon pull into the lot. The smell of hot chocolate and pine trees immediately sends warmth throughout my body. The area is lit up in Christmas lights, with decorations of Santa and his elves scattered nearby.

It's been two years since I've been back here to pick out a tree with my family, and I missed it. They don't have stuff like this in LA, or at least not that I know of.

There's a stand with hot chocolate and a gift shop at the base of the large hill by the entrance. This is always our first stop, no matter what. If we're getting a Christmas tree, we might as well have the whole experience. Ugly Christmas sweaters, hot chocolate, marshmallows. Everything that makes the holidays so special.

We go up to the stand at the front of the farm to pay for our food and drinks, and then we go over to grab what we'd like.

Rome gets a cup from the stack behind the hot chocolate and fills it to the brim from the dispenser. "How many marshmallows do you want?"

"At least six."

He hands me the cup with eight marshmallows inside. "Thanks, Rome," I say.

"No problem."

Rome fills another cup for himself before taking the can of whipped cream and adding some to both mine and his.

"Thank you," I say before taking a sip.

I miss the cold winters and the experience of drinking hot chocolate in the snow.

I look up at Rome, realizing he's been staring at me for quite a while. "What?"

He leans into me. "Here." He takes his thumb and swipes some whipped cream from my nose before licking it off his finger.

"Thanks," I say, melting a little at his touch. "Look. They've got a ton of cookies laid out."

Chocolate chip, M&M, sugar, and, best of all, snickerdoodles.

"How many do you want?"

"All of them, obviously." But I don't put quite that many in my bag.

He looks at me like I'm crazy. "We can always make more later. You know that, right?"

"Yes, but no one can make them like they do here. I need to treasure these until I can get them again next year."

He laughs and shakes his head. "Don't ever let anyone tell you fame has changed you. It hasn't."

I'm not quite sure what to say to that, so I say nothing at all.

We sit down on two nearby stools. Rome scoots his a little closer to mine and offers me a bit of his chocolate chip cookie.

"It's good," I say. "But nothing beats a snickerdoodle."

I hold out mine for him to try. He takes a small bite, careful not to eat too much.

He shrugs. "It's good."

"Good?" I prod. "Just good?"

"It's great," he amends.

"Much better."

Once we're done eating, we make our way up the hill. There are tons of sections for the different kinds of trees, but I generally know what I want.

"Do you need a tree too?" I ask Rome.

"No, I'm good."

"You already got one?" Rome's never been the kind to decorate for the holidays. Not since his mom passed.

"I don't really celebrate Christmas at my apartment."

"Why not?"

"It's not worth decorating for just one person."

"Oh, Rome."

I can't imagine how hard things are for him living in the town where he spent most of his life without his parents. With their memories following him everywhere.

I wanted to be there as he packed up his mom's things and moved across town to his first apartment. Hell, I wanted to use my first paycheck to help him cover his mortgage, so he wouldn't have had to sell the house. I know my parents checked in on him sometimes, brought him food, made sure he was alive, and reported back with updates. But it wasn't enough.

"Are you sure you don't want to get a tree? I can help you decorate it."

Just by the look on his face, I can tell my idea doesn't sit well with him. "How about I just help you with yours?"

A compromise.

"I'll take you up on that."

"I'd expect nothing less."

"Okay," I say. "Let's go find one we like."

We walk over to the collection of them on the other side of the hill.

We spend a few minutes walking around the area, examining each tree.

"You haven't found one you like yet?"

"I'm waiting for it to come to me!"

I don't exactly know a ton about Christmas trees, but I always know when I find the perfect one.

The first time my parents took me to the farm with them, that I remember, I was six years old. I was quite clueless and didn't really know what I was looking for, but wrapped up in the excitement of the day, I fell into this one beautiful Spruce tree. My parents immediately had it wrapped it up and took it home. From that day forward, I've always picked the family tree.

I can't say this tradition has moved forward into my own home. Sierra and I would use the same fake tree and have someone decorate it for us. She never cared much about the holidays and saw a pretty tree as an Instagram opportunity, but it's always nice to do when I'm back home. Something special for just Fertsville.

We walk around for about ten more minutes.

"This one!" I shout, pointing to a tree as Rome comes to find me.

"You're sure?"

"Yes. One hundred percent sure."

It's a beautiful spruce tree that's the perfect length and width. I can already imagine it now with lights wrapped around it and presents underneath.

It'll look wonderful in my parent's living room.

"Okay. As long as you're sure."

He returns from the office area set up in a Santa hut with an ax.

"You got this?" I ask him.

He looks at me like I've just asked the dumbest question of all time. "I got this."

I go over to pay before we make our way back down the hill, Rome carrying our tree.

"You need my help?" I ask him, gesturing to the tree, but given my lack of upper body strength, I know I won't be of much assistance.

"No," he says. "I think I can handle this."

When we finally make it to his truck, Rome puts the tree down, prepping to tie it on top of the car. "Why don't you turn the heat on while I get this done?"

He tosses me his keys. I get the car started, the heat pumping, and then make my way over to the passenger seat.

We spend the first half of the ride in comfortable silence. Rome puts his hand on my thigh as he drives, and I keep a goofy smile on my face, thinking about how nice it was to spend a day with him like this.

But we pass by Jeff's parents' house on our way back from the farm.

I think Rome can sense my awkward energy, so he reassures me. "My best memory in this house by far is the night I fell in love with you."

My heart stops for a second. "You fell in love with me that night?" That was one of the worst nights of my life. But I guess also one of the best, considering it was when we started dating.

"Yes," he confirms. "I remember the exact moment I knew."

"Was it before I puked my guts out or after?" I ask.

He laughs. "Surprisingly after."

I look at him, mouth hanging wide open. "That's so embarrassing."

He gawks at me. "What's embarrassing about it? My love for you?"

"No! The fact that I threw up all over your friend's carpeted floors and embarrassed us both in front of everyone."

"You didn't embarrass me. You can't be embarrassed when you don't care about other people's opinions."

I think we can agree to disagree on that one.

"What made you decide you loved me?"

Rome, who normally seems so calm and collected, now seems kind of nervous. "It was the build-up of everything that had gone on that night. When I came to your door, I felt something I had never felt before. You looked so beautiful, the most beautiful girl I'd ever seen."

He tucks a strand of hair behind my ear.

"You were willing to try new things that night. It was out of your comfort zone, but you came anyway. I wasn't expecting you to, and to be honest, I felt kind of bad for asking. But you wanted to fit in with the people I hung out with. You wanted to play pong with me. You drank until you made yourself sick, which I obviously didn't want, but I don't know, I guess I found it endearing? I saw you sitting on the bathroom floor, looking at me like you wanted to sink into the walls. I could tell you were embarrassed, but I didn't care that you'd just puked your guts out. That's the moment I knew. I was absolutely in love with you."

I can hardly breathe.

Suddenly I'm right back in high school. Seventeen and madly in love with Roman Torres. I was convinced I'd marry him one day. There was no one better for me.

"Rome," I gasp. "I don't even know what to say."

He puts a hand on my cheek. "You don't need to say anything, Pen. I just wanted you to know."

CHAPTER
forty

"Holy Ground (Taylor's Version)" by Taylor Swift

June, Five Years Ago

*I*t might have been a mistake to blow my entire month's paycheck on this ticket to fly home for the weekend, but I couldn't help myself. This is so beyond worth it. I look out the window at the clouds—I cannot wait to land.

After ten months of auditioning, doing background work, and waitressing in LA, I've finally been cast. *A lead role in a TV show, no less!* My initial reaction was to pick up the phone and call Mom, but it'll mean so much more if I tell her in person.

My dad is the one who picks me up from the airport, as Mom doesn't even know I'm coming yet.

"I've missed you so much, Dad," I say as I get in the car, hugging him awkwardly across the seat of his old Chevy van.

"I can't wait to hear this exciting news you have to tell us."

"I want to tell you together over dinner."

He laughs and puts a hand on my knee. "Whatever you say."

In just under an hour, I'm back at my parent's house for the first time since moving to LA.

I've missed a lot about this house. The fact that there are multiple rooms, to begin with. It may not be a mansion, but it's ours. It's the perfect size for us.

Right now, I'm living in a decent area in a tiny studio apartment. It's not as bad as it could be, but I'm definitely homesick. All I've got is a small kitchen setup, my bed, and a nightstand. It's not too bad, though. And now that I'll be making more, maybe by the end of filming, I'll be able to afford rent on a bigger place in my building.

Since my mom's not home yet, I take the opportunity to borrow my dad's car and drive to Rome's house. A million thoughts run through my mind.

I knock on his door as obnoxiously as possible, unable to contain my excitement. I've missed him an unbelievable amount. Rome and I haven't spoken much since I left for California.

All I want is to wrap my arms around him. Feel his lips on mine. Not have to wonder about what it would be like to be with him again. Know for myself.

"Pen?" he says, opening the door, shocked for a moment before wrapping his arms around me and twirling me around. "Pen! Oh my God."

Our lips meet for what feels like the greatest kiss we've ever had. It's frantic. It's loving. It's sweet. It's incredibly beautiful.

I've missed him. He can make my anxiety disappear with just a single kiss. My love for him hasn't gone away over the time we've been apart, if anything, it's gone stronger.

He pulls me into his arms.

"I missed you so much," I say. "So, so, so much."

"What are you doing here?" he asks. "Did things not work out?"

"It's actually quite the opposite."

"Tell me!"

"I booked my first big role!"

"Oh my God, Pen. I'm so happy for you." He dances me around the foyer. "What's the part?"

"I'm going to be the lead role on ATN's newest drama. It's all about this murderous sorority girl. I'm really excited about it."

He kisses me yet again, but this one is short-lived.

"I'm so proud of you. I always knew you could do it, *mi cielo*. You're so amazing."

"That means so much to me, Rome."

"You better believe I'll be home watching every single murderous episode. I'll be supporting you for the rest of your career."

"Thank you."

I want to tell him that I love him. I want to tell him how much he means to me. How much I care about him.

"How's everything been going for you?" I ask, wiping my eyes.

"Here, come in." He moves to the side. "I'll tell you everything."

CHAPTER
forty-one

"mirrorball" by Taylor Swift

December, Present

*M*urray calls me around nine o'clock the next morning. I'm a little surprised, given that LA is three hours behind Fertsville, meaning it's only five in the morning for him, but I know what this means. More bad news.

I just don't know what could be worse than what we've already faced.

"Hey," I say. "What's up?"

"Aspen, I'm about to send you a link to a series of tweets containing personal pictures of you that were taken from your boyfriend's phone."

The air is knocked out of my lungs. "What?"

"After your old friend did that interview, people were trying to find as much information on him as they could. It seems someone hacked his iCloud account and found a series of pictures of the two of you taken throughout the years."

I don't think I've ever experienced such an invasion of privacy.

I open the link he's sent me to see pictures of Rome and me. So many pictures. Some are innocent, from our time together in high school. Others were taken in the last couple of years when I was supposedly in a relationship with Keith or the other guys I was rumored to be with.

The first few aren't so bad. There are a few selfies of us out in town and funny candids he's taken of me. But then there are the scandalous few.

Selfies of us in his bed. Mirror pictures of us in his bathroom in the apartment, with him topless and me in my underwear. To make matters worse, they're all time-stamped. Everyone is going to assume I was still seeing him while I was "with other people."

We didn't document our time together much, but we did take a few pictures. Ones we thought we'd be the only ones to see.

"What can we do?" I ask breathlessly. "We can sue, right? We can make them take these down. Rome…"

Oh my God.

Rome.

He's never going to forgive me for this. Never.

If he wasn't going to be able to get a job in education based on his fight with Cane, these pictures are gasoline thrown on that fire.

Now the first thing people are going to see when they google his name are these raunchy photos of the two of us.

I'm famous. Within a couple of years, something new and more exciting will happen in my life. I'll book more projects. People won't remember exactly how everything went down. These pictures won't be the first thing people see.

But for Roman?

"I have to go," I say. "I have to call him. He's going to freak out."

"Aspen, I know this was an invasion of your privacy. I know you're likely hurt, but I'm growing concerned. Young girls follow you and listen to their music. How are you going to sell concert tickets when–"

"Don't you think I know that? You think I wanted this to happen? You think I wanted these intimate moments out into the universe?"

Parents aren't going to want to take their kids to see my shows. They're going to think of me as more of a slut than they already do. They're going to view me as the kind of person who would purposely try to poison their kids with sexual content like this.

I'm directing a show with children at a *church,* for God's sake. I can't even begin to fathom how their parents are going to take this. If they didn't like me before, they're going to hate me now.

"It's okay," Murray says, his tone finally turning softer. "It's all going to be fine. We'll figure out a plan. I'll call an emergency meeting with the rest of the team to figure out how to approach the situation. Take some time off. Get off social media."

"Okay," I reply weakly. "I have to go."

I need to talk to Rome. I have to explain what's going on before he finds out from somewhere else. But this isn't something I can do over the phone.

I throw on a pair of leggings and a hoodie and get into my rental car, sweat dripping as I struggle to catch my breath. My stomach is churning.

"Hey, Pen," Rome says as he opens his door. "Is everything okay?"

Nothing is okay.

"I don't know how to say this. I'm sorry. I'm so, so–"

Rome puts his hand on my shoulder and guides me into his apartment, then sits me down on his couch. "Breathe, please. Tell me what's wrong."

"Pictures," I tell him. "They found your pictures."

"What?" he asks, confused. "What pictures?"

"All of them. Someone hacked into your iCloud."

His expression turns from confusion to shock to anger in a matter of seconds.

"Show me!" he says. "I don't believe this." I pull up the link Murray sent me.

I watch as he takes it all in. The intimate pictures of us across Twitter. The invasion of privacy I still can't believe is happening to us. All of the retweets and comments about how awful a person I am for cheating on Henry, Robert, Zachary, and Keith, as these pictures were taken over the years we've been together. Just as I'd assumed they would.

This wouldn't have happened if I hadn't brought Rome to New York with me and introduced him to the world.

Besides, it was reckless to document our time together. Stupid, even. But at that moment, neither of us could have imagined that pictures like this would get out.

No one in the press had any clue who Rome was. He's the safest, most trustworthy person I know. I was never concerned that he would share them with anyone or post them somewhere. He respects me far too much.

But now, that poor decision-making has blown up in my face.

"You've got to be kidding me! This is illegal. How are people just allowed to post stuff like this?"

I try my best to present like I'm calm. Like all of this isn't freaking me out just as much as it is him. "It's the internet. I'm famous. Things like this are bound to happen, but–"

"No," he says. "Things like this don't happen to me. People are going to google me, and the first thing they're going to see are these goddamn pictures. Do you know what they're going to–"

"I know what people are going to do! I'm sorry. I'm sorry. I shouldn't have asked you to come to the Blitz. I shouldn't have run the risk of this happening. What else can I say that will make this better?"

Rome doesn't even dignify my apology with a response. He simply rises from the couch and begins to pace. "I cannot believe this. Have your parents seen these?"

"I don't know." They weren't home when I left, so I guess that's a conversation for later.

But my parents must know I'm not a virgin. I used to stay over at his place when I'd visit.

"What if the kids' parents see this?" he asks. "What if they find out?"

"I can't pretend I have all the answers. Most of them are ten or younger. I doubt they have Twitter or unfiltered access to the internet. If their parents find out, then we'll just have to handle that as it happens."

He scoffs. "You might be fine living a life where you're not entitled to privacy. A life where your decisions aren't your own. A life where you get so nervous you can hardly breathe, and you let your own management berate you for things that aren't your fault, but I never chose to live this way. These people are crazy. Your supposed fans don't seem to care about you. I mean, I don't know how you do this. It's too much, it's–"

"Okay!" I say, unwilling to hear his harsh words anymore. "Okay, I get it."

Rome could never live in my world. He doesn't want *me* to live like this.

It hurts to hear Rome list all of the reasons he thinks I'm pathetic for being in the industry, but I love my job. I live for my career, and I refuse to give up my livelihood because of people on the internet.

"You know, I'm a victim in this too," I say. "Those pictures aren't just of you. You're not the only one who gets to be upset about this situation. But you're right. You never wanted to live like this. It was wrong of me to bring you into a lifestyle you had no desire to be a part of."

Rome looks at me with an expression I struggle to place. It's a while before he says anything.

He looks away from me suddenly and stalks back over to the kitchen. "I don't think I want to talk about this anymore. I think we need to take some time apart."

"Yeah." I sniffle. "Maybe you're right."

I stumble out of his apartment and into my car, then shove my key into the ignition.

I'm unable to look my parents in the eye as I walk through my front door ten minutes later. I'm praying they haven't heard about the pictures yet; it's only been about two hours since they were leaked.

"Morning, Penny," says Dad.

"Hey, Dad. Hey, Mom," I say quietly. I cross the room and sink onto one of the seats at our dining room table.

"Is everything alright?" Mom asks.

Tears are streaming down my face as my parents rush over to the table.

"Aspen, honey," Mom says. "Tell us what's wrong."

"They hacked into Rome's iCloud, Mom. All of our private pictures. Things we'd never want anyone else to see. They've been leaked onto the internet."

Mom looks over at Dad and then back at me, placing her hand over mine. I can tell this subject is making Dad uncomfortable.

"I'm so sorry, Penny," he says. "How did this happen? Have you spoken to him about it?"

I nod. "Speaking to him just made things worse."

I've caused irreparable damage to my career. And there's nothing I can do about it. What goes on the internet stays there forever. Taking legal action isn't going to solve this problem.

Nothing will.

I run my hands through my hair. "He probably never wants to see me again. How is he ever going to get hired as a teacher after this? The fight at the Blitz Ball was bad enough."

Mom puts her hand on my shoulder. "I'm sure he's mad right now, but eventually, he won't see things this way. He'll recognize that you're a victim in this just as much as he is."

"I signed up for this." I stand up and back away from them. "He didn't. I don't know why I thought things could be different."

Why I thought that I might actually get the best of both worlds for once.

Dad grimaces. "I won't pretend to know all of the ins and outs of celebrity or how you can work through this together. But he loves you, and you love him. And in my book, that counts for something."

"But it isn't enough."

Leila calls me about two hours into my self-inflicted hibernation. I know she's seen the pictures the second I pick up the phone. The careful tone she greets me with is a dead giveaway.

"Hey, Aspen," she says apprehensively. "How are you doing today?"

"If you want to ask me about the pictures, just go ahead and ask," I reply. "I'd honestly rather talk about it than dance around this and pretend like I don't know you've seen them."

"I'm so sorry," she gushes. "I know you're probably feeling like shit right now. I didn't look at them! Just the headlines."

I appreciate her loyalty, but it's not like it makes a difference.

"In a few years, people will realize how stupid they're being right now," she says. "Why should anyone care so much about how you conducted yourself in your past relationships? Sure, cheating is bad, I know that more than anyone, but–"

"I never cheated on anyone," I interrupt. "It's all made up. I was never with any of those guys in the first place."

"Oh my God, I'm so sorry for assuming," she says. "I should've known you'd never do that. I just hate seeing so many people attack you like this when I know you deserve so much better. You're an amazing person. Far better than whichever dumbass did this to you."

I take in a breath. "Thanks, Leila. That means a lot, seriously."

CHAPTER
forty-two

"I miss you, I'm sorry" by Gracie Abrams

June, Five Years Ago

$\mathcal{W}$e walk together to Rome's room to sit and talk. I've missed the times we used to spend on the phone until we fell asleep. Or after school, debriefing our days until I had to go home. I've been so homesick these past few months. It's hard to believe I'm actually here. But I am here in Rome's house with my hand in his.

"So, tell me about how things are going. How's your mom?"

"She's been better," he says softly. "It's been an adjustment for her, you know, not working anymore. She worked so hard to become a paralegal, and now she's not even up to going to the grocery store sometimes."

"I can't imagine how hard that must be for the both of you right now."

He shrugs. "I just want to see her get better. I want to see her happy again."

"If you need anything," I say, "I'm always just a phone call away. I don't want you to feel alone."

He smiles weakly. "Thanks, Pen."

"Which courses have you been taking at Fertsville Community?" He'd told me about a few classes he wanted to take in education last summer before I left.

"Actually," he begins, before taking a pause, "I dropped out."

"You did?" I ask, not sure what to make of this.

"I got a job at the grocery store. We have to pay the bills somehow while Mom is undergoing chemo."

I wrap my arms around him and squeeze him tight. "I'm so sorry. I don't know what to say. I wish I could help you guys out, but I'm barely able to afford rent on my tiny apartment."

"It's okay, Pen," he replies. "I'd never ask you to do that. I'll take care of this, don't worry."

I feel terrible that he has to put his dreams on hold and take on responsibilities that he shouldn't have at nineteen years old.

"I'd like to see her, if that's okay. If she's feeling up to it, maybe you guys can come for dinner with me and my parents tonight?"

I've missed Rosa too over these past few months, so it'll be nice to see her again. Maybe getting out of her house will even bring her a bit of joy during this difficult time.

"I'm sure she'd love that," he says.

"That's great, Rome. I'm happy she's feeling a bit better."

He reminds me of what I'm still struggling to believe has finally happened. "Besides, I'm sure she'll be thrilled to hear your amazing news!"

"Awesome," I reply. "I'm excited."

CHAPTER
forty-three

"Sign of the Times" by Harry Styles

December, Present

$\mathcal{R}$ome and I need to talk before we see each other in front of the kids, so I go over to his apartment about thirty minutes before we're set to start. This is going to be a tough conversation to have. I know he's feeling angry and stripped bare. But I'm angry too.

Angry at the universe for constantly kicking me when I'm already down. Angry at Rome for acting like all of this is my fault when I'm a victim too. Angry at the fact that I've done what seems to be irreparable damage to my career, and the media won't let me forget it.

Parents of a few of the kids in our show have already called my dad and expressed their discomfort in having their kids directed by Rome and me. Luckily, he was able to reassure them that they had nothing to worry about, but it cuts deep that my LA issues have seeped into my hometown life in such a drastic way. It's no longer silent whispers in the hallway about me being a homewrecker. It's people openly calling my father to tell him what an awful influence I am.

I've had to try my best to block out all of the new death threats and social media posts commenting on what's happened. Though there are some people saying that it was wrong for someone to leak intimate pictures of us, everyone is still in agreement that I'm a terrible person for "cheating" and being with Rome while in other relationships.

I want to come clean about the fact that I was never actually with any of the men named, especially not Keith. But doing so would mean telling the world that I'm a liar who let them believe false narratives solely for my personal gain. While it's not the worst crime in the world, I don't need any more reasons for the public to grow further disillusioned with me.

So Murray and I crafted a vague statement addressing the photos and shared it with each of my socials.

> In light of the recent images of me circulating around the internet, I wanted to make a statement. No one deserves to have their private life out in the open. I never intended for any of my young supporters to see anything like this. As for the rumors, whenever there is a lack of information about the private lives of celebrities, the media likes to construct stories of their own to fill the gaps. These stories are very far from the truth. I apologize for the damage this has caused and urge those who put these on the internet to consider the harm they've done to not only me, but a good man, innocent of the accusations.

We knew it wouldn't fix everything, but at the very least, it's a start.

"Rome!" I call, knocking on his door as my hands quiver from the cold. "It's Aspen. I want to talk."

He opens it a few moments later in a hoodie and gray sweatpants, his curly hair still damp from a shower. "Hey."

"Hey," I reply, holding out a box of chocolate chip cookies I brought as a peace offering. "I brought these for you. I know you like the grocery store ones."

He smiles weakly and takes the cookies from me, bringing them over to his kitchen counter.

"Thanks."

Walking into his one-bedroom apartment, I take in everything, something I was too flustered to do when I was here three days ago. It still looks as it always has, small and a bit dusty. Rome always keeps it super clean, but the paint color, cramped space, and awful furniture all make for a not-so-nice living space.

Being back here reminds me of all the nights we spent wrapped up in each other, in his bedroom, or on this couch. All the times I came straight from the airport, unable to contain my excitement to see him.

"I'm really sorry about how everything went down," I begin as I rub my hands down my jeans. "I know this has messed with your life in so many ways, and that it might be hard for you to get hired for jobs. Trust me. I never wanted this to happen. I've always just wanted you to be happy. If I would have known–"

Rome shakes his head and puts his hand on my shoulder. "I'm so impressed by you, Aspen. This wasn't your fault. I shouldn't have made you feel like it was. I don't know how I'd ever get used to any of this. You are a stronger person than I am."

Rome and I drive to rehearsal together. We didn't see the point of taking two cars, plus it meant we could prep.

We start with notes, then run the show from top to bottom. Millie is learning to get along with those outside her posse and actively participates when we play a theater game.

Ella does her song for everyone again, and it's beautiful. I can tell she's been practicing. She was definitely the right choice for Mary.

Although Miles and Ron, two of the prophets, are having a little bit of trouble sticking to the script, everything seems to be working out in our favor. It's nothing we can't fix in two more rehearsals.

Rome and I are waiting for the remaining stragglers to leave the building when I get a text.

"Rome!" I call as I cover my mouth. "Oh my God!"

"What?" He takes the phone out of my hands, reads the message, hands it back to me, then checks his own.

"Pen–"

"We have to go! Now!"

I stare back at the text, now blurred from the tears in my eyes.

> **Mom:** On the way to the hospital. Dad fell at work. Come ASAP.

"Okay," he says. "Breathe, *mi cielo*. Go grab your stuff. I'll start the car."

> **Aspen:** we're on the way.

I rush off toward the back of the auditorium, grab my bag and the few things I'd brought with me, and meet him in the car. Unlike me, Rome is calm as he drives us to the hospital, which is one town over, about twenty minutes away.

"What if he hit his head?" I ask him as I call my mom for the second time. "I've been telling him he should be cutting back. I—"

"Pen," he says. "Please. I will get us there as fast as possible. Don't start creating scenarios in your head. You know that'll do nothing but upset you even more."

I would argue, but I feel like I'm about to puke and don't really have that kind of energy.

I take the aux cord and plug it into my phone. I need music to calm me right now. He strokes my thigh as he speeds down the highway.

We pull up to the hospital a few minutes later. We've barely parked before I jump out of the passenger seat.

"We're here for Mark Moore," I tell the woman at the reception desk breathlessly.

"Aspen!" I hear Mom call from her seat on the other side of the waiting room.

"Mom!" I am relieved to see her. "What's going on?"

We rush toward each other, and she throws her arms around me in a warm embrace. "I don't know much other than that they brought him into surgery, and they'll tell me more when they can. I wasn't with him when he fell. He was working at the shop with Lennie, who called nine-one-one."

I look into her eyes. "They haven't told you anything at all?"

"No," she says.

"Well, let me go try and talk to someone. Maybe they can tell me what's going on." I look around for someone who looks like they might be in charge.

"Pen, Linda," says Rome. "Why don't you guys go sit down? I'll ask around and grab you guys some food."

"No, I should try and talk to someone maybe—"

"Relax, Pen. You're clearly going through a lot. Plus, if he's in surgery, the doctors need to focus. They won't have much time to answer your questions."

"And they'll answer yours?"

"Please, *mi cielo*. Just sit down and trust me. Take care of your mom. Everything's going to be okay."

I might have a better chance at getting answers, given most people in this hospital probably know who I am, but my mother needs me right now.

Mom and I sit together while we wait for him to come back. She's crying like I've never seen her cry.

"Mommy," I say, wrapping my arms around her. "Did Lennie tell you anything else?"

"No." She sniffles. "Only to come over here as soon as possible, and that Dad was in an ambulance."

"He didn't tell you what happened?"

Her hands tremble as she wipes her eyes. "He didn't see. Your dad was in the back."

"Did you get a chance to speak to him before he went into surgery?"

She simply shakes her head.

Rome comes back a few moments later.

"Did you find out anything?" I ask.

He shakes his head. He's got two cups of coffee and bagels. He hands one to my mom, her favorite kind, an everything bagel. And gives me my favorite as well, cinnamon raisin.

"Thank you so much, Roman," says my mom.

"It was the least I could do."

"No," I say. "Thank you, really."

He nods at me. "You want to talk about anything now, or do you just want me to sit with you?"

"You just being here is enough."

Rome sits in the chair next to me. I lay my head on his shoulder and place my hand on his lap.

It's a while before we hear any news about Dad.

"Anyone here for Mark Morre?" a doctor asks.

"Yes!" My mom and I jump up at the same time. "That's us," she finishes.

The doctor nods. "I take it you're his wife?"

"That's me," she replies. "Linda Moore."

The doctor nods again. "Your husband is asking to see you now."

"He's okay?"

"He's okay. I can tell you more if you follow me."

The two begin to walk off toward the hallway, leaving me one step behind them.

My mom turns to face me. "Aspen, honey, why don't you stay out here for right now while we discuss his condition?"

"Why can't I hear this?"

"Aspen, now is not the time to argue with me."

"Okay," I reply meekly, sulking back to the waiting room, Rome following close behind.

I sink onto the chair, covering my face with my hands.

"I'm sure they'll let you in, in a minute. You already heard the doctor say that he's okay. That's all you can ask for right now. You've gotta give your parents a little space."

I turn to look at him and sink back into my chair. "How can you be so calm right now?"

"You think I'm not worried? I am. But I'm trying to stay calm for you."

He pulls me closer, transferring a tiny bit of his calm to me.

"I need you to tell me everything's going to be okay."

"Everything's going to be okay, *mi cielo*." But even Rome's got an edge to his voice right now.

About an hour passes before my mom finally comes out to talk to me. Her cheeks are tear-stained, and her eyes are puffy.

"Mom?" I say, nervous about what she might be about to tell me.

"Aspen, honey, do you want to come see your father now?"

"Yes!" I jump up from my seat. Rome stands up too and follows behind me.

"There's something we need to talk to you about," she tells me slowly.

"Is it bad, Mom? What's going on?"

She still looks as if she's in panic mode. "Not without your father."

My mom leads us down a hallway, and we take an elevator a few floors up. Her reaction tells me that Dad's injury is likely something beyond him simply pushing himself too hard.

My stomach is in knots by the time we reach his hospital room.

"Dad!" I exclaim before slowly approaching him and carefully wrapping my arms around him.

"Penny," he says. "Hey."

Dad is hooked up to a couple of IVs and lying in a hospital bed. The machines are beeping at a steady rate, so I try to calm myself as much as possible.

His face looks mostly fine, aside from a couple of bruises and scattered cuts, but I can see purple bruises darkening both his arms. Though the rest of him is covered, I can only imagine how his injuries look underneath.

"What happened?"

He sighs like it's no big deal. "I fell off of a ladder in the back. It's nothing too serious, just a few broken bones. That's why they had to operate."

"Nothing serious? You had to get surgery, Dad!"

He shakes his head. "It's okay, Penny. I'm the parent. I'm supposed to worry about you, not the other way around."

I kiss his forehead. "Are you okay?"

"Yeah, Penny," he says. "I'm okay."

"I was so worried about you. I love you so much," I say, my voice breaking.

He hugs me even tighter. "I love you, too."

I can finally take a breath after holding it since what seems like yesterday. I look over at Rome, who smiles.

"Listen, Penny," Dad says, clearing his throat. "I have something I need to tell you."

"Yes?" I say immediately. "You can tell me anything."

He looks around at my mom, sitting in a chair across from us, then back at me. He's silent for a moment, and all I can hear is the quiet beeping of the machines he's connected to.

"I was diagnosed with Parkinson's disease."

"What?" I ask breathlessly. "When?"

I almost don't believe him. I've been home for weeks. We've had a million heart-to-hearts, he's had a million opportunities, and yet he never said a word?

"About six months ago," he replies. "It's still early, but it's slowly progressing."

"Why didn't you tell me?" I ask gently, trying not to sound as hurt and upset as I'm feeling on the inside. This isn't about me.

He shrugs. "You had a lot going on, and I…."

"I would have come home in an instant. Don't you know that?"

"That's why I didn't tell you. That wasn't necessary."

"If you would have told me then, this never would have happened. You wouldn't have been doing things in the back office by yourself. I'd have hired double the staff. I'd have kept you—"

"This is why I didn't tell you, Penny." He begins to raise his voice. "I'm your father. It's not your job to worry about me like this, and it's definitely not your job to help support my business."

"Ugh!" I breathe, moving away from him and beginning to pace. "You act like I'm some stranger on the street who's treating you like a charity. I'm not. I'm your daughter, and I care about you. *Let me help you.*"

"Aspen," my mother says sharply. "I refuse to sit here and watch you berate your father like this in a hospital room. He's been through a lot in the last twenty-four hours. I suggest you go outside and collect yourself."

I want to say something else, but the words won't come out. So instead, I follow Mom's advice and walk out of the hospital room and into the sterile, white hallway without a clear path or direction to go in.

"Pen!" Rome calls.

I can already tell from his tone that he's pissed too. I look back at him. "Not you too."

"She does have a point."

"Did you know?"

Rome always looks the same when he lies. "Did I know what?"

He's got to be fucking kidding me.

"You knew?" He's spent the last month and a half pretending to be a friend to me while lying right to my face? "How could you know my father was sick and not tell me?"

Rome glances away. "He wanted it this way. I—"

"When did he tell you?"

"Pen—"

"How long did you know that Dad had Parkinson's disease and kept it from me?"

"Five months," he replies evenly.

"Five months."

Five months ago, I was playing shows in New York, Philly, and Pittsburgh for my first few weeks on tour. Five months ago, I could have easily come home and spent time with my family.

Not to mention, Rome's had time to think about this. He's had more than enough time to make the right decision and fucking talk to me. He chose not to.

"He wanted it this way, Aspen. He didn't want you to know."

He didn't want me to know?

But he wanted my ex-boyfriend to?

"Yeah, thanks. I got that much."

Rome scoffs. "You can't seriously be mad at me over this."

"I absolutely can." Nurses are bustling by, flashing me disapproving looks, but I can't bring myself to care. "You shut me out of his life."

"You wanted me to go against his wishes?"

"How would you feel if the situations were reversed? I would have done it for you."

"That's the difference between me and you, Aspen. Both my parents are dead. If I could go back and do one more thing they'd asked me to do, I'd do it. You can be so selfish sometimes. Your father is lying in a hospital room, clearly hurting, and all you can think about is yourself. Why didn't they tell *you*? Why *you're* not the center of attention right now—"

"It's not about that, and you know it! I care about him."

"Then care about him enough to respect what he wants. How he handles his illness isn't up to you, Aspen."

"Since when do you know my own dad better than me?" I manage to spit out. "He's my dad!"

"Well, he's the closest thing I've got."

There's nothing I can say to that.

I think about returning to my Dad's room and spending more time with him. But my brain is in such a fog right now, I don't think I can stomach it. I don't want to upset him or Mom any further. I don't want to cause any more issues for him than he's already suffered.

I'll talk to him eventually. I just need a little while to process things on my own.

"I'm calling a car," I say, opening the Uber app.

"I'll drive you home."

"No," I reply sharply. I can't stand to be around him any longer. To look him in the eyes, knowing that he's lied to me like this.

"Aspen—"

"No! I want to be alone."

By alone, I mean I just need to get away from here. I text Leila letting her know it's an emergency and asking if I can spend the night at her place.

She accepts immediately.

I stomp away without looking back.

Fifteen minutes later, I'm standing on her porch.

"Hey," she greets me as she opens her door. "What's wrong?"

"What's not wrong?"

"Aw, honey," Leila says. "Come in."

CHAPTER
forty-four

"Come Back...Be Here (Taylor's Version)" by Taylor Swift

July, Five Years Ago

$\mathcal{I}$ stare down at my phone for what feels like the hundredth time today.

> **Rome:** Happy first day on set! I know you're kicking ass out there right now. I'm so proud. Make sure to call and tell me all about it.

I want to respond, I really do, but I just can't bring myself to do it.

The truth is, I don't fit in here. If these last few months of working, auditioning, and feeling lonely didn't prove that, my first day on set certainly has. Almost everyone in the cast has worked with our director or ATN in some capacity before. They've all been in this industry for years and seem to know what they're doing. I don't know much about how to behave on a set or how to get through a scene without feeling unsure of myself and screwing things up. I don't know any of my fellow castmates, and they all seem to know and like one another.

I'm the lead on the show, and everyone—including me—seems to think I'm the least qualified person in the room.

I miss Fertsville more than I've been able to admit to anyone. My parents are already worried about me living so far away. Rome has so much faith in me, and he's confident that we made the right decision by breaking up so I could move to LA and focus on my career.

He's stuck paying the bills back home and taking care of his mom while I'm supposed to be having the time of my life out here, starring in a big-budget TV show.

I can't text him now. I can't rely on him, not only because of how much I miss him and how homesick it'll make me, but because he's got enough on his plate already.

I can't burden him with problems that don't even begin to compare with his own.

So here I am.

Stuck navigating my way all on my own. I could use some emotional support right now.

I could use a friend.

CHAPTER
forty-five

"Beautiful Lies" by Birdy

December, Present

$\mathcal{R}$ome and I pull into the church parking lot at the same time the next morning. I consider waiting in my car for him to go inside to minimize the risk of us having to talk about last night, but it's no use. He's already spotted me.

I left Leila's about twenty minutes ago, and I am not in the mood for him to talk to me right now. I was up half the night, overwhelmed with emotions. I felt bad because there could be some truth to what Rome was saying. Maybe I was acting selfishly. I should have been concerned about Dad rather than the fact that Rome had kept a massive secret from me.

But I wanted to be there for him. If I had known about Dad's diagnosis, I would have come home from tour in an instant. I understand his reason for not telling me, but I can't help but struggle to let my anger go.

"Aspen," he calls out to me as I walk across the lot. "Stop."

I don't listen, so he runs up to me instead.

"Your mom called," he says, putting his hands in his pockets. "She said you didn't come home last night."

I turn to look away from him. "Not that it's any of your business, but I was at Leila's house. Mom knew."

Rome speaks up after a while. "I'm willing to admit the ways I was wrong last night. Seems like you're not there yet."

He can't be serious.

"You just never get it, do you?" I ask. "Not everything is the same, Rome! This situation is completely and utterly different from yours. You lied to me and then turned it around on me when all I wanted to do was be with my dad. If I had something going on with me, and I didn't tell you, and then saw you every day for *months,* would you be upset? Angry, even?"

"I..."

More and more cars are pulling into the lot.

"We're late," I say abruptly, realizing the time. "We can talk about this later."

Or never.

The kids all pile in from the hallway, eager to get our final run-through finished before dress rehearsal. We've yet to put together all the parts, so it's definitely a big day. They'll get to watch each other and work off the energy of their peers. I'm excited. Plus, it'll be a nice distraction to take my mind off Dad.

"How are we feeling today?" asks Rome.

"Good!" they all reply.

"Who's ready to kill this show!"

They all whoop and cheer. "Then let's get started!"

KIMI FREEMAN

The run-through goes even better than I expected. Everyone remembered their harmonies. There were only a few noticeable line mess-ups, and the kids stayed mostly quiet on the side, minus the clapping and cheering, which we don't mind.

Millie has managed to be nicer to the other kids and seems happy enough with the small solo singing verse Rome, and I gave her.

The only part with a few problems is the closing scene. Since it's still fresh, there were a lot of spacing mishaps and timing issues, among other things.

But overall, I'm sure happy with all the work everyone has put in.

Rome and I award the kids with a standing ovation. "Good job!" he says.

"Yeah, guys," I say, "you were all excellent."

"You know what I think this means?" Rome asks the kids when we've still got forty-five minutes left in rehearsal.

"What?" they all ask.

"We're having an ice cream party!"

Ice cream party?

"You never ran this by me," I whisper.

"You're against having an ice cream party?"

I'm not *against* it per se, I just don't like that he went behind my back to plan this when he knows we still have things to get done.

"While I'd love to spoil you guys and have some ice cream, there are a few things we need to work on."

"Like what?" he asks. "They were great."

"The final scene could use work," I say, putting it as nicely as possible.

"I say we need a break." And obviously, everyone agrees with him.

"*Roman*." I use my sharpest possible tone. "let's talk outside for a second, yeah?"

"The kids deserve a break, Pen," he says once we make it into the hallway.

"They can take a break once the final scene is stage-ready."

This show is extremely important to me. Dad's been directing it for years, and the whole town loves it. I want to make him proud and show him that he made the right choice by asking me to help him out this year.

I also want a chance to prove to all of the parents that were judging me and unsure of my ability to direct their kids that I could handle it and make the show better than it's ever been before.

"Fine," he says evenly. "You can work on that. I'm gonna go upstairs and get the ice cream ready."

And with that, he stalks away.

I head back into the rehearsal room.

"Okay, everyone," I say, trying to muster as much energy as possible. "Let's get to work on that final scene, yeah? Then ice cream."

We work for about twenty more minutes, walking through spacing and running through lines multiple times. The kids don't seem to want to work with me, so it takes me double the time to clean things up, as I'm constantly having to ask them for more. I know they aren't exactly having a blast right now, but it's what we needed.

After the third time through with no mishaps, I think we're good to go. "Who's ready for some ice cream?"

They all cheer and follow me up the stairs toward where Rome's got everything set up. He has vanilla, chocolate, cookie dough, and strawberry. He lets each kid decide on the number of scoops they'd like. He's even got sprinkles, rainbow and chocolate, and gummy bears set up as toppings.

"Can I have a cup?"

He nods and scoops up cookie dough ice cream, my favorite, and adds chocolate sprinkles and gummy bears.

"Thanks," I say.

"You're welcome, *mi cielo.*"

I want to forgive Rome. And eventually, I will. But I can't bring myself to forget what he said to me not too long ago.

Selfish. I make everything about me.

At first, I wondered how he could possibly see me the same way all those people who don't know me do. Use the same language the media uses to scrutinize me and show the world why they should hate me.

But now I'm starting to believe he may have been right.

At least in one respect.

I need to speak with my dad.

I circle the block a few times before I pull into my parents' driveway. I know that the longer I avoid my problems, the longer it's going to take for things to be okay again, so I bite the bullet and go inside.

"Mom! Dad!" I call, opening the door. "I'm home."

"Penny!" Dad shouts from upstairs. "Come up here."

Here we go.

I take a seat on the edge of his bed. "Hi, Dad. How are you feeling?"

"Eh, I'm okay. Your mom just went out to get my favorite sandwich for lunch. They've got me on painkillers, so there's not much to complain about."

That's Dad for you.

"There's lots to complain about," I argue. "You were seriously injured."

He simply smiles at me. "But I'm okay."

"I sure hope so."

Dad takes my hands in his. "I need you to understand something, Penny. I didn't do this to hurt you. My not telling you about all this had nothing to do with how much I thought you cared about me and everything to do with how much I know you do. You have a life to live, and so do I. You don't need to spend yours worrying about mine."

Tears threaten to spill from my eyes. "You don't get how it felt, Dad. To get that text from Mom saying you were in the hospital. I had no idea what was going on or why you were hurt and what was happening. Everyone else knew. Everyone but me."

He shakes his head. "Honey—"

"I had to see you lying in that bed, not knowing how this could have possibly happened to someone who used to be so careful. Falls are serious. And they're a hundred times more likely to occur because of this disease."

His gaze fills with understanding. "And I'm going to make a plan to cut back more than I already have. I've had Roman at the shop—he's been a big relief in helping me do less."

It's good to know that Rome is supporting him in this way.

I scoot over a little farther onto the bed and give him a gentle hug, careful not to bump into any of his casts.

"I'm sorry for how I acted yesterday," I tell him. "You were hurting, and I shouldn't have treated you like that. It wasn't about me. But I felt like you were cutting me out of your life, cutting me out of what was happening to you, and that hurt."

He strokes my hand with his thumb. "It's easy to get blinded by how much you care."

I take in a deep breath. "I love you, Dad."

"I love you too, Penny."

We lie together in silence for a moment before a question comes to mind.

"Why did you tell him?" I ask, referring to Rome.

He strokes my hair. "Believe it or not, that's not why he came to work for me. I'd always liked the kid and needed someone who spoke Spanish to help out after Mario quit a few months ago. He was in the market for a new job, and this was a good fit for him. Eventually, I told him the truth, and he became one of my main supports around the shop."

"And you told him not to tell me?"

"Yes," he replies. "That man loves you, Penny. He'd do anything for you. And he'd never do anything he didn't think was best for you. He knew that I would tell you when the time was right."

"You both kept secrets from me. By telling Rome instead of me, you made me feel like I was less important to you. You made Rome keep something from me, and that wasn't fair to him, either. But he should have told me."

"Oh, Penny. That wasn't what I intended at all."

"I know. I know that now."

He nods like he understands. "Just talk to him."

"Trust me," I say. "I have."

"That's all I can ask."

We stay in bed watching silly Christmas movies on TV until Mom gets home. She smiles from the door as she sees us lying together.

"You guys look cozy."

I smile. "Hey, Mom."

She scoots into the bed next to me and gently kisses my forehead.

"I'm sorry about last night," I say.

"Oh, Aspen. I'm sorry too. Keeping secrets never turns out well."

"It's okay, Mom. I love you."

"I love you too, honey."

Dress rehearsal goes even better than our last run. I can tell each of the kids practiced after our last rehearsal. The harmonies are clear, their voices are strong, and they know their lines. Seeing them with props and in costume just makes this experience all the more surreal.

As Ella takes her place center stage, I'm slightly nervous for her.

But it turns out I had nothing to worry about. She's absolutely breathtaking again.

I catch Rome just as he's about to leave for the night.

"You were right," I confess. "I was acting selfishly that night. I shouldn't have made Dad's injury about myself. You didn't have to tell me. Not if he didn't want you to. He shouldn't have put you in that position in the first place."

"You just care about him and wanted to be there. I'm sorry if I made you feel bad about that. That was wrong of me. I can't believe I–"

"No, no," I say. "I think your words were exactly what I needed to hear."

CHAPTER
forty-six

"Would've, Could've, Should've" by Taylor Swift

January, Five Years Ago

$\mathcal{I}$ haven't felt like myself these past few months in LA. It seems I've fallen out of touch with the person I used to be, so much so that I no longer know where to find her. Drinking isn't me. Partying isn't me. Showing up late to the job I worked so hard for isn't me.

I'm going to take this week to collect myself and come back to work stronger. With a good head on my shoulders. Maybe it'll take returning to my roots to do this.

I've never been more excited to come home. I miss my parents. I miss the comfort I felt in my home. But something about being back here also feels empty.

I don't want to tell my parents about Keith's betrayal. They won't want me to return to set and have to see him every day. But I worked hard to secure a lead role on *Soon After*. And I'll be damned if I let anyone take that away from me.

So once I land and make it to the door, I go to Rome's instead.

I don't know what I'm going to say to him. I don't know how to tell him what's happened. I don't even know if I want to.

But I want his comfort right now. I want to feel the safety he made me feel all those months ago.

I keep thinking back to what feels like the holy ground where we once stood. And I can't help but wonder if I made a mistake, leaving this town to follow my dreams.

"Rome," I say loudly, knocking on his front door. "It's me."

I hear his rushing footsteps. "Pen, oh my God! What are you doing here?"

"I requested two days off. I'm here for the weekend."

He hugs me, and I bury my head against his chest. "Fuck, I missed you."

I smile but don't look up at him. "I missed you so much."

"Come inside," he says, grabbing my hand and leading me through the doorway. "Mom's not gonna be home for another hour. Fill me in."

I shake my head as we walk up the stairs. "I don't have much to say."

We make it to his room and sit on his bed. "There's got to be something. You're the lead in an ATN TV show! How's that going?"

It feels nice to sit on a bed after I've been avoiding mine for the past few weeks, opting to sleep on my floor instead.

"It's going."

I can't bring myself to think about my lapse in judgment right now. All of the ways I've let both him and myself down by putting my career at risk.

Rome grimaces. "I don't like seeing you like this."

"Seeing me like what?" I ask.

"Unconfident. Closed-off."

I tuck a strand of hair behind my ear. "I'm sorry. It's not on purpose. It's just been—rough."

"I get that. I understand."

Besides, Rome has been going through so much over these past few months. I should be focused on him.

"Enough about me. I can't imagine how you've been doing. Tell me about you."

He sits up. "Things are okay. I'm still working at the grocery store."

"Okay," I reply. "How's your mom?"

"She's been better," he tells me. "She's struggling through chemo. It's hard to see her like this."

"I wish I could be here for you. I don't want you guys to feel like—"

"Stop. It's okay. You don't need to feel bad for me."

"Feel bad for you?" I stare at him. "I don't like to see you struggling alone."

He's silent for a moment, the air growing thick between us.

"Well, I'm not alone this weekend," he says.

Rome shifts closer to me before kissing me gently on the lips. I try not to show how this gesture makes me feel. What it reminds me of.

He lays me back on the bed and places a hand on my chest, which brings me right back to a day I'd give anything to forget. He places a kiss on my neck, but by now, nothing he can do will calm me down.

I need him off me.

Now.

I jump off the bed and start making my way toward the bathroom.

But Rome stands in my way.

"Pen!" he says. "What's wrong? Tell me what I did." His tone softens. "Please, breathe. You're scaring me."

I sink down to my knees and try to steady my breath, but it's not working. "I can't. It's not—"

Rome takes my hand and places it on his chest. "Here. Focus on my heartbeat. Try to match it."

And eventually, I'm able to calm down.

"Pen," he says, cupping my face with his hand, "are you ready to tell me what happened?"

CHAPTER
forty-seven

"Superheroes" by The Script

December, Present

My phone buzzing on the nightstand around midnight awakens me. I already know the person calling is likely in LA, given how late it is here. I toss and turn for a minute longer, but I eventually pick up the phone to see a missed call from Murray and a link to yet another earth-shattering, career-altering interview.

Cane has done a tell-all interview with *the American Post.* I don't want to read it, but I have to.

Following the breakup of the internet's OTP and the media destruction of America's sweetheart, Aspen Moore, American Post reporter talks with the man at the heart of it all, The Disasters lead singer, Cane Dawson.

By now we've all seen Sierra Wong's Instagram posts about both her ex-best friend, superstar Aspen Moore, and now ex-boyfriend Cane Dawson.

I read it again: *ex-boyfriend Cane Dawson.* Well. That was fast.

> Today reporter Diane Wilks sits down with Cane to hear his side of the story.
>
> **Diane:** Hi, Cane. It's nice to see you again.
> **Cane:** It's nice to see you too.
> **Diane:** So, what's life been like since you and Sierra broke things off?
> **Cane:** Definitely a lot quieter. I've moved back in with one of my close friends actually, Keith Haverton.

Sierra never told me Cane was friends with Keith. I guess she must have assumed it would make me hate him, which she would be right about. Now it makes sense why Cane would lie about me and destroy our friendship. He was doing it to protect his best friend, Keith.

> **Diane:** What would you say was the main cause for your split?
> **Cane:** Sierra was always psychotic about making sure I wasn't cheating on her, way before Aspen did what she did.
> **Diane:** Psychotic. That's a pretty strong label to use.
> **Cane:** Well, she was constantly asking where I was and was insecure about my female friends. It was exhausting, really.
> **Diane:** So, you'd say Aspen didn't have as much to do with it as Sierra thinks she did?
> **Cane:** I wouldn't quite say that. I mean, she was definitely a

major source of stress for both of us. The fight she started at the Blitz Ball didn't make things better.

Diane: Can you tell us exactly what happened?

Cane: While the details are still a little foggy, I can try my best. Sierra and I went over to Aspen at the start of the event to wish her well and make sure she knew we didn't want any drama during the night. She made a snarky comment toward Sierra and me. Being the boyfriend I am, I defended my girlfriend. But then her new boyfriend went completely psychotic on us, and Aspen encouraged him. It was awful, really. He almost broke my nose.

Diane: Completely psychotic, wow.

I have to take a break for a moment. This is unbelievable. *The American Post* is blatantly spreading lies about me, and nobody thought to reach out to me for a response? Although it doesn't seem like my word means anything to anyone anyway.

Diane: Let's circle back to something you mentioned earlier. You're living with Keith Haverton now. As Aspen's ex, what does he make of all this?

Cane: He's honestly not surprised. The two had a thing going on for quite a while, but Aspen made him out to be some monster when that just wasn't the case. She even told Sierra that he'd raped her.

My hands tremble, and my vision becomes blurry. Blinking, I look up toward the ceiling, fighting to breathe. I never went public about the rape, and I never went to the police. And now Cane...or Keith...has taken that out of my control. I don't understand. Are they trying to discredit me so I won't ever go to the police? Is that the endgame?

> **Cane:** Being her friend, Sierra obviously believed Aspen, but even I felt something was off with her story. Sierra insisted I cut him off. But when Aspen came onto me, Sierra finally saw her true colors.
> **Diane:** Wow. And to think we were in the dark.
> **Cane:** She's managed to keep so much of this hidden. It honestly amazes me.
> **Diane:** Well, thanks for sitting down with me today, Cane. It's always a pleasure to have you.
> **Cane:** It was my pleasure, Diana.

Bile rises in my throat as I shut the app, closing the interview. I don't even know what to think anymore.

I don't get how anyone could befriend someone as slimy as Keith. I don't know how I didn't see it earlier.

He had all the telltale signs of being a grade-A asshole. Keith was rude to waitresses, constantly made anti-feminist comments, and didn't have one good thing to say about any of his supposedly crazy exes. He couldn't have been more clear if he'd waved a giant red flag in my face. But I didn't care. I had just started on *Soon After* and was still heartbroken over Rome. I needed a friend more than anything.

Keith seemed perfect at the time.

He was my costar and knew the industry far better than I did. He'd already gotten his big break as a teenager and had worked with ATN on other shows. Keith helped me feel at home on set and fit into a world that was so different from the one I'd grown up in.

He'd let me come over to his penthouse and pour me drinks as I told him how much I missed Rome. At first, I didn't want to drink, considering my only experience with alcohol, but Keith told me I'd have to learn anyway—it was a staple in the entertainment business. So even though I was three years below the legal drinking age, he got me into all sorts of LA bars and clubs.

He'd help me memorize my lines, and we'd go out to dinner afterward, but I never suggested anything beyond friendship. I didn't understand that he could be seeing our relationship in a completely different way.

Keith was with me the first time I blacked out. Unbeknownst to me at the time, he thought my inability to stand up for myself meant that I was up for the taking.

But as the months went by, I started to put myself back together. I wasn't looking to be with anyone, but I'd also accepted that I couldn't be with Rome. I just wanted to rediscover who I was and put myself first. Keith, though, had other plans.

He waited until we were alone, and I was tipsy. When I wouldn't give him what he wanted, he assumed he could take it. And I didn't even know he already had.

I was so blacked out that night that I couldn't have given him consent. I wouldn't have done that. And he knew it. Yet Keith rubbed that in my face as a reason why he had the right to do anything he wanted with me.

He would have succeeded a second time if Karina hadn't knocked on my door when she had. I had never seen that side of him before. A side that was so ugly, it made me question everything I thought I knew about him before. I'd never once in my life been truly terrified. Not until that night.

Despite this, I couldn't quit the show. I was the main character, and it was only season one. Things had just started picking up. I'd be ending my career before it even started. There was nothing I could do, and no one I could tell.

So, I handled it on my own.

I was quiet. I didn't put myself out there too much. I didn't drink. I quit smoking. I didn't do anything to ruin my perfect image.

I moved out of my apartment, unable to look at my own bed the same way. Luckily Sierra and I were becoming close, and she was in the market for a new roommate. I remember the day like it was yesterday, curled up in a ball on my bedroom floor, not knowing where else I could sleep.

My couch reminded me of him. My bed reminded me of him. Everything reminded me of that sickening feeling inside me.

I had to look the man in the eye and act as if I loved him for another year and a half. I had to kiss him. I had to see him all the damn time. I had to fight with the network not to give us any more sex scenes, so I wouldn't relive the traumatic experience. Everything was already too much.

I eventually became numb. I'd disassociate whenever we were in the same room. It was slowly killing me, but I let it happen.

I didn't tell anyone except Rome about what Keith had done to me. Not until I told Sierra, who eventually convinced me that after three long seasons, it was time to go. Rome had always believed me, but he never pushed. He never did anything I didn't want him to do. And I love him for it.

The public is going to think whatever it wants to think about me. But there's only one person whose opinion of me has never changed.

And I gave him up for a career I'm not even sure is worth it anymore.

I can't believe that this secret I've been keeping from the public has finally come to light. I don't worry about doing damage control with my family. I don't think about calling Murray back and asking him how I should handle this situation. For once, I do something that I want to do.

I pull out my phone, open the notes app, and craft a message for my five million followers.

Hey Guys.

Cane Dawson's interview with American Post has just recently come to my attention. Not that I owe anyone an explanation, but I wanted to come on here and quickly address the situation. Keith Haverton manipulated and raped me when I was 18. Older, he harassed me and tried to force me into a relationship when I was nowhere near ready to be in one at the time. He's now convinced Cane, and probably many of you, that I would lie about him when he knows the atrocity he's committed. In these past few weeks, I've been labeled a homewrecker, whore, psychopath, and terrible person. When in reality,

I did none of the things the media has accused me of. I never came onto Cane. I never tried to destroy my best friend's relationship. And now, personal photos of me have been leaked on the internet, bringing me back to the way I felt during this traumatic experience. When is this going to stop? When will we give women a chance to write their own stories without being labeled a whore or a slut? I'm tired of fighting rumors. I'm tired of being afraid to live the way I want to. I urge you all to support women—not just in your own life, but those in the media. We are real people who face real struggles. In short, respect women. Respect people. Be kind.

    Aspen

I wake in the morning feeling better rested than I expected. Despite my better judgment, I brace myself and scroll through Twitter to see what people are saying about the article. And the responses are nothing like I thought they would be.

There are thousands of retweets of tweets posted by girls discussing their interactions with Keith. All the women he assaulted at clubs or parties, the waitresses he harassed, and the strippers he forced into blow jobs are finally telling their stories.

According to every social media platform out there right now, Keith Haverton is in the number one spot on the internet's shit list. And it's about damn time he made it there.

Karma.

What a beautiful thing.

There are even a number of people talking about how awful Cane was for outing my experience and for dragging me into his breakup in the first place. He took this a step too far, and now no one believes his story.

But for once, it isn't about what the public believes. I know my story. I don't need anyone else to believe it.

My manager Dean calls, and I hesitantly answer the phone.

"Aspen, hey," he says. "How are you doing?"

For once, I have a simple answer. "Good. I'm doing well. But there was actually something I wanted to talk to you about."

"Anything," he says. "Absolutely anything."

I know what the world is expecting of me. But I just don't know if I can live like this anymore. I'm so focused on what other people want, what I'm *supposed* to do.

It's not about how popular I am, how many awards I win, or anything outside of myself. Because what does any of that matter if none of it means anything to me?

When is it my turn to do what makes me happy?

If I keep going down this path, that time will never come.

"Talk to the label," I say. "I want to do an indie album next. Not pop. I even have a new song to play you guys."

"Oh, okay," he says, only mildly enthusiastically. "Great. Take some time. Whatever you need–"

"Thanks, Dean. Talk soon."

A moment later, my phone rings. It's Sierra. I shouldn't pick up, but there are a few things I want to say before I cut her off for good.

"Aspen!" she says, sounding super surprised that I picked up. "I—"

"No. You don't get to say anything. But there's a lot I want to say to you. You fucked up. You know that. I know that. In what world would I ever sleep with your boyfriend, Sierra? I've been drying your tears for three years, and you didn't even have the decency to pick up your phone when I was trying to explain? And you told your boyfriend something that I *never* wanted anyone to know. That shit was personal. I would never tell anyone your secrets. Not even now, in revenge. I trusted you, but you know what? You're not worth my time. And you're not worth my energy anymore."

I hang up the phone. That was more therapeutic than a year on a psychiatrist's couch.

CHAPTER
forty-eight

"Box of Memories" by Georgia Webster

April, Five Months Ago

*I*t never gets any easier, leaving the arms of the man I've come to know better than anyone else on the planet. The word goodbye never gets any easier to say. I never really want to board that plane, but I always do.

My life can feel that way sometimes. Like I'm just going through the motions. Like nothing really means anything. I've gotten so used to the monotony of my daily routine. But when it comes time to return to the one place that will always feel like home...

It's been months since I returned to Fertsville for Christmas, and I've missed my hometown in a way I struggle to understand. I love what I do. Most days, I love what I'm doing in California, but something about being home feels like a kind of peace I can't get in LA.

They say you'll never find forever the first time, but I don't believe that's true. I found it the first time. And I keep finding it, over and over again.

So no, it never gets any easier to leave Rome, to untangle myself from his arms, with the words, "I love you" and "Just tell me to stay" on the tip of my tongue.

My love isn't always enough.

It's not today. It wasn't yesterday. But I can't lie and say that I don't hope that someday, it might just be.

CHAPTER
forty-nine

"'tis the damn season" by Taylor Swift

December, Present

$\mathcal{M}$y dad is the first to see me downstairs making coffee around nine-thirty the next morning. Leila texted me about an hour ago, letting me know she's always here to talk, and I let her know I'll definitely want to catch up once the show is over.

I walk over to the cabinets in search of a mug as Dad turns to face me. "I read an article about you earlier, and I saw the tweet you wrote last night."

I go completely still.

By the time the dust had settled and Keith was out of my life for good, it was too late to tell my parents. I knew they'd be hurt if they found out I hid this for so long. I recognize the irony here.

"Oh," is all I can say.

"I'm so sorry that happened to you, sweetheart. Maybe one day we can sit down and talk about it."

I let out a deep exhale. He's not mad at me.

I'm kind of mad at myself for ever thinking he would be. He's not like that. He's not like *me*. And I know this.

Maybe one day, I will want to talk to him about Keith and how everything went down from there. Maybe I'll tell him about what Rome and I have been through and all the shit that's been going down with Sierra.

"Thanks so much, Dad," I say. "That means so much to me. I'm sorry I didn't tell you."

He kisses my cheek. "I understand why you didn't. I just feel terrible that something like this happened to you. I love you so much, Penny."

"I love you too, Dad," I look down at my phone and check the time. "I'm gonna run over to Rome's before the show starts."

He kisses me lightly on my forehead before letting me go. "Okay. See you soon."

I quickly run upstairs to my parent's room to find my mom still lying on her bed watching *Jeopardy*.

"Hi, Mom." I walk over to her side of the bed and give her a hug. "Good morning."

"Aspen," she says softly, tears welling in her eyes. "How are you doing?"

I tighten my hold around her. "I'm okay, Mom. Really. I'm fine."

"I would have been there for you, honey. I wish you would have told me."

"It's okay, now. I promise."

She nods. "I love you so much, Aspen."

"I love you too, Mom," I say once we finally pull away.

My phone buzzes next to me, and I see it's a call from Rome.

I check the time. "I have to run to the church for a quick final rehearsal. But I love you so much, Mom. I'll see you later."

I pull into the church parking lot about twenty minutes later. Rome's car is already parked.

"Rome!" I call when I'm inside the auditorium.

"Pen," he says breathlessly. "You didn't answer my call."

"I wanted to talk in person."

He squeezes me tight. "I love you so much, *mi cielo*. You're so strong. I love you so much."

I don't know what to say. I don't know what this means for us, our relationship, or anything else. But I do know the kids are waiting, and that after this production, we'll have all the time in the world to figure it out.

"I love you too."

We hold a quick rehearsal with the kids, running only the scenes that were sloppy during dress rehearsal.

"Thank you all so much for getting up so early today and really showing up," Rome says once we've finished. "You're all going to be absolutely amazing. Feel free to go take a break in the lobby, but make sure you or your parents get you made up and costumed by twelve."

A few of the kids wave at me, Ella included, and I wave back. Then they all rush out to get ready for the show.

My parents arrive at the church a few minutes later. They're dressed in their Sunday best, with wide smiles on their faces.

"Hey, guys!" I say. "I'm so excited for you to see what we've done with the show this year. I hope you'll be proud."

"Always," says Dad. "We're always proud of you."

At a quarter to eleven, the kids and their parents soon start to return, fully dressed in hair, makeup, and costumes.

One of the parents approaches me. "Hi," she says. "I'm Vanessa, Ella's mom. I'm not sure if you've seen me around."

Vanessa looks just like her daughter, so even if she hadn't told me, it wouldn't be hard to guess she's Ella's mom. Her hair is black and curly like her daughter's, and her skin is the same shade of brown.

"Yes!" I say. "Hi, I'm Aspen."

"I just wanted to thank you for all the work you've done for my daughter. She talks about you all the time. My husband and I have really begun to see a change in her. She's so much more confident."

That's all I ever wanted to do for her. To be the mentor I wish I'd had when I was her age.

"That means so much to me to hear. I've absolutely loved getting to know her over these past few weeks. She's been an absolute pleasure to direct."

It's also nice to know that at least one parent believes I've influenced their child in a positive way.

Vanessa smiles and nods. "I'll let you go. I'm sure you've got a lot to do before the show."

Walking through the hallway, I overhear Millie speaking with her mother while she's finishing up her makeup.

"I can't believe we even showed up to this thing," says Millie's mom as she adds a bit of blush to her daughter's cheeks. "I mean, we pay for voice lessons, and you're not even a lead role?"

"Mommy, can we please not do this now?" Millie begs, tears welling in her eyes. "I tried my best. I already told you that."

Her mom huffs. "All I'm saying is that if you're just going to waste our money like this, then maybe—"

"Hi again, Larissa," I say. "Would you mind if I stole your daughter for a moment?"

She waves us off. "She's all yours."

"What do you want?" Millie asks me, her eyes still wet with tears.

I put a hand on her shoulder. "I just wanted to tell you that you're amazing and that you're going to do great tonight. It doesn't matter whether you're an angel or Mary or a tree. You're a talented girl, and you can shine in any part you're given. Don't let anyone discourage you. Don't let them dim your light."

She wipes a tear off her face.

"Now go out there and have an amazing show, okay?"

She hugs me. "Thanks, Aspen. I will."

Seeing Millie like this reinforces what I was already coming to realize. She's just a sweet kid with a mother that puts far too much pressure on her.

Rome shoots me a text asking me if I can run upstairs for some of the extra programs he left in the office when he was printing them.

When I make it to the office, I can't find them, so I open his computer to print a few more.

There's a document already open. It's a collection of letters he wrote to me over the years. The document is over twenty pages long, and each entry has a date and time.

I scroll all the way down to the bottom and see an entry he left for me this morning.

KIMI FREEMAN

Dear Aspen,

I don't know what else to say other than I'm so proud of you. When I saw that article, I was shocked. I couldn't believe that dick would go and expose you like that and publicly lie about you.

I haven't checked the news much over the years, but it's like I can't stop looking at the headlines now that everything has gone down with us. It hurts me when people say these terrible things about you. It hurts to see those headlines of people calling you a cheater or an awful person. I know you better than anyone else, and they would love you if they knew you too.

I never saw myself living in California, and I never saw myself settling down with someone famous. Leaving Fertsville feels almost as wrong as it did to move out of the only house my parents ever purchased for themselves. The last one we lived in. I never imagined my life outside of this town, and I honestly always imagined you like how you are when you're in it. But now I've seen this other side of your life. I've seen you handle everything these people throw at you like a fucking champ, and I'll regret it for the rest of my life if I never tell you that I love you and that I want to spend the rest of my life with you. Fuck the paparazzi. Fuck the press. Fuck everyone else who doesn't matter.

I hope one day I'll find the strength to send this to you. Maybe that day will be today.

Roman

332

I absolutely melt inside.

I rush down the stairs, but by the time I do, Rome is waiting with the rest of the kids for me on the stage of the auditorium.

"Did you grab the programs?" he asks as I run over to him breathlessly.

"Shoot! I'm so sorry. I totally forgot."

He chuckles. "Don't worry about it, Pen. I'll ask your dad to get them before the show starts."

I flash him a small smile. "Thanks."

"We're about to start letting people into the auditorium because the lobby's getting full," says Rome. "So let's get you all backstage."

"How are you feeling?" I ask Ella once we make it to the wings.

"I don't know," she says. "Kind of nervous."

"Don't be nervous," I say. "You're going to be great. I spoke to your mom earlier. She's super nice."

"Yeah," she says. "I tell her all about you!"

I nudge her arm. "I heard."

"It's time to make the opening announcements," says Rome a few moments later.

"Already?" I ask, checking my watch. There are still about ten minutes until we're due to start.

"The auditorium is full," he says, moving the curtain over and pointing to the large crowd. "Why not?"

"Okay," I tell him. "Let's get started then."

The audience bursts into applause, and the lights go down in preparation for the very first scene. Rome and I walk down the small staircase on stage left and make our way to center stage.

"Hey, everyone. I'm Roman Torres."

"And I'm Aspen Moore," I add. "We wanted to take the time to thank all of the children involved in this production and their parents for raising such amazing kids."

Rome looks over to the wings. "You guys have all been a pleasure to work with, and we hope to see you again very soon. Thank you for such an incredible experience."

I never imagined how much I'd come to miss this group of kids, but the thought of not seeing them again makes me really sad. I'll miss Joey and the way he always cheers each of his fellow actors on so enthusiastically. I'll miss the way Lucas always has a new fact to tell me about bugs, even if they're sort of gross. I'll even miss Jamie, the incessant nose-picker who's nowhere near shy about it.

I look over at Rome. "Without further ado, we present the annual Fertsville production of the Very First Christmas!"

I'm absolutely blown away by the massive amount of talent that lights up the stage. Everyone came in today and put forth their best selves.

Ella receives not one but *two* standing ovations during "O Come Little Children." She is so poised and sounds so beautiful, she takes my breath away.

There are so many people I used to know in this audience. Rina and some of her old friends. Some of the guys from the football team. A bunch of kids I went to high school with. It's surreal to see them all in the same room again, just like that day at the talent show. I thought I might feel sick to my stomach, but I don't. I feel sort of... *indifferent?*

Throughout the show, I am extremely aware of Rome next to me. Of his movements, when he claps, when he laughs, when he smiles. I keep looking over at him, catching his eyes, and looking away.

And then it's over. All that work for one night's performance. We climb onto the stage after the standing ovation, and Rome raises his voice above the applause. "Thank you guys so much for being here tonight!"

We get the kids lined up once we've made our way backstage. "Come on, guys. We've got to get you to your parents in the lobby."

They all rush up to bring me into a group hug, which absolutely warms my heart.

Ella runs up to me after everyone has gone and gives me another big hug. "Thank you so much, Aspen. This has been the best few weeks ever!"

I smile. "Thanks, Ella. I'll walk you out to your parents."

We find them toward the left side of the lobby, with huge smiles on their faces. Ella runs up to each of them with a hug as they congratulate her.

"If you guys would ever like me to give her a voice lesson, let me know. We can totally set something up."

"Thank you," her father says. "That means so much." Her mother hands me her phone, and I put my number into it.

I give Ella one last hug before I go. "Thank you for a great few weeks, Ella. I'll see you soon."

She squeezes me tight. "I'm going to miss you."

Yeah. "Me too."

I look over to Rome as he talks to a few parents in the corner. I'm so excited to start the rest of our forever together. We've finally made it out of the woods. I just need to ensure he's on the same page—because I'm never giving him up again. Never.

❄

I rush into Dad's arms as I see him from across the room. He pulls me in for a brief yet meaningful hug. "The show was amazing, Penny! Way better than I've ever done."

"Thank you so much, Dad. I had a lot of fun doing it."

My mom hugs me too. "Absolutely beautiful."

"Thanks, Mom."

Rome comes up behind me and puts an arm around my shoulders.

"Hey," I say, turning to face him.

"Hi," he replies, his smile wide across his face.

"Roman," says my Dad, "you guys put on a great show."

"Thanks, Mark. I really appreciate that."

Mom smiles at him. "You'll have to come out with us for a celebratory dinner tonight! You guys certainly deserve it."

"Of course I will."

"Perfect," I say. "Can you guys give us a few minutes before we leave? We can meet you at the restaurant."

"Yes, of course," Mom says. "We'll be on our way."

I turn toward Rome as my parents walk away. "Rome, I–"

Before I can say anything substantial, I see Leila coming toward me from across the room.

"Not to interrupt you guys or anything, but that was fucking amazing!"

"Thanks, Leila. I really appreciate that."

"Well, I should run," she says, winking. "Seems like you guys want to talk. But call me in the morning, yeah? We should hang at my place."

"Sounds good," I reply. "Love you!"

"You too," she says back.

"I've always liked her," comments Rome.

"I love you," I blurt. "Not in an 'I'll always care about you from afar' kind of way, but in an 'I don't care what it takes, I'll do whatever I have to do to be with you' kind of way. I can't see my life without you, Rome."

"I don't know what to say, Pen, other than I love you too. In every kind of way."

"I read what you wrote about me," I confess.

"You looked at my computer?"

"I did."

Rome smiles at me before taking my hands in his. "I'm sorry that I didn't tell you how much I love you sooner. I'm sorry that it took spending all of these weeks together for me to realize that I'm willing to put aside my fear of what's outside of this town to be with you. But I hope you understand that now. I hope you understand that I'm willing to do whatever the hell it takes to be yours forever."

My heart melts.

I know we still have logistics to work out. I know figuring out how we make our forever work will take some time and a lot of planning. But none of that matters because we know that we're each other's endgame. And that's all that matters to me right now.

I press a gentle kiss to his lips. "I'm just happy to be with you."

We're about to start walking toward the exit when someone calls out my name.

"Aspen!" shouts Rina, coming up behind us. "What an interesting performance you put on tonight."

Passive aggressive as always.

"Yeah," I reply. "Thank you."

She looks over at Rome. "I had no idea you guys were back together. Does this mean you're moving out to LA now?"

Rome looks straight at me.

I haven't really considered where we'll go once I need to get back to work. I haven't signed any contracts yet, so I can always stay here if Rome doesn't want to come with me to Cali.

"I think I'll stay here in Fertsville for a while."

"Oh," she says, realization crossing her face. "I get it. Hollywood is not for everyone. Some people just weren't made for that life."

"No, actually. It's not that at all. Some things are just more important than money or fame. Way more important." I can't believe it's taken me so long to realize that.

"Well, listen," she says, totally ignoring what I just said. "We should totally catch up soon. I—"

I cut her off right there. "No, actually. I think I'm all good with catching up. And thanks for that interview you gave. It really showed everyone what a dear friend you are to me. You see, I have thicker skin than you'll ever know. Do a million interviews. Drag my name through the mud as much as you want. I'm done."

She's too stunned to speak.

I nod at her and casually walk toward the exit, Rome following close behind me.

"Holy shit, Pen," he says, drawing my attention back to him. "That was badass."

"Was it?" I felt it was pretty badass too.

He pulls me into him again. "You know how hot you are when you're angry, right?"

"You should make me mad more often." I plant a gentle kiss on his lips.

"Noted," Rome replies.

Everything is finally coming together.

I've repaired my image. I finally stood up to the girl who gave me hell throughout the formative years of my life.

And I have him. The man I'm going to grow old with. The man I'm finally going to wake up next to every morning. The man who, after all these years, is mine once again.

"I love you so much, Rome. I'm sorry that it took me so long to come to my senses, but I can't wait to spend the rest of my life loving you. They'll be the easiest years I'll ever spend."

Rome leans over and whispers in my ear, "Let's hurry up and get to the restaurant. I have many plans for you tonight, none of which I can do in public."

"We better move fast then. We've got to make up for so much lost time."

CHAPTER *fifty*

"Karma" by Taylor Swift

February, One Year Later

Thank you so much, Karina. This looks amazing." I absolutely love the smokey eye and eyeliner look she's done today.

"No problem, Aspen. You look gorgeous."

"All thanks to you," I reply. And really, it's the truth.

It's been about a year since Rome and I got back together. And it's been one of the best years of my life.

We bought a house in Allentown about two months after we got back together and stayed there for a few months. After that, we purchased a condo in LA and traveled back and forth while Rome applied for colleges, and I began working on my next project.

Rediscovering the depths of Rome has felt like finally finding daylight.

I released my second studio album, *changes,* in August.

It was a feat convincing my label that a change in sound would be good for them, not to mention me, but it was the only way I would sign a contract for another album. I realized how important it is for me to stay true to myself. And lately, I've been putting myself first.

There are many songs on the album that are extremely vulnerable for me, but I thought it was important to share some more personal parts of myself with the public after being painted as someone I wasn't for so long. I wanted to take control of my own narrative, and music was the best way for me to do that.

I spent a few more months at home, writing songs by myself. One of my fan favorites is "Old," a song I wrote about what Keith did to me. It wasn't a single or anything, but my fans have grown attached to it, and they've been begging me to add it to the set list for my upcoming tour.

While it definitely scared me to give so much of myself to the public, the very people who criticized me for something I didn't do, I had to do it. I had to let people see me for me.

My album nearly broke the record for the most streamed album in a day. Three of my songs hit the Hot 100, and my lead single, *it still hurts*, held the top spot for nearly eight weeks. Being nominated for a Cobalt award is just the icing on the cake.

In fact, I've been nominated for three awards. Album of the Year, Song of the Year, and Best Female Artist. I'm not expecting to win any of my categories at the awards ceremony tonight, but just being nominated is a huge accomplishment.

My stylists and I picked out a hunter-green, floor-length gown for the evening. It's got thicker straps and a more structured top, similar to a corset. We paired this with a smoky eye look, with pops of green glitter and a nude lip. My hair is down with a few curls.

Unlike last time, Rome's got his own team helping him get ready.

His suit is custom-made, and I picked it out myself. It matches my green dress perfectly.

"Fifteen minutes!" is called out from the other room.

"You can come in now!" I call, giving myself a once over before facing the door.

Rome opens it, and my jaw drops.

Now tailored, the suit fits even better than it had before, clinging to his body more perfectly than I think any item of clothing has fit anyone. The green pocket square and trip on his white shirt are the exact same shade as my outfit.

I've always loved his curly hair, but it looks so much more defined today due to the way he was styled. And I'm totally obsessed.

"Holy shit, Pen," he says. "You look gorgeous."

"You always say that!"

"Only because it's true."

"Well, you look amazing too. I've never seen anyone pull off a suit so well."

He kisses me on my cheek, careful not to ruin my makeup.

We head to the car from our hotel, the paparazzi cameras flashing as we do. Rome's gotten better with them now. He doesn't bother them if they don't bother him. Sure, there have been times when they've asked invasive questions or gotten in my face, but now he knows to stay calm and ignore them.

"You finally gonna tell me anything about this performance of yours?" he asks once he shuts the car door.

"That would completely ruin the surprise." And this surprise is a big one.

I've only told Leila, and that's just because I find it impossible to keep anything from her nowadays.

I'm doing a performance of my second single off the album, *since forever*, a song about our relationship over the years. It's one of the most emotional songs I've ever written, and it took me months to complete. Rome is obsessed with it, which is why I've chosen to play it tonight.

But I've opted not to tell him my plans for a few reasons. If I told him now, I'm sure he'd encourage me against it. He prefers to stay out of the spotlight, but I think if done right, this time could be worth it. Besides, he hates when I give him credit in interviews for the success I've received on my new album. He inspired almost all of it, and I give him props for that, which he detests.

But today, if I win a Cobalt award, it'll be all about me. Which means he has no say over who I thank.

I walk the red carpet by myself, posing for at least twenty minutes. I spend another thirty in interviews, most asking the same few questions.

"What inspired your new album?"

"How does it feel to make this sort of comeback?"

"What do you have to say to all of the people who doubted your character?"

And to these, I always have the same answers.

"A lot of things, really. While I won't go into many details of my personal life, the man in my life has been a huge source of inspiration."

"It feels great! I love that people love the record as much as me. It means the world."

"I appreciate the people who've stuck by me. I appreciate those who have come to support me. That's really all I have to say about that."

By the time I'm done, I have to head backstage. There are still a few things we need to go over before my performance, which is opening the awards show.

"Bye, baby. I'll see you later," I say, kissing him on the cheek.

"Bye," he says. "I'm excited to see you perform."

As he should be.

I typically have a massive amount of nerves before I go on stage and struggle to calm down, but I'm not really feeling those tonight. I'm not thinking about who in the audience I need to impress or staging that I need to remember. All I'm thinking about is me, my guitar, and singing to the love of my life.

I take my place on the stage and look up as the spotlight hits me. This is my moment. And I'm more than prepared.

I know the lyrics to this song like the back of my hand. I've never played it live, but somehow I nail every chord and line like I'm doing it for the millionth time.

When I'm done, the audience erupts in applause, which warms my heart.

As I make it back to my seat during the break, Rome is beaming.

"There are so many things I would do to you right now if there weren't a thousand cameras in this room."

I laugh. "You can still kiss me if you want. But be careful not to ruin my makeup. I might have to go back on for my acceptance speech."

He kisses me softly. "You will have to go on. Because you *will* be giving your acceptance speech."

"Whatever you say."

My stomach is in knots by the time they begin to announce my first category. I can hardly hear as they call out the names of the other nominees.

"And the winner for Album of the Year goes to..." the announcer, an up-and-coming reality star, pauses for dramatic effect. She opens up her envelope. "Aspen Moore!"

Oh. My. God.

"You're joking."

I cannot believe this album actually won. I wrote these songs for myself, and yet they're being appreciated in such an amazing way.

"You did it, *mi cielo!*" Rome shouts as he stands up and kisses me. I know the cameras are watching. So does he. But we no longer care.

I walk up the stairs and onto the stage, still in shock.

"Wow. I can hardly believe I'm standing in front of you all today. Thank you so much. I have so many people to thank for this incredible honor. All my fans, those who have supported me throughout my career. Everyone who streamed the record, all my wonderful collaborators. Thank you so much. To my parents, I love you guys tremendously. Thank you for giving me the world and putting your faith in me. To my amazing best friend, thank you for being the first to listen to this album, and for being there for me always. And lastly, thank you to my wonderful boyfriend, who's here with me tonight. You've inspired so much of this record and have taught me what it means to be loved and cared for. I cannot wait to continue on this amazing journey with you by my side. I love you forever. Thank you all for helping me to get where I am today, and have a wonderful rest of your evening!"

The audience erupts into more applause, and my face starts to hurt because I'm smiling so hard.

Rome whispers in my ear once I'm back in my seat, "I'm so proud of you, Pen. I love you so much. I wake up every morning wondering how the hell I got so lucky that you want to be with me. I'll be yours until I take my last breath. I cannot wait to make you my wife."

The air escapes my lungs. "Was that a proposal?"

"No," he says firmly. "When I propose, you'll know I'm doing it."

EPILOGUE

"King of My Heart" by Taylor Swift

May, Four Years Later

*Y*ou almost ready to go?" I shout from the bathroom sink. I'm almost done with my makeup. I just have to finish my lipstick.

"Yeah!" Rome calls. "Give me a second."

"Don't worry. We don't have to leave for another twenty minutes."

Life's been good these past few years. Like, really, really good.

Rome's about to graduate with a master's in education from Lehigh University, and I can't wait to support him in the way he always supports me. My extended family has driven from Ohio to see him walk the stage, and my parents are coming too, obviously.

I saw my extended family last when we married in January, about four months ago, and it was the best day of my life.

The ceremony was small, with under twenty guests, as only our closest friends and family were in attendance. My dad walked me down the aisle, and Leila was my maid of honor. It was almost surreal getting to live the dream I'd had for so long. But it was finally coming true, and I couldn't have been more thankful.

We've been splitting our time between Allentown and LA for a while now. It's hard not getting to see each other every night or even every week, but now that Rome's finished school, we're probably going to sell the Allentown home. Instead, we'll buy one in Fertsville and come back once a month or so.

Rome enters the bathroom and smiles at me. "Wow, Pen. You get more and more gorgeous every day."

He says charming, sweet, and incredibly cheesy things like this to me on a daily basis, but over the last few years, I've definitely grown fond of this quality.

My heart swells. "Thanks, baby, but you're the most handsome man I know. I'm proud to call *you* my husband."

He cups my face and kisses my lips. "You think we have enough time to—"

"No. Absolutely not. We tried that once. Do you remember what happened?" He completely destroyed my makeup *and* ruined my hair just twenty minutes before we had to leave for a talk show.

"It was an accident!"

"Nope. I'm not falling for that again. You'll just have to wait until tonight."

He groans. "Fine. I'll wait."

"I have some news for you, anyway. News I think you'll be very excited to hear."

He perks up.

"What is it?" he asks. "Are you up for another award?"

"No! Nominations don't come out until tomorrow. There's something else." The Cobalt Awards are not even something I want to be thinking about right now.

"What?" he asks.

I pull my pregnancy test from the drawer beside me. "Look." Two lines.

His mouth drops. "Oh my God! Pen, does this mean…"

"Yes!" I shout, unable to contain myself. "We're going to have a baby."

I throw my arms around him, and he peppers my face with kisses as he lifts me into his chest. "Please tell me you're not joking."

"Of course, I'm not joking! Aren't you excited?"

Rome's been begging for a baby since our one-year anniversary. Obviously, I wanted one just as much as he did, but I wanted to wait until we got married, he finished school, and life settled down a bit.

I suppose nature has perfect timing.

"This is one of the best days of my life, *mi cielo*. You don't know how fucking happy you've just made me."

He puts me down and bends to his knees, planting a kiss on my belly. "I cannot believe you have our child growing in there."

Neither can I. I'd dreamed of this day forever, but that's where I thought it would always stay. In my dreams.

I place a hand beneath his jaw. "I hope our children grow up to be just like you."

He stands and kisses me again. "I hope we have a beautiful baby girl. I want her just like *you*."

"If we do, I know what we should name her."

"What?"

"Rosalia." After his mom.

I can see the tears welling in his eyes. "I love you so much, baby. You're everything to me."

"I love you too, Rome."

He kisses me one more time before saying, "It's probably about time to go."

"Okay," I reply. "Let's head out." I grab my purse and lip gloss, and we head to the car.

"Should we break the news tonight during dinner?" Rome asks.

I don't even have to think about my answer to this.

"Yes. If my parents weren't obsessed with you before, they're sure as hell going to be obsessed after tonight."

Rome's not the only one who's been begging for a child.

He squeezes my hand from the driver's seat. "I love them too. And now we can finally give them grandchildren."

All the more reason for us to buy a house in Fertsville.

I look over at him and smile. "Looking back, the public attack on my reputation ended up being the best thing that's ever happened to me. It's brought me to you, and I can't help but feel thankful to everyone who played a part in it all those years ago."

"We would have ended up together eventually. We just needed to lose each other before we could find our way back."

There he goes. Always finding the right words. Melting my heart in the best way possible.

"Roman Torres, you can be a damn poet when you want to be."

He plants a quick kiss on my cheek. "Aspen Torres, I'll be whoever you want me to be, as long as it puts a smile on your face."

Roman Torres.

After all that we've been through, we deserve all the happiness we can get in our lifetimes.

ACKNOWLEDGMENTS

Tis the Damn Season was born in the summer of 2022 in a one hundred and thirty square foot dorm room in Providence, Rhode Island. I was in the midst of a summer program and a month shy of turning fifteen. The idea of writing a novel based on Taylor Swift's same-titled lyrical masterpiece had struck me a few months back, but it wasn't until school let out and I was done with all my homework that I got bored and decided to start the project.

I can't thank you all enough for picking up this book and reading it. It's hard to believe that after about a year of working on this novel nonstop, it's finally made its way into the hands of readers. I hope you enjoyed reading it as much as I did writing it.

I'd also like to extend a big thank you to all the people who made this book possible.

Thanks to my dad, siblings—LJ, Andrew, Brian, Jason, and Nicole—and my brother-in-law, Andre. I love you all, whether you read the book or not.

To Sarah, my twin flame, in the word's most literal sense. I love and thank you for all the times you listened to my rants about this novel. I know it must have been annoying, but I suppose it all worked out in the end.

I thank Erinn Salge, my mentor, and only real creative writing teacher. I would never have written a decent novel without your guidance and support. I can't count the number of ideas you came up with for this book, and I can't thank you enough for inspiring so many brilliant plot points.

Thanks to no other than Taylor Swift for writing not only "'tis the damn season", but the wonderful songs that have gotten me through all of my hardest days.

And last but certainly, not least, I thank my wonderful mom. I wouldn't be where I am today without all the sacrifices you've made to give me all the opportunities in the world. I appreciate you more than anything.

ABOUT THE AUTHOR

Kimi Freeman writes heartfelt contemporary romance and is an avid lover of all things dance. A northern New Jersey native, she is often found enjoying a toasted cinnamon raisin bagel or taking trips into New York City, a short distance from her hometown. Her stories are swoon-worthy, fun and always guarantee a sweet happily ever after. Follow her on her social media platforms for updates and additional information.

Find Her Online

authorkimifreeman.com

@kimifreeman_

@kimifreeman

@KimiFreeman